Fafleen ... an immense pool of liquid fire, clearly fueled by the volcano itself.

―ⱽⱽⱽ―

She paused on the edge, hesitant about disturbing such a magical place.

"Ask, Daughter." The old dragoness, the Ancient One, had entered and stood silently behind the younger dragon.

"I would see those I know from the Realm who are here with me."

For a second, the pool bubbled fiercely, then smoothed into a red mirror, showing the crystal form of Myst trapped within the mind net.

"Myst, can you hear me? asked Fafleen.

Myst nodded.

"Where is Lealor?"

A shrug of crystal shoulders answered Fafleen.

"Not trapped with you?" Fafleen's talons clenched. "Then Lealor is unprotected!"

Myst's head drooped. Fafleen's slow breath of realization fogged the pool. When the mist cleared the scene had changed.

The dragon saw Lealor standing in a garden admiring the flowers with an older woman.

"Lealor!" Fafleen called, but she got no response . . .

―ⱽⱽⱽ―

ALSO BY CAROL DENNIS

DRAGON'S KNIGHT
DRAGON'S PAWN

DRAGON'S QUEEN

BY CAROL L. DENNIS

WARNER BOOKS

A Time Warner Company

WARNER BOOKS EDITION

Cover illustration by Janny Wurtz
Cover design by Don Puckey

Questar® is a registered trademark of Warner Books, Inc.

Warner Books, Inc.
666 Fifth Avenue
New York, NY 10103

W A Time Warner Company

Printed in the United States of America

First Printing: December, 1991

10 9 8 7 6 5 4 3 2 1

To Richard
The wind beneath my wings

And to Andrew Craig Davidson
The newest reader in the family

Prologue

SILVER moonbeams illuminated the snakelike form as it moved over Lealor's wrist. Its glassy body reflected the moon-blanched colors of the covers. Lealor's red hair fanned dark against her pale features. In the air outside the tower window, a vortex of shadows whirled, then stabilized into the form of a huge dragon.

Wyrd had returned to Realm.

Lealor slept on, even as the voice of the huge saurian hissed, "Come, daughter." Silently, the glassine form of Myst, the only daughter of Wyrd, sped for the open window and freedom from her charge.

"Am I free to go now, father?" she asked.

"Are you so eager to stop protecting this Jarl-child?" Wyrd replied, amused that Myst chose to stay the same miniature size she wore when she disguised herself as a bracelet on the arm of Lealor. Myst hovered before her father's face as if she were a hummingbird.

Wyrd softly exhaled a jet of flame, turning Myst into a pink figure as she basked in the glow of his affection.

"How nice," she said. "I often feel the chill clasped around Lealor's wrist."

"Is the task you have set yourself so onerous, youngling?" Wyrd's voice spoke the dragon mindtongue directly to his daughter.

"It was not exactly my wish to be born a talisman," Myst gently reminded Wyrd.

"Yes that is so. Twenty years ago I created you and your brothers to act as guardians to the children of my companion, Jarl Koenig."

Myst wondered if her father was at last becoming old. She had never known him to meander on about things they both remembered well. Still, she gave him her respectful attention.

"The peril of the Shadowlord hung close to those Jarl cared for. The guardian bracelets freed his human mind to address the rescue of his wife and to confront the Shadowlord once again." Wyrd lowered his head in shame.

"Do not feel sadness, father. You could not destroy the Shadowlord without endangering those you had sworn to protect—including that terrible infant, Baloo, the Bright One."

"Does not the small Bright One rest within Achaeasun?" A look of surprise was an impossibility for a dragon, but Wyrd's eyes widened at Myst's opinion.

"Several times word has come that he is restless. Then Mirza rides Ebony, her dragon friend, to Achaea and sings a song to lull Baloo to sleep once more."

"I have been remiss. I should have watched Baloo's development."

"Oh, he is fine. It has been five years since he last woke."

"Have you decided whether to stay with Lealor, daughter?"

"Yes, father. I will stay. Until your search for the Shadowlord is successful, I must remain. My brothers are still companioning Seren and Argen. I would not leave my charge until I am certain she is safe. It would shame me. My teasing brothers would remind me of it for thousands of years.''

Wyrd looked carefully at Myst. It saddened him that of all his children, she must be the one to be unable to speak to her charge. If only Lealor had not refused Myst when he had offered her the protection of a talisman! Watching Lealor grow up, Wyrd had learned much more about humanity. Had he understood human children, he would not have invoked dragonlaw to silence his daughter. Both Myst and Lealor had suffered from his prideful command that Myst must never speak to Lealor, only protect her from magic. He nodded, and spread his wings preparing to leave.

"Don't forget," Myst reminded him, "that Lealor and I are leaving Realm to act as gatewatchers for a year."

Wyrd nodded, wondering if he should tell Myst of his strong intuition that danger awaited Lealor. He abandoned the impulse, and rose into the air, fading into nothingness as he reached the top towers of the building. He comforted himself with the thought that facing peril built character in the young.

Chapter
One

LEALOR stood within the mosaic of the star, smiling at those who had come to see her go to her first post as gatewarden on another world.

The Courtyard of the Gate had never been large and now it appeared full to bursting with well-wishers. Lealor looked around, nodding to the silent wavers and calling soft goodbyes to her more vocal friends. Her father looked agitated, but her mother was calming him. Andronan and Cibby, her Realmish great-grandparents, radiated their pride in their only great-granddaughter. Andronan's white robes and beard shone in the early morning sunshine while Cibby's hair, gathered in a generous bun, had a few wisps flying away in the faint breeze.

"Be good, my dear," Cibby mindspoke a last admonition.

"Of course." Lealor answered her aloud. Lealor's grandparents had disappeared through a gatemalfunction years before she was born, so she thought of her great-grandmother as the grandmother she had never seen. Lealor found it almost impossible to believe that her grandmother was an extremely powerful witch. Cibby had taught Lealor to use her own talents in spite of looking like an old woods granny. "I promise, grandma," she offered mentally just as she had when she was a little girl.

Lealor's momentary reversion to her childhood amused Cibby. She hoped being gatewarden far from home would satisfy her granddaughter's yearning for independence. There was something so lovable about Lealor that Cibby, like the rest of those who had known Lealor since she was a child, sometimes treated her as if she were much younger than her actual age. She waved a hand and Lealor heard a faint plop as a magic provender bag joined her pile of baggage.

"Thanks, Gram," Lealor said.

"It's in case you get hungry for some goodies while you're away." Cibby gave her a wink.

"Don't forget me while you're gone," Fafleen, the young dragoness, called from her perch on the balcony. She fluffed her pale-blue scales and blew a delicate smoke ring. Her long, narrow tail twitched slightly from the excitement of seeing her friend leave.

"I won't," Lealor promised, feeling relieved that Fafleen's parents and brother had not come. Tons of dragon flesh hovering over Lealor had never appealed to her. Then too, young Fafnir, Fafleen's big brother, still had to gain control of his flame which shot out in all directions in moments of excitement. Her mother or father threw a protection spell around everyone if he forgot to aim the flare upward. Still, it was nice not to have to worry.

"Sure you wouldn't be wantin' a little company, bein' away so far and all?" Rory, her self-appointed leprechaun guardian, wheedled mentally. The silver buckles on his shoes glinted from a recent polish, although his brown pants and jacket were the same as ever.

"Why, I'll be back before you can miss me. After all, it's

only for one year. What could go wrong in such a short period of time? You know how easy it is to be a gatewarden. My parents wouldn't let me do anything dangerous. Don't be afraid for my welfare.'' Lealor smiled gently at her oldest and best friend. She knew she would miss his swift popping in and out to see her.

"Afraid? Now how could you think such a lackwit thing! Have you already forgotten everything I've taught you?'' Rory drew himself up to his full two-foot height and stood, arms akimbo, a veritable classic picture of an outraged leprechaun.

"Sorry.'' Lealor apologized. "I know leprechauns are never afraid of anything, no matter what. It's just about the first thing I learned from you.''

"Humph,'' Rory snorted. "It's getting too big for your mortal britches you are.'' Mollified, he waved before he winked out.

Lealor caught his last thought, "Too many mortals around for comfort. They'll be trying to steal my pot o' gold next.''

No one but Cibby and Lealor noticed the tiny teardrop that shimmered in the air before it splashed wetly on the ground.

"Now you will be careful, won't you?'' Mirza mindcalled softly, knowing Lealor would never forgive her if she spoke out loud.

"Bright One's sake, mother, I'm all grown up. I even graduated from vet school back home on Earth before I volunteered for this job. You know how short-handed we are since Argen discovered the *Book of Gates* that lists the worlds that have portals and how to activate them.'' Lealor's thoughts were sharp.

"Try to be patient with your mother,'' Jarl warned his headstrong daughter privately in mindspeech, putting his arm around Mirza's shoulders. "No matter how old you grow, you'll always be her baby.''

"Yes, dad. I'll try.'' Lealor thought to herself that being out from under Mirza's smother love was one of the big attractions of being a gatewarden on Aurora. She was sorry to be leaving her family. Still, she couldn't help the flame of happiness that wavered inside at the thought of being an adult, on her own—at last.

"Are you sure you have everything you'll need?" Mirza asked, eying the huge pile of baggage piled at her daughter's feet.

Remembering her father's warning, Lealor stifled her first thought and said, "Of course, mother. What could we possibly have forgotten? You insisted on my taking the magic medikit in case of injury, a ton of books to read, preserved rations, perishable items . . ." Lealor ticked things off on her fingers as she named them. She planned to give them to the poor as soon as she reached Aurora. If they have any poor there, Lealor thought to herself. A temple complex housed the gate on Aurora. Being in the care of the temple guardians was preferable to staying on Realm where everyone looked out for her welfare.

"I'm well provisioned," she told her anxious parent. Her foot tapped on the lumpy pack nudging her knees. "I even have that full-room decorator's setup you insisted I take in case I don't like my room or get tired of the way it looks." She smiled at her parent reassuringly. Lealor thought to herself that once she was off Realm on her own she'd never use half the supplies her mother had gathered for her. After all, Aurora was a civilized world. It was not one of the places which had dropped out of the gate system over the centuries since the Old Ones built the gates.

That was her mother. Prepared for fire, flood, and famine when it came to her children. She was bad enough with Seren and Argen. They were men, so Mirza finally gave in to their pleadings and let them do their own packing. Doing their own packing was just one of the things Lealor envied her brothers.

Seren and Argen had made friends of their talisman bracelets. Lealor never stopped regretting her refusal of Myst, the glassine dragon who curled around her wrist, forever silent as the dragon Wyrd had commanded. Seeing the daily interchange between her brothers and their dragon bracelets had rubbed a raw spot inside Lealor. Her quick refusal had branded her as headstrong forever. Bright Ones in a basket, she had been only seven when she told the magical dragon Wyrd that she didn't want a bossy bracelet. In all his centuries of life, no being had ever said no to a request from him. A cold chill went over Lealor as she remembered the event in detail. She'd been lucky. A dragonmage like Wyrd had the power to transform her permanently into anything he chose, or blast her to the Black Universe. Her father's face had looked so odd. That was her only clue to her danger. Thank the All she'd remained silent when Wyrd commanded his daughter to protect Lealor, but never speak.

"Are you ready to go?" Lealor mindspoke to Myst who gently clung to her wrist, silent as usual. Over the years, the human and the dragon had worked out a primitive form of wordless communication. Myst reprimanded with a flick of her tail, making Lealor feel like she was being snapped with a rubber band. If Lealor framed a question, Myst could nod yes or no. Myst could tighten on Lealor's wrist to warn her of danger or suggest she should consider her actions more carefully. Lealor knew what a weak substitute they had for the rich exchange of ideas her brothers shared with Soladon and Nyct, their dragon bracelets. One of the plus factors of being away from her family was not being reminded almost daily of her folly so many years before.

Lealor had visited Aurora once before pledging to be gatewarden, so it wasn't difficult for her to begin visualizing where she wanted to go.

A loud thump disturbed her.

"Hey, you weren't going without giving me a chance to say goodbye, were you?" The rather pudgy young dragon who joined his sister Fafleen on the balcony peered down at her with one saucer-sized eye only inches from Lealor's nose.

He curled his tail around his blocky golden body and used the end of it to polish some tarnish from his scales.

Lealor ignored the dagger-sized teeth in the dragon's huge head. "Er, of course not—" Lealor began to lie politely, wishing dragons used mouthwash as she got a whiff of partially digested kippers, of which the dragon was fond. Privately she swore to herself, using the kind of oaths her parents didn't suspect she knew. If that wasn't just her luck! Trust Fafnir II, the densewit, to arrive just as she was about to leave.

"I'd have been here sooner, but grandfather takes a while to get ready to pop in, as it were," the dragon explained.

Fafleen gave a ladylike snort at her brother's remark, carefully directing the tiny flame skyward.

Lealor hid her smile. Talk about each child in a family being different! Probably young Faf would never get the *Dragon Chronicles* learned. His younger sister Fafleen had already memorized the hundreds of books that composed the history of dragons and their laws. Young Faf collected gold like a pack rat and hid it, under the fond delusion that his parents didn't know about it. His hoard was stashed in a dozen caves on Realm, waiting for his parents to declare him an adult. It was his hard luck that his mother was a stickler for the old ways and insisted on his continuing his studies. Faf would be older than his grandfather, Old Fafnir, before his mother would see him as an adult.

"Grandpa's coming," Fafleen warned in embarrassment.

Both Mirza and Jarl got ready to intervene in case the old dragon misjudged his landing space. Cibby, ever practical, wasted no time in putting a protective spell over everyone in the courtyard.

Bless her, Lealor thought, grandmother was always certain that safe was better than sorry. Lealor doubted the old dragon would notice the spell. He was really ancient.

A vast form shimmered over the crowd, drifted slowly to

the spire, then slid to the balcony. It groaned with the weight of three dragons. Fafleen firmly anchored her grandfather's tail with one claw, and hid a pained look.

Lealor could sympathize with her. She knew how Fafleen hated to look foolish, and a brother and grandfather like hers almost guaranteed it.

Mirza cast a stabilizing spell over the building seconds before her dragon friend Ebony, the mother of Fafleen and Fafnir, arrived with Fafnoddle, the young dragons' father. The senior Fafnirs noticed the stress on the balcony and sensibly perched on a nearby pair of towers.

"We won't stay and hold you up, Lealor," the sensible Ebony promised, noticing Old Fafnir shedding scales on the courtyard. She levitated a small box into Lealor's hand. "Just a little remembrance," the dragon said.

"Why, thank you." Lealor felt guilty for wishing at first that the dragons had not come. They were her parents' and her brothers' friends. They had fought the Shadowlord in the final battle on Realm, years before Lealor was born. If it had not been for their aid, perhaps every being on Realm—and who knew where else—would be the slaves of the mastermage. Lealor had only met him once, and she still suffered silently from his curse. The words rang in her ears still: "If ever you attempt to turn yourself into another form than the one that is honestly yours, you will stay in that form forever."

She shivered, hoping no one would notice the goose bumps that raised on her arms as she remembered. The Shadowlord had also sworn her to secrecy. Lealor had not dared to break her promise in all the years since her vow. Although she had studied magic and searched for the counterspell, she had never found it. At first, Cibby and Mirza had commented on the young girl's refusal to shape-shift. As time passed, they decided shape-shifting was just a phase Lealor had gone through and then outgrown. They didn't know how often Lealor longed to allow her flesh to flow into another pattern. Nor had they any idea of how many times she cried herself to sleep. She felt imprisoned in the human form she was doomed to retain against her shape-shifting instincts.

She wrenched herself back into the present. Old Fafnir was offering her a small gold coin with his unsteady claws. Fafleen had a tight grip on his tail to keep him from falling headfirst into the courtyard. So great was the weight of the old dragon that Young Faf had coiled his tail around a projection on the balcony and sat on his sister's tail to keep her from joining the crowd of humans below.

"Thank you, sir," Lealor said, pocketing the tiny coin. She noted that Fafnoddle waved a taloned paw just before the coin grew much heavier. She smiled, thanking him for increasing the size of the coin with his magic. "Thank you all for coming, but now I must go to begin my adventure," Lealor told them.

Sunward, Baloo the infant Bright One heard her words. He had escaped from Achaeasun, his home, and was visiting Realm without anyone's knowledge. People and dragons interested him. He knew from past experience that if Mirza discovered he had left his sun-nest she would take him back and sing him to sleep. He wished Mirza would stop treating him like a baby. He liked Lealor and she had mentioned adventure, hadn't she? Baloo had also overheard her thought about wanting to break the Shadowlord's spell so she could shape-shift. Hmmm, Baloo thought.

"I fix!" He whispered to himself, twisting the gate's power before he whisked himself to a far place only he knew how to find.

Before she could finish her sentence or visualize her destination, Lealor disappeared.

"Malfunction!" Fafleen hissed angrily as she flew into the powerfield just before it dispersed.

Ebony hissed her distress, while Mirza stood in shocked silence. People and dragons stood as if spellbound, watching Fafleen also disappear. Everyone had experienced the strange ripple of energy as Lealor and Fafleen vanished. All the gate users knew they were in deep trouble. What they didn't know was what to do next. An empty feeling settled over them as it dawned on them that Lealor and Fafleen were gone—perhaps forever.

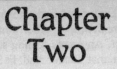

Chapter
Two

L EALOR looked around at the trees which ringed the cracked tiles of the gate mosaic on which she stood. Fafleen narrowly missed her as she, too, landed on the faded patterns of the gate.

"Fafleen! What are you doing here?"

The dragon hissed in distress. "Wouldn't it be better to question what we are both doing here?" Fafleen carefully pushed aside a few of the bundles that formed Lealor's baggage. She settled herself more comfortably while she waited for an answer from her friend.

"Where is here? would be an even better question," Lealor suggested.

"I wasn't the one visualizing the destination, you know," Fafleen replied, with some justification.

"Surely you don't think I had anything to do with this!" Lealor gestured to their surroundings.

"Well, the possibility had entered my mind." The dragon uncurled her tail carefully, letting it stretch into the trees that surrounded the gate.

"Believe me, I had nothing to do with arriving here." Lealor looked around them. "You don't recognize where we are, do you?"

"Egg's sake, no." Fafleen shook her head in a human way.

"How did you get here?" Lealor queried. "The last I knew, you were draped over the balcony, bidding me dragon's departure."

"At last a sensible question! Quite sensible," the dragon approved. "I felt—" Here, Fafleen paused to reflect. After years of human contact, she still had difficulty sometimes in conveying her thoughts in human languages.

"Yes, go on," Lealor urged, looking up while the dragon stretched her head high as if fresh air might help her to find words to speak.

Fafleen lowered her head to Lealor's level. "It was something strange. . . . Almost as if something . . . or someone . . . interfered with the gate power. I swear I heard the thought 'I fix.' But that's impossible. It reminded me of someone . . ."

"Yes, and I know who!" Lealor interjected.

"You do?" Fafleen's eyes grew to dinner-plate size.

"Did you ever get to meet my mother's pet Bright One?" Lealor asked. She didn't stop to think how incongruous it was to call a being with the potential of wielding the tremendous power of a Bright One a pet.

The dragon closed her eyes as an aid to remembering. "Baloo?"

Lealor nodded.

"Loot and plunder!" Fafleen burst out in imitation of her brother's colorful vocabulary.

In spite of their predicament, Lealor chuckled. She knew

what a trial her unscholastic brother was to Fafleen, a born scholar like her mother. How insulted she would be to learn she sounded just like him.

The dragon lowered both eyelids and glared at her human companion. "I caught that thought!" she said.

"Now, Faffie." Lealor took a step backward and hoped she could placate the dragon before she was incinerated.

"Faffie, indeed." The dragon snorted a little fire, but skyward, to show she was mollified somewhat.

"I've been to visit Aurora and, believe me, this isn't it. Do you recognize this world from any of your studies?" Lealor looked around her as if she could see through the vegetation that formed an almost impenetrable barrier around the abandoned gate.

"Let me take a short flight to check out the area from the air," Fafleen said. "This isn't any place I ever read about, but maybe from the air I can see some landmark or something that would be helpful."

A cool breeze made Lealor shiver. "Unless the sun of this world rises in the west, it won't be long until nightfall. I'd like to find some shelter for the dark hours. Keep a watch for a cave or something close, will you?"

The dragon wasted no time in words, but raised her wings and then brought them down in one mighty gesture that seemed to pull her into the air. Lealor wished dragons would remember how fragile humans were as she struggled to stay upright in the draft of the dragon's first wingbeat. She felt lighter here than she did on Realm. Perhaps Faffie had startled herself with her easy ascension, Lealor thought charitably.

Following standard gate practice, Lealor lugged her baggage out of the path of any incoming traffic. It was one of the first things new gatewardens learned: Clear the gateway immediately. There was no sense in moving into the woods. It would just make it harder for the dragon to find her when she returned. Lealor piled up some packages to form a rough seat and collapsed gracefully on top, prepared for what might be a long wait. Nobody understood dragontime because their sense of time duration was very different from humankind's. Even her brother Seren, who might as well have been born a dragon himself, considering all the hours he spent with his dragonoid friends, didn't understand. He found himself occasionally taken aback by the dragon's idea of what a "little while" was.

Now that Lealor relaxed, she was more in tune with the world around her. She noticed the prickly feeling you get when someone is watching you. It would have been relatively easy for her to cast a spell to make the unseen visible. One of the things she had decided before she left Realm was that she would not use magic. Other people managed just fine without any hocus-pocus and there was no reason why she had to use her witchy powers. Now that she was here—and who knew how long it would take until she could return home—she might as well begin the way she had planned. She looked at her wrist circled by Myst, her dragon guardian. She felt the familiar pang of regret. She was reasonably intelligent, she had the healing gift as well as an affinity for animals, and she looked exactly like her attractive mother. Why wasn't she satisfied with what she had instead of wanting more? She didn't begrudge her brothers their dragon-bracelet companions, but she did wish Myst might speak with her. That wish paled in comparison to her desire to shape-shift. It was a constant ache, denying her true nature. The Shadowlord's threat that any further shifting would become her permanent form had made her a quiet, thoughtful person, never able to be fully joyful.

Turning up on the wrong world was the start of an adventure. Lealor meant to stay long enough to find out what this world was like. Judging from the state of the gate, it was one of the worlds that had been "mislaid" during the years when humankind had learned to use the gates the Old Ones had abandoned. It would be nice to be able to reintroduce a world to the gate system all by herself. First, Lealor knew, she had to find some shelter for the night. If worst came to worst, she could stay here near the gate with Fafleen. Although the dragon was only half grown, it would take a pretty formidable beast to attack a dragon.

A white bird with brilliant ruby eyes flew by and perched on a branch near Lealor. It bobbed briefly and tipped its head, watching her, but she knew it wasn't the bird that made her feel that she was being observed. Without a second thought, she whistled a few notes and called the bird to her. It flew to her hand as if compelled.

"Don't be afraid, birdie." Lealor reached into her pocket and offered a few seeds in the palm of her hand. She had never outgrown her habit of carrying tidbits in her pockets for her animal friends.

When the bird finished eating, Lealor tossed it gently into the air and smiled as it flew away into the green forest.

Lealor felt the prickles again. Where was that secret watcher? Suddenly she knew. He was behind her! She turned quickly and caught a glimpse of a little man peeking from a nearby tree bole.

"Hello," Lealor said softly, working a little magical spell that made her speak the tongue of this world without thinking. Then she remembered she had promised herself not to use any magic. Her visitor reminded her of Rory, except he was larger. She didn't want to frighten him away. He probably knew all about the area. His information might be more helpful than anything Fafleen saw from the air.

A slight pinging noise preceded the appearance of the little man before her. "Human, I suppose," he muttered to himself as if Lealor wasn't sitting there right in front of him.

She nodded in polite acceptance of his evaluation.

"Well?" he asked sharply.

"Well, what?" Lealor queried in return.

"Humph!" The little man snorted. "Humans are a dangerous lot. Berdu, perhaps you'd better just vanish before she tries to capture you.''

''Oh, I wouldn't do that.'' Lealor felt distressed and it showed.

''And why not?'' He put both hands on his hips and leaned forward until his nose was only inches from Lealor's own.

Lealor was glad she had remained seated. If she stood she would tower over the man by two feet or more. ''Because it wouldn't be kind,'' she replied.

''Kind!'' The man jumped back a foot. ''And when, pray tell, was any human kind to old Berdu?''

''Are most of the people you meet here in this woods unkind humans?'' Lealor became concerned. She didn't mind spending time among uncivilized people, but she drew the line at unkind barbarians. If humans were unkind, she needed a place to hide until she could figure out how to get home. Although, she admitted to herself, if she could lay hands on that terrible infant, Baloo the Bright One, she might give him a good spanking for delivering her here without so much as an if-you-wouldn't-mind. He might think her action unkind.

''Berdu is all alone. No humans are friends with him, so Berdu doesn't show himself to most humans.'' He looked at Lealor with piercing green eyes. ''But you—you seem different, somehow. How'd you get here?'' He glanced around carefully, running a hand over his long white beard which only missed dragging on the ground by an inch or so. ''Sitting here on the old star. Used to be a gate. Yes, Berdu remembers. Used to be a gate to faraway places a long time ago. Very long time ago. Humans forgot this gate. Berdu watches. None of his people come any more. Poor Berdu. Berdu . . .'' He shook his head.

Obviously the little man was very old. Lealor felt sorry for him, but she understood he had lost the train of thought he had been following. She gently reminded him she was there by speaking. ''My name is Lealor.''

"Le-a-lor? Funny name for a wicked witch. Even for a pretty wicked witch."

"I am not wicked!" Lealor jumped up in her own defense without thinking what effect it might have on Berdu.

He promptly disappeared.

"Berdu! Where are you, Berdu?" Lealor called and turned around, searching for him.

"Oh, I'm still here, missy. I'll just stay invisible until I find out what kind of a wicked witch you are."

Lealor longed to stamp her foot at Berdu's stubbornness, but she realized she had to convince him she didn't mean him any harm. "Berdu," she said, in the tones which always produced compliance from Rory, her leprechaun friend. "I'm lost. I don't know anyone here except you and you keep calling me wicked. Can't we be friends? I promise I'll never hurt you, or take anything from you that you don't want to give me, or lock you up, or . . ."

"Careful what you promise. Promise breakers come to a bad end." A shaking finger materialized to her left, but the rest of Berdu stayed invisible.

Lealor hid her smile. "Back where I come from, it's not considered polite to hold a conversation without being visible." Berdu pinged into sight with his finger still waving an admonition. "And where I come from, young one, it's not considered polite to correct your elders. Why," Berdu said, with the first smile Lealor had seen on his face, "I bet you haven't even seen your third century!"

Lealor's laughter pealed out. "Sorry. You're right," she apologized. "Can we be friends?" She held out her hand and waited.

Berdu took a step forward and placed his warm hand in hers. "Agreed." Then he stepped back hastily. "No nasty witchy tricks. Promise!"

"Cross my heart." Lealor smiled at her new friend.

A cloud crossed the face of the descending sun, darkening

the clearing where they stood. The darkness reminded Lealor of her need for a place to stay. And where was Fafleen?

"Berdu, is there anywhere around here where I can find shelter?"

"Not at my place!" Berdu sputtered. "Not big enough for a giant. Not big at all. Little! Hidden! My secret!" he ended belligerently.

"Of course I wasn't suggesting you would take me in for the night. I'd just like some place safe to sleep. What if it rains?"

"Your ringlets will be stringlets!" Berdu chuckled. "Ringlets to stringlets. Magic!" He stopped, suddenly silent for a moment. "Never use magic. Calls trouble. The bigger the magic, the bigger the trouble—tiny little spells clutter up the place until they call . . ."

"Call who?" Lealor never knew when her friend was going to drop a piece of important information.

Berdu put a finger before his lips in a gesture that commanded silence. "Bad. Not to talk about. Abandoned cottage that way." He pointed with a gnarled finger. "Next to the river in the oak grove, used to be magic, but not anymore. Never, never, no more. Bad happened there long ago. A good place now."

"No one lives there now?" Lealor didn't want to get into any trouble with the local people if she could avoid it.

"Good people lived there, but all gone now. All gone because—"

The huge shadow that was Fafleen soared over them. Berdu looked up and vanished.

"Oh, dear! Berdu!" Lealor called to no avail. Berdu had really disappeared. "And just as he was getting to the really interesting part." Lealor fumed a little, but calmed herself as the dragon landed. It wasn't her fault the little man was so apprehensive.

"There's a village several miles to the north," Fafleen

announced. "Farther north it looks like there's a big city, but it's so far away I couldn't see it very clearly. I thought it was just as well if I didn't go flying over. You know how touchy some ignorant humans can be if they see a dragon aloft."

Dragons were all alike in some ways, Lealor thought to herself. It never occurred to them that they were lacking in tact. They just blundered on, saying what they thought. Lealor wondered how dragons in stories ever got the reputation for double-dealing and deceit. All the dragons Lealor and her family knew were forthright to a fault. They said exactly what they thought and let the scales fall where they would.

"Yes, I know, Faffie. Did you see an abandoned cottage that way in a grove of oaks?"

"Lealor, just when I begin thinking of you as sensible— for a human, that is—you say or do something really stupid." The dragon fluffed her scales in exasperation.

"Sorry. Don't tell me. You couldn't see the cottage because it was under the trees? Right?"

"Much better. Logical."

Lealor hoped the dragon wasn't going into one of her lady dragon liberation speeches. Every dragon she knew had some individual quirk. Old Fafnir was into loot and plunder. Ebony, Faffie's mother, was a rabid historian. Lealor heard her in her mind's ear, "Those who don't know the *Chronicles* are doomed to repeat the errors of the past." Fafnoddle, Faffie's father, was an avid amateur magician and gardener. And what could anyone say about young Faf? He was a dragon materialist. Not for him the glory of the past, the wisdom of his kind, or the magic his father took such delight in. All he ever thought about was gold and how he could get more. Fafleen was a scholar like her mother, but she had lived in the shadow of her brother's sparse intellectual accomplishments so long, it had warped her into a real dragon's libber.

"Well, I met someone called Berdu. You frightened him away, but before he left he told me there was an abandoned cottage over in that grove of oaks by the river." Lealor pointed to make sure the dragon knew which direction she meant.

"Yes, I know the grove you mean."

"Would you be willing to airlift my luggage over to the cottage?" Lealor looked at the sun. It was quite close to setting.

"Surely. You had better get started if you want to get there before dark. Human feet are never as rapid as dragon wings."

Lealor ignored Fafleen's smirk as she grabbed several of the largest bundles and took off for the grove. Left alone, Lealor lost no time in hurrying after her friend. Fafleen would have to make several trips, and Lealor wanted to be at the cottage before it got any darker.

She could just make out an overgrown path in the deepening twilight. Fafleen passed her, going back for another load. She was flying rapidly. If she finished quickly she could settle in for the night herself. A few minutes later Lealor noticed her airborne friend flying back to the cottage. Lealor hurried on. She had quite a way to go and Fafleen's flight would last at least fifteen minutes, judging from her previous trip. She skirted a clump of bushes, hoping the path would continue on the other side. She looked at the sky. Stars were beginning to be visible. She stepped back on the path with relief, almost feeling her way along in the gathering darkness.

She stopped abruptly when she heard the noise ahead of her.

"Who—who's there?" she questioned, afraid to move from the path.

A deep growl which sounded very unfriendly answered her. It came from the path just ahead, between her and the cottage she hoped to reach!

Chapter Three

LEALOR took a deep breath. The animal—she couldn't see what kind—sounded large. She sensed waves of pain. She had a natural rapport with animals, but this one was big and hurt. Even humans were hard to get along with when they were in pain. It was so dark she couldn't see what to do. So she stood there, calming herself. She knew animals could sense when people were afraid and nervous. Lealor worked hard to appear calm and to project friendliness. She said softly, "I won't hurt you." At the same time, she mindcalled Fafleen as loudly as she was able. Then she waited.

"What do you want?" Fafleen answered her mentally.

"I need a little help, here," Lealor mindspoke calmly. The animal growled again. "Now!" Lealor mindcalled in what would have been a yell if she had been speaking. To heck with dignity, she thought to herself.

"How rude! It wasn't necessary to mindblast me, you

know," Fafleen said conversationally from above where she hovered. "I started coming the minute you called and I was almost over you anyway."

"You could have told me that," Lealor said quietly. Thanks a bunch, she thought to herself. "We've got a hurt animal down here."

"We have? How did I get involved in your do-good scheme?" Fafleen's thought carried some resentment with it.

"Let's not split hairs—" Lealor began mentally.

"Rabbits? A good idea. I'll go hunting for some," Fafleen said enthusiastically.

"Don't be dense, Faffie," Lealor said. "That was a metaphor. I meant let's not argue over small things."

"I'd have said it was a pun—"

A low growl interrupted her.

"Fafleen von Fafnoddle, help me."

"What do you want me to do? That bear seems quite cross."

"Bear? Then you can see?"

"Of course, dear girl. After all, dragons could hardly live in caves without good night vision. Mother was always feeding me balanced meals so I'd grow up big and healthy. Naturally I can see."

"Well, bully for you," Lealor said. "Try to shine a little light down here, won't you?"

"Why didn't you use mage light? I know Grandma Cibby taught you how."

The last comment distracted Lealor enough to wonder why it didn't seem at all strange to her that Fafleen and her brother called Cibby, who really was Lealor's great-grandmother, grandma. She put her errant thoughts in order and said, "I didn't want to startle the bear. Remember, I can't see him."

"Are you sure you really want to bother with him? I could take care of him for you. He looks delicious."

"Fafleen! Shame on you."

"It's all your fault. All that talk about rabbits. It's well past mealtime and I'm starving. This baggage handling is hungry work.''

"Just hold on until we can get to the cottage. I'll feed you from the provender bag grandma gave me before we left.''

"Promise?''

It was amazing how something as large as a dragon could sound like a human child. Lealor had a tendency to forget that intelligent as Fafleen was, she was still almost a baby by dragon standards.

"Cross my heart,'' Lealor said gently. "And now, a little light, please.''

A jet of flame illuminated the night sky above the girl and the bear. Then it went out.

"What happened, Faffie?''

"I'm just tired out. I'll try a little mage light.'' A soft green glow shone down on the bear.

"Much better. Thanks.'' Lealor approached the bear, wondering why he hadn't made a sound while the dragon hovered above them. He hadn't seemed like a coward and she didn't suppose he was able to mindspeak like the animals on Realm. For a moment she was afraid he was dead. Then she touched his head gently. He had fainted.

"He's out like a blown candle,'' Lealor said aloud.

"Then could I eat him?'' Fafleen said hopefully.

"No, you can't.'' Lealor hid her exasperation. Now all she would hear was "I'm hungry'' every ten minutes or so until she fed the dragon. She ran her hands over the bear's body, feeling for damage. His paw was curled under him. It was in a trap.

"Can you help me open this?'' Lealor asked.

"Do I have to? It's made of iron. I hate the stuff,'' Fafleen grumbled.

"All right. Just get me a stick a couple of feet long about this big around.'' Lealor indicated the size with her hands.

"And then we'll eat?''

"As soon as you carry him to the cottage,'' replied Lealor.

Fafleen hissed her exasperation. "All right."

The light disappeared, leaving Lealor standing in the dark. The bear made a noise. She stooped beside him, running her hands over his head in a soothing gesture. "It'll be all right, bear. Lealor is going to help you get well. Don't you worry."

The light returned and a stick plonked beside Lealor, who jumped. "Fafleen! You could have warned me."

"How was I supposed to know you'd forget all about me? You didn't forget you promised to feed me, did you?"

"No, Faffie. I didn't." Lealor sighed. She was feeling tired and hungry herself. She rose and poked the stick at the trap several times until she felt the teeth loosen fractionally when she pushed down. Muttering a prayer that the trap and the bear wouldn't bite into her, she finally pried the trap open. "Now, Faffie. Grab the bear and carry him to the cottage."

"He's so heavy—" Fafleen began.

"I'll put a levitation spell on him so he'll be easier to carry. Hurry. This trap may close again any minute."

The dragon clasped the bear in her talons and rose into the air. "All this nice, fresh meat," she mind thought, flying off into the darkness.

"Don't you dare eat him!" Lealor called, letting the trap spring shut.

"I promise." Fafleen reluctantly sent the thought.

"Dragon's honor?" Lealor mindspoke.

"Human blood and bones, Lealor." The dragon snorted.

"Fafleen, you know your mother would have your hide for an ill-bred remark like that. Promise me again and don't forget."

"Yes, I promise. Dragon's honor."

Lealor heaved a sigh of relief. Dragons were hard enough to manage at any time, but a hungry young dragon at night when she felt exhausted herself was the limit. Now if only she could shift into the form of a bird or anything that could travel faster than a human. She wanted to shape-shift so badly. For the thousandth or perhaps millionth time, she regretted her promise to the Shadowlord not to shift her shape. It wasn't as if she had a choice at the time. She had been only seven when he cast the spell that would keep her in any shape she shifted to forever. Sometimes she wondered if she shouldn't just choose some shape and shift into it and have the whole sorry mess over. If she had to stay in some shape, she guessed she would prefer to be a dragon . . . then common sense came to her rescue. She felt tired and worried. She hurried on, blundering down the path. Didn't this misbegotten world have a moon? A cold wind blew. Above, almost as if her thought were being answered, the clouds parted and pale-blue light shone along the path. She made much better time with the light. She slogged on through the underbrush.

Finally, just as Lealor was about to give up and call Fafleen to come to her, she got to the river. "Bright Ones give me strength," she muttered. "You'd know the cottage would be on the other side of the water." She looked around. No sign of any easy way over. She didn't want to use magic unless she absolutely had to and she knew she would dry out eventually. She took a deep breath, ready to plunge into the water. She put her foot out and felt herself grabbed by the back of her pants. Before she could even frame a thought or yell to Fafleen for protection, she was on the other side.

"Now can we eat?" Fafleen asked plaintively, dropping Lealor within a few inches of the ground so she landed with a thump.

"Bright Ones in a bucket!" Lealor said, making the phrase a curse. "Don't ever lift me like that without warning me, Fafleen."

"You wanted me to wait until you were soaked?" Fafleen asked. "Temper, temper. What do you suppose your mother would say if she caught that thought?" Fafleen shook her head in a surprisingly human gesture. "And you were correcting the way I talked!" The dragon cocked her head and sat squarely in front of Lealor. "Don't I get an apology or thanks or anything?"

Lealor gritted her teeth and smiled politely. She wasn't able to see the expression on Fafleen's face, but she remembered dragons could see at night so she smiled. Fafleen moved to the side to allow Lealor to pass.

"You're welcome."

Lealor stamped her way to the cottage door. Damn dragon, she muttered to herself. Oh, dear, she was even more tired then she had thought. She knew the only reason people swore was an inadequate vocabulary. It was also ridiculous. She really didn't want anything bad to happen to Fafleen, who was probably her favorite dragon of them all. She had to do something about being so exhausted. She had a bear to help, a dragon to feed, and a shelter to get ready before she could sleep. She could always start doing without magic tomorrow, she told herself. She lifted her arms in the moon's pale-blue light and willed moon magic into energy. It wasn't much, but it would help for a while.

She pushed the cottage door open. Adequate in size, but filthy, this room had not held anyone for years, yet it was still weatherproof. She entered, feeling acceptance. Now why would that be? A spell? Her witchy senses explored. Yes, an old spell protected the building. She had promised herself to manage without magic, but she was just too tired to clean tonight, when a wave of the hand would take care of everything. She'd definitely start not being a magic user tomorrow. With a gesture, the room sparkled. "Not bad," Lealor muttered to herself. "Good as grandma could do it, I bet."

"Now can we eat?" Fafleen asked, putting her head next to the doorway. She was too big to enter the cottage. "You didn't forget, did you? I'm awfully hungry."

"Can you find the magic provender bag?"

Fafleen turned her head for a second and then thrust the bag into the room, holding it by one talon. She knew only Lealor could make the bag work.

"That was fast," Lealor commented.

"I took the liberty of locating it while you were coming," the dragon admitted.

"And what would you like for dinner?"

"Well, I'm kind of homesick. Do you suppose I could have eight or nine bushels of steakfruit?"

"Eight or nine bushels? Are you sure you can eat that much safely? I wouldn't want you to get sick tonight. One patient is enough at a time."

"You don't want me to starve, do you? I'm still growing," the dragon explained.

Lealor couldn't help chuckling. Of all the problems she expected to have as a gatewarden, this was one she never could have foreseen.

"It's not funny," Fafleen said, looking injured. "I suppose I could break my word and eat the bear, but I did promise . . .."

"Just tip the bag up and the steakfruit will come out, Faffie."

Lealor could hear the steakfruit being chewed. She didn't bother watching. Dragons were never neat eaters. She didn't think anything could diminish her own appetite, but she wasn't taking any chances. Outside the door, she saw the magical package that would decorate a room. She brought it in, and wished for the cottage to be furnished just as it was before someone abandoned it. She made the proper magical wave of her hand. A brief puff followed. The room was rather rustic, but comfortable. Lealor didn't waste time looking around. She reestablished the levitation spell on the bear and pulled him gently into the room. She put him beside the hearth. Even her gentle pat didn't rouse him.

His huge skin hung loosely on his body. His nose was hot, too. "Dehydrated, I bet," Lealor muttered. She saw a pot on the other side of the hearth. "This should hold water." She carried the pot to the door and handed it to the dragon, who was still chewing vigorously. "Are you still eating?"

"It's not my fault," Fafleen protested. "Mother read about

chewing your food thirty times and made me promise I'd eat correctly."

"That's a good idea. While you're chewing, take this bucket to the river and fill it for me, please," requested Lealor.

"I'm still eating."

"Take another bite, then, and get me the water while you're chewing."

"If I do, can I have dessert?"

"Yes, I promise."

"Anything I want?"

"Just get me the water and you can have anything you want for dessert."

"Deal," the dragon said, dropping gobbets of partially masticated steakfruit from her mouth.

"Don't talk with your mouth full," Lealor admonished the dragon, who skimmed along the ground with the bucket in her talons. She returned in less than a minute.

Lealor poured some of the water into a dish for the bear to drink. The rest she set over the fire which had come into being when the cottage was bespelled.

"Lealor," the dragon called from the door.

"Yes? What do you want now?" Lealor checked the water in the pot. It wasn't hot enough to clean the bear's swollen paw.

"You promised," Fafleen reminded her.

"Promised?" Lealor said. Only a small part of her mind was on her conversation. She came out and picked up a bundle of linens her mother had insisted she take along. It was one of the things she thought she'd be able to give away when she reached her destination. Was there some universal law that mothers always had to be right? She wondered as the dragon handed her the magic bag.

"Dessert," Fafleen demanded.

"What would you like?" Lealor regretted her rash promise. She would bet an old dragon's hoard that Fafleen's dessert order would be unusual. Whatever the dragon asked for, she would grant the wish and hope Fafleen would never tell her mother what Lealor had fed her.

"Ten triple-layer chocolate cakes with double fudge frosting."

"On top of all you already ate?"

"I'm not through yet. I want a ring of smoked kippers on each one for topping." Fafleen could see Lealor was having second thoughts. "You promised!"

"All right. So I did. In the interests of saving you from a tummyache, how about three cakes?"

"Seven," the dragon bargained.

"Five," Lealor countered.

"Done."

Lealor reached into the bag and pulled out the first cake.

"Just toss it here," the dragon ordered.

One by one, Lealor brought out the cakes and threw them into the air. Fafleen's long neck snaked out and her opened mouth caught every one. The dragon lifted her neck into the air like birds do after a drink of water and belched loudly.

"Fafleen!"

"I couldn't help it. I'm pretty full, you know."

"And whose fault is that?"

"Why, yours. My mother would never have let me eat that much at one time. She doesn't want me to get my full growth too fast."

"You didn't see fit to tell me that before I fed you," Lealor said. She made a mental note not to let the dragon's size make her forget her real age. "It's time for you to go to bed. Where do you plan to sleep tonight?"

"In that big oak tree over there. I'll stay close in case you need some help."

Lealor, who had been quite put out with Fafleen's gluttony up to this point, felt touched by her consideration. "Goodnight, Faffie," she said quietly.

"—Er, Lealor?" the dragon said. "Could I have one more thing? Then I'll go straight to sleep. Dragon's honor."

"More food?"

"Oh, no. I'm quite full now. I wouldn't want to stretch my stomach. Could you reach into the bag and get a teddy bear for me to sleep with—just for tonight, 'cause I'm kinda homesick."

Lealor noticed that ordinarily the dragon spoke excellent English, but now that she felt tired she sounded like a little girl. "Of course," Lealor said, reaching into the bag and producing a huge pink teddy bear with a white bow around its neck.

"Thank you. Pink's my favorite color." Fafleen took the teddy bear and clutched it to her like any human child. "Goodnight," she said. Then she flew to the old oak. Leaves rustled. "Night again," the dragon whispered.

The gentle snore of the sleeping dragon drowned out Lealor's reply. "She really is an exhausted dragon," Lealor said to herself as she entered the cottage and shut the door. She could bring in the rest of her belongings the next morning.

Now, to clean the bear's paw. She turned and looked upward into two large, glaring eyes.

Chapter
Four

THE bear stood in the center of the room, reared to his full eight-foot height. He swayed, and his injured paw dangled limply before him. He opened his mouth to roar his displeasure.

Lealor made a warding gesture. She drew in a breath. The room had augmented her spell. It surprised her, but she felt the addition to her warding as a kindness. She was almost sure this cottage was what remained of a former gatewarden's home. Since all gatewardens were trained in healing, this probably wasn't the first time the home increased a spell to help a healer work on an injured animal.

Lealor knew the bear did not like being trapped indoors, but he needed her skills. She sensed waves of pain from the furry, brown body. "All right, bear. Let's get this straight once and for all. I'm the doctor, you're the patient. As soon as you're well enough to leave, I'll let you, but for now, you need my help more than you need to get out of here."

The bear tipped his head to the side as if he was struggling to understand her. He swayed again and almost fell.

"Now, my foolish pooka, you stretch out here where I had you so I can tend that paw." As she spoke she put her hands on the bear and pushed him gently. The levitation spell had not entirely worn off, so he was easy to move. Soon she gently bullied him into his former position. She kept talking as she worked over the bear, as much to reassure him as to reassure herself.

"Pooka. That's what I'll call you, I guess."

The bear growled softly.

"You don't like Pooka? Do you have a better suggestion?"

The bear looked at her with pain-filled eyes.

Lealor rested one hand on the bear's head in sympathy. She offered him water and he lapped it weakly. "Well, Brownie seems a bit mundane and Bear Mountain is a little awkward. No," she said as she prepared a basin of warm water and the cloths to clean the wound, "Pooka sounds too small. I guess I'll just call you Pook. Now, this may hurt a little, so I'm going to cast a teensy spell to keep you from feeling much pain." Lealor sat on the floor beside the bear. She muttered and gestured, then took the bear's paw into her lap, which she had covered with a clean cloth.

The bear growled softly, as if warning her.

"Don't be such a baby. I haven't even started cleaning yet. I'll have to see how much damage you've done to yourself." Lealor kept on talking as she worked. She didn't expect the bear to understand her, but her talking did seem to soothe him somehow. She mindtouched the wound. Festered. She cleaned it gently and started the healing process, imagining healthy flesh where the trap had left wounds. Her hands shook a little as she finished. She felt so tired. She cast herself into a light trance and checked the wound and the bear's whole leg. She sighed with relief. The bear's eyes looked at her with an almost human look of inquiry. "We were lucky. I got it before the infection spread."

The bear dropped his head in what almost seemed like a nod of agreement. Exhausted, Lealor failed to notice the nod. Her hands added a healing powder and wrapped the paw. She had done this many times in the veterinary clinic on Earth where she had worked. Her body was on automatic. She fetched the bear a pill and coaxed him to take it. "Good bear, Pook," she congratulated him when she finished. "This is your water dish. Try not to tip it over. Now, you stay there until morning, you hear? I expect you'll be much better when you wake up tomorrow."

Lealor took a cup from the cupboard on the wall. She filled it with milk from the provender bag. Next, she reached in and retrieved an apple. She crunched away for a moment, considering the sleeping bear. It was an effort to chew. She was simply too tired to eat any more. She decided she would rest on the cot in the corner for a minute before checking on her patient again.

She set the provender bag in the corner and stretched out on the cover of the cot. It was small, but comfortable, Lealor thought briefly. "So tired," she murmured before she fell asleep.

The fire on the hearth flared briefly, blown by the tiny draft of air that accompanied the opening of the door. The moonlight fell across the floor, making a gigantic shadow of Lealor's visitor. The bear's eyes opened. He watched as the intruder entered the room and looked around. When the shadowy figure approached the sleeping Lealor, Pook limped silently until he was behind the figure. The firelight illuminated the glassine form of Myst. The visitor showed an inordinate curiosity about the bracelet. Pook waited, taking no action, until the intruder reached out to touch the bracelet. Before any contact, the bear's giant paw shot out, claws extended, and pulled the intruder away.

Pook pushed the intruder down on the floor and stood over him with one paw above his chest. He rumbled softly.

Firelight flickered over Berdu's face. "You stupid bear,"

he whispered. "I wasn't going to hurt her or take anything. I was just curious, that's all."

Pook moved his paw so that it didn't threaten Berdu. He watched as the little man rose from the floor. When Berdu tried to approach Lealor for the second time, Pook positioned himself between them. He shook his head from side to side in an unmistakably negative gesture.

"Move, you hulking brute," Berdu whispered. "I want to take a better look at that bracelet."

Pook stood guard as immovable as a boulder. Berdu gestured him away, but the bear ignored him. The little man tried to walk around Pook, but the bear used his body to block Berdu.

"You fool! She's an obvious witch. You're not old enough to remember what happened the last time folks around here tried to use magic. Bad things. Evil. No place to hide. All changed. All gone. No more. Poor Berdu. The last, the very last . . ." Berdu shook his head. "Oh, dear. So bad. Alas. Power gone. All changed . . ."

The little man stood, lost in memories of the past. Pook used the time Berdu spent in reverie to push him gently to the door. When the door closed behind him, Pook positioned himself directly between it and Lealor, sighed, and slept.

Across the room on Lealor's wrist, Myst relaxed her vigilance a fraction so she could dragonnap through what remained of the night.

The moon shone brightly over the cottage as if to guard it from any shadow of evil. The forest itself rested, waiting for the first rays of the morning sun to gild the cottage.

Pook raised one sleepy eyelid when Lealor arose and fumbled her way around him to the door. Her fists rubbed her eyes. She stretched and yawned, outlined in light, unaware of the bear's watchful gaze.

"No different from home," she murmured to herself. "Mornings come too early as usual. How can anyone enjoy them if they're not awake?" She turned and saw the bear looking at her with his large brown eyes. "Oh, so you decided to stay! I left the door ajar so you could leave if you wanted to. I'll make us some breakfast after I wash up." She propped the door open with a chair before picking up her towel, washcloth, and soap. "You might want to go out too, this morning," she said pointedly. On the one hand, talking to the bear was probably a waste of time. On the other, she always talked to animals as if they could understand her. If nothing else, it soothed them.

Somehow, she felt as if this bear was different. His eyes seemed to hold human intelligence. The bear was quite handsome, for a bear. She could almost imagine the strong square jaw and soft brown eyes he would have if he were human . . . She gave herself a mental shake and proceeded out the door. She had too much to do. Standing around imagining the might-have-happened only wasted time. She scolded herself as she hurried down the path to the water.

She returned to the cabin to find the bear gone. "Oh, dear," she said. "I hope he has the sense to return. I need to look at his paw again."

A soft woof from the doorway told her the bear had not gone far.

She turned and smiled. "Oh, there you are. Shall we eat now, or do you want me to look at the paw first?"

The bear proved his intelligence by shuffling to the corner where the provender bag sat. He nosed it gently.

"It's all right. You may pick it up and bring it to me if you want, Pook," Lealor told him, impressed in spite of herself by the animal's actions.

The bear shook his head with disgust as he heard her call him Pook. Then he picked up the bag and carried it to her in his teeth.

"Thank you," she told him, wondering if he had been someone's pet. "I'll get you a nice bowl of cereal—" she began.

The bear growled softly.

Lealor raised her eyebrows.

Pook growled again.

"Fussy, aren't we?" Lealor teased. "Now how can I find out—Oh, I know. I'll name some things and you can nod to me. Okay?"

Pook lowered his head in agreement.

"Very well. Berries, biscuits and honey, fish, eggs . . ." Her eyes widened as the bear's head moved up and down vigorously at each mention of food. Lealor continued, curious to see if he really understood her. "Big fat grubs?"

Pook signaled a definite negative with his head.

"Cookies?" Lealor tried again, and got another affirmative motion. She put her hand into the bag, rapidly producing the items which she placed on the table. The bear came over, favoring his hurt paw, and sat on the floor. The top of the table was in easy reach of his mouth. He began to eat ravenously, yet neatly.

Lealor sat to eat her cereal and berries. As she finished her meal with a piece of steakfruit from the bag, Berdu entered the cottage.

"Good morning, Berdu. Come in," Lealor said unnecessarily since Berdu had already seated himself at the table.

"Morning," Berdu replied, eying her steakfruit hungrily.

"Would you like some breakfast? Or have you already eaten?" Lealor asked.

"Already ate," Berdu said and hastily added, "but I could always manage an extra bite or two," when he saw the girl begin to clear the table. "What's that?" A long, bony finger pointed to the steakfruit Lealor offered to Pook.

"Oh, it's just some steakfruit." Lealor offered him one.

"Don't mind if I do," he said, finishing the fruit in two bites. "Well?" he asked, obviously expecting more.

Lealor, astonished to see a person that small eat so fast, reached into the provender bag and pulled out a large bowl, filled to the brim. She placed it near Berdu. "Help yourself," she said. Then she watched as he picked up the bowl, tipped its entire contents into his mouth, somehow managed to swallow all of the fruit, and burped loudly. "Not bad—for a snack. Unusual flavor. Don't think I ever ate anything like these before. Steakfruit, you say?"

"Yes. In my" —Lealor paused in thought— "country, they are everyone's favorite fruit. So large, you know, and with no pit or seeds."

"How do you grow new ones, then, if they have no seeds or pit?"

"I have a few starts of the steakfruit plants, but I really don't know. They were created by Fafnoddle, a dragon friend of my family's—"

"Dragon created? Magic! No dragons seen in these parts for years . . ." Berdu seemed to lose himself in thought. He muttered disjointedly. Lealor couldn't catch everything he said, but some phrases made sense. "Weren," Berdu muttered. "Shape-shifters. Magic users. Bad times. Dragons all gone. Bad magic. Magic bad. Dragons. Gone. Weren. Enemies. Trouble." He looked at Lealor. "Never use magic. Dangerous. Berdu knows. Berdu remembers. Berdu remembers dragons . . ." Then he snapped out of his trancelike state. "Dragons?"

"Yes. Dragons. At least, a few. Fafleen, my dragon friend, is here with me."

"Here on Widdershins with you?" Berdu's eyes widened.

"Yes," Lealor answered her agitated guest. Widdershins, she thought, what an odd name for a world!

"Dragon! Here? Now?"

"Yes," Fafleen's voice came through the window. "I'm hungry, Lealor. Can you feed me some breakfast?"

Berdu shrieked once and vanished.

"Oh, dear." Lealor rose from the table and took the provender bag outside with her since Fafleen was too large to fit into the cottage.

Pook left the table as well. He stood in the door of the cottage and watched, fascinated, as Fafleen poured a never-ending stream of edibles into her cavernous mouth. She ate without swallowing or pause. Finally, after several minutes elapsed, the dragon lowered the bag and returned it to Lealor.

"I wouldn't want to overeat," Fafleen explained. "Mother wouldn't approve."

"I should guess not," Lealor said. "And in the future, I expect you to chew your food."

"Pish tush. Dragons don't have to chew their food. Our digestive systems are built for swallowing prey whole if we want to—"

Lealor interrupted her, not wanting to be the recipient of a long lecture on dragonly anatomy and life style. "Manners."

Fafleen blew a puff of smoke upwards. "You sound just like my mother."

"Never mind who I sound like. You know I'm right."

Fafleen seemed inclined to argue the point, but she stopped in astonishment as Pook uttered a warning growl. "My goodness, another country heard from," she said. "And who, pray tell, do you think you are?"

Pook growled again. He limped over to a spot midway between Lealor and the dragon.

"Quite the protector, aren't you?" Fafleen hissed her amusement. "Imagine a bear doing battle with a dragon! It would be no contest, bear."

"Pook," Lealor corrected.

"Named him, did you?" Fafleen lowered her head. With her jaw on the ground, she was eye to eye with Lealor. She blinked her eyes like a simpering maiden. "Oh, my dear, you're not getting fond of him, are you? I mean with your witchy powers you could always zap him into a handsome young man. If all he did was growl like the hero in those barbarian books, he would be the strong, almost silent type—"

"Faffie Fafnoddle!" The pink-cheeked girl faced the dragon in exasperation. "I never!"

Seeing her truly embarrassed, Fafleen ignored being called

Faffie and reassured her. "Of course not. I was just teasing. Can't you take a joke?" Little wisps of smoke drifted upward as the dragon chuckled gently.

"It was kind of clod witted. More the thing I would have expected from your brother than you."

Fafleen winced. "Point taken. Bright Ones forbid I should sound like him." She blinked once. Then she said, "If dragon minds were all like his, none of us would ever find the doors to our caves so we could come outside to eat."

"Oh, come on, now. Even though he's no great literary light, he's still a pretty nice dragon. Don't exaggerate his weak points."

Fafleen snorted steam in the air, wilting some tree branches that were overhead.

"And he's still young. He may mature into a more thoughtful dragon later." Lealor wondered how she had ever got herself into the position of defending young Faf, who was not only ignorant, but seemingly gloried in his stupidity. Any mental acuity he possessed ended up spent in planning how to get more gold for the mini-hoardes he had stashed all over Realm, and Bright Ones only knew where else.

"We can only hope to be so lucky," Fafleen said.

Pook, who had listened to this exchange, watching first one and then the other speaker, relaxed. The dragon really was the friend of the girl, odd as the situation was. He huffed in satisfaction before wandering away from the cottage.

"Wait!" Lealor called. "Your paw! I didn't get to change the bandage on your paw."

Pook kept on going. He disappeared into the woods.

"Oh, fiddle!"

Fafleen's eyes twinkled. Humans were a never-ending source of amusement to dragonkind. "You want me to go and get him and bring him back?"

"Not now. He's got the sense to return when he's ready." Lealor looked into the sea of greenery where the bear had disappeared. "He's not limping much this morning. I guess I did a good job last night, even tired."

Fafleen ruffled her scales and shifted from one foot to the other, for all the world like a child who needed to use the restroom. "Er—uh . . ."

"What's the problem?" Lealor looked at her dragon friend and smiled.

"Well—" The dragon paused, undecided.

"You may as well tell me, Fafleen. You never look like this unless there's something on your mind. I can see it's worrying you."

"All right. Remember last night when I returned from my flight?"

"Yes. Go on."

The dragon raised and lowered her wings before settling down close to Lealor. "There were mountains to the west. Some of them might have caves. It's the perfect place for dragons to live—if there are any dragons left in these parts."

"Dragons had to exist here at one time. Berdu mentioned them at breakfast this morning."

"Why hasn't he ever stayed around to meet me? Every time I come around he disappears. Is it my breath or what?"

The dragon's injured tones carried a whiff of partially digested breakfast. In spite of this, Lealor said, "Oh, no. I'm sure that's not the reason. He's such a strange little man. He's afraid to use magic and he usually disappears if dragons are so much as mentioned. Whatever his problem is, I'm certain it has nothing to do with you, personally."

"I'd like to go exploring today. I don't want to leave you all alone and unprotected—"

"Bright Ones forever!" Lealor broke in. "This is just what I was so happy to leave home for. I wanted to be an adult, not everybody's child. Surely you can understand that, what with your folks forever glorifying every random fact your brother manages to absorb and totally ignoring your mastery of literally hundreds of entire books—including the *Dragon Chronicles* with the entire history of dragonkind listed, date by date—''

This time it was Fafleen's turn to interrupt. ''All right, all right. I'm sorry if I treated you like a child. I didn't mean to, you know.''

''I'll be just fine. Truly I will. Besides, Pook will return after a while. You saw how protective he was. I really don't need two gigantic bodyguards when I am out here alone in the woods.''

''And you have Myst to guard you as well.'' Fafleen nodded toward Lealor's bracelet. ''I almost forget about her because she can't talk. Imagine a dragon oathbound to silence! I'm glad my father didn't do that to me.''

''Yes. I've often thought how unfair it was. There's nothing I can do about it. My brothers' talismens are their friends, but Myst and I don't even know each other because she promised her father not to speak to me. She could have taught me so much . . .''

''Dragons are good sources of information. If I can find any, perhaps I can answer some of the riddles about this place.'' Fafleen rested her head on the ground so she was eye to eye with Lealor.

''That's a great idea! It would be a good idea to know more about Widdershins before I meet the local people.'' She could see her reflection in Fafleen's silvery eye. Seeing eye to eye with a dragon was quite an experience.

''What do you plan to do about returning home? They'll be worrying about us both. I've never attempted to transport myself from one place to another instantaneously because mother always said I'd stunt my growth. This does seem to be an emergency, and I do think I can do it.'' Fafleen scratched her chin reflectively.

''Perhaps, if we get into a real jam, you might have to fly home. The gate worked once, and I may be able to get it to work again. Dragon travel is kind of dangerous. Your folks haven't given you any practice flights or anything. I'd rather save your special traveling abilities until we really need them. After all, things are pretty peaceful here. Let's wait.''

''That's a good idea. I'd like to meet some new dragons and have a few adventures before we have to go home to our mothers.''

Lealor made a face at the idea of returning to their parents. ''I want to gather enough data about Widdershins to bring this gate back into the system. Each of my brothers has found new worlds for the system. I don't know of any reason why I can't do the same.''

''Good.'' The dragon flexed her muscles preparatory to takeoff. ''Look out below, I'm going up!'' Fafleen sprang into the air with the first beat of her huge wings. ''I'll return this evening. Save some steakfruit for me,'' she called as she barely cleared the tree branches above them before she arrowed west.

Lealor waved one last time and then turned and entered the cottage. ''Now what shall I do first?'' she muttered to herself. It was an old habit she had retained from childhood. Her brothers had done things together, but she was ''the little one'' in the family and usually played by herself.

Because she had promised herself to try not to use magic, she spent an hour tidying up the cottage, trying to remember where she placed the supplies she brought with her from home. ''Maybe mother has something. If she had not helped me pack, I'd probably find there were a lot of things I wished I had brought. What is it about mothers anyway? They always have to be right. It must be some type of maternal magic that goes with the job.''

She saw a fly buzzing at the open window. It didn't come in. ''I wonder what's keeping it out?'' she said. She walked over and put her hand up to the window. She could see sunlight and feel a gentle breeze, for there was no screen. The fly buzzed, blocked by an invisible barrier. ''Hmmm.'' Then she extended her senses and noticed the shimmer of magic. "A very competent person set this spell. It's quite old, but it still works. Sunlight triggers it. I bet moonlight makes it work at night. Clever. I'll have to remember this." The disappointed fly buzzed away.

Sunlight glinted on Myst, her dragon bracelet, turning the talisman into a rainbow-hued circlet. It was rare for Lealor to notice her bracelet. Usually, Myst called attention to herself only when she warned her wearer to think before doing something potentially dangerous. Between those times when Myst tightened on Lealor's arm, she almost forgot about her.

"Myst," Lealor softly addressed her bracelet. "I need to talk to you a bit. You know I'm trying to manage without magic . . ."

The tiny dragon head moved up and down, indicating she knew.

"Well, I wondered if you could become invisible. You're very beautiful and people think you're an unusual piece of jewelry. They notice me because of you. I'd like to be very ordinary during my stay here. No magic, nothing special that anyone else couldn't do with training. You do understand, don't you?"

Myst closed her eyes in resignation. If Lealor wanted her invisible, then no one should see her. It broke her tiny dragon's heart. Somehow, she'd always hoped that Lealor and she would make a pair, have the special bond that had developed between her brothers and the girl's. Now she accepted the death of that hope. She would not act until her charge was within seconds of disaster. Lealor wanted to manage without her and so she should. Myst hardened her dragon's heart. No longer would she ache to speak with Lealor. She would guard as her father bid her. Nothing else.

As Lealor watched, Myst faded into nothingness. Only the slight feeling of weight remained to remind Lealor of her guardian.

Pook returned and Lealor tended to his paw, which was

responding to her treatment remarkably well. A slight limp was all that remained of the injury that would have killed the bear if she had not helped it. She felt good about that.

The day passed rapidly. Lealor didn't even think of Myst. She wouldn't realize what she had lost until it was too late.

Chapter
Five

B Y the time the sunset gilded the waters of the nearby river, Lealor had explored the area around the cottage. She looked anxiously towards the west, squinting as the sun blinded her.

"If that isn't just like a dragon," she muttered to Pook, who had returned and followed her as if he were a large dog, except he took short journeys to forage in the mass of berry bushes that flanked the rear of the cottage. Pook had discovered them. His happy woofing noises had led Lealor to the patch. The bushes were badly in need of care, but nevertheless produced a bumper crop of juicy fruit. Lealor filled a container for dinner and made a mental note to take cuttings back to Realm with her.

"Where is Fafleen? If anything happens to her, I'll be dead meat—literally—when her mother and father find out." She never stopped to consider how ridiculous it was for her to worry about defending a ton or so of healthy young dragon who could have gobbled her up in one gulp if she so desired.

Pook reared up on his hind legs and growled.

"What is it?" Lealor asked.

Pook dropped to the ground in a rush and hobbled over to knock Lealor down and stand over her, growling. Lealor looked up into the bear's ferocious face, wondering if she was going to become his dinner.

"Pook, let me up, you big lump!" Somehow, even in her undignified position, she managed to sound indignant and in control of the situation.

A shadow blocked out the sun for an instant, and Fafleen power-dived almost on top of them. She was in such a hurry that her talons actually skidded on the grass and her nose was within inches of hitting the ground. Lealor sputtered and Pook growled.

"Faffie von Fafnoddle, explain yourself!"

The dragon paid absolutely no attention to the words. Instead, she began speaking at a breakneck pace.

"Oh, Bright Ones in a bucket, you'll never, never, never, ever, never, ever guess what I've found in those mountains, Lealor—you'll be so proud of me and at last I've done something my older but obnoxious brother has never accomplished—my parents will have to admit I've done something really worthy for once and for all—and maybe even let me become an adult officially—"

"Bright Ones indeed, Fafleen! Slow down! I can't make talon or tail of what you're trying to tell me. Go back to the beginning and tell me again. And for Bright One's sake, this time slow down!"

This impassioned speech lost something because Lealor was still flat on her back half under Pook, who had finally stopped growling. He nuzzled Lealor, leaving bright-red berry juice over her face.

"Let me up this instant, you overgrown—"

At this point, Pook carefully put a gigantic paw on Lealor's middle. She felt protected and not hurt. She did get his point.

"May I please get up? I appreciate your trying to save me from being squashed, but Fafleen would never do that to me."

Fafleen watched the lesson in courtesy with interest. "It never hurts to be polite, my mother says. And besides, I did make that landing a little too fast."

Pook made a noise that sounded suspiciously like a snort.

Fafleen peered at him. She was a bit nearsighted from all the reading she did in the dim light of caves. No one dared to tell her about it. "Lealor, are you sure this bear can't talk? I have a funny feeling in my scales about him. He's much too bright to be an ordinary bear."

"I've never heard a word out of him myself," Lealor said, reaching over to ruffle the fur on Pook's head. "Now, what is this wonderful news that almost annihilated us all?"

"Teeth and talons! I've made a find!"

"You mean you've found some dragons willing to help us get home?"

"Something more important than that." The dragon blew three perfect smoke rings in the air and looked very satisfied with herself.

If there was anything Lealor hated it was a smug dragon. Her friend showed definite signs of getting too big for her scales. "If your mother saw those rings, you know, she'd probably forbid you to read for a whole day. You must have spent hours practicing. All that smoke isn't good for your lungs, you know."

Fafleen ignored her comment and continued. "I found a cave!"

"Well, goody for you. Do you propose we move there?" Lealor wondered why dragons took forever to come to the point.

"Not just any cave. It was a treasure hoard, but long abandoned."

"Gold and jewels aren't going be very useful unless you

plan to pay someone to help us.'' Lealor felt disappointed. Usually her friend was a very sensible creature, but she seemed to have lost her wits over an old cave. Surely she wasn't old enough to start thinking about nesting—or was she? Admittedly, dragons grew faster than humans. Her brother was so fixated on treasure, he hadn't started scale chasing. Girls were usually ahead of boys in the romance department. Fafleen was definitely female, so maybe . . .

"Better than gold and jewels." Fafleen snorted a jet of flame upward, careful not to start a forest fire. "Books! Old books full of stories and history I never heard of before.''

"Congratulations, Fafleen. Your folks will be proud of you. I hope you made certain that you're not intruding on any dragon's lair.'' The whole adventure was too good to be true. That a bibliophile should discover some abandoned library just didn't seem real.

"And best of all,'' the excited dragon continued, "there's a really old copy of a book that I think is the *Dragon Chronicles*.''

"You think? Are the cover and title pages gone?''

"No, they're there, all right. I just can't read them.''

"Why not?'' Lealor was astounded. Fafleen read a dozen or so languages and spoke several fluently.

"I can recognize a few of the symbols, here and there. They look like some of the very oldest symbols of dragonkind. I've found an unimaginably ancient copy of the *Chronicles*. Mother will be wild to find out about it.''

Since Ebony and Fafnoddle, the dragon's parents, had the second largest library on Realm and had been book collectors for years, Lealor felt Fafleen's opinion was understated. In fact, Lealor had heard her brother Argen lamenting that scholars from the university went to the dragon's cave to study since Ebony wouldn't hear of lending her books. Once she got a book in her possession, she never let it far out of her talons. Argen himself had traveled to her cavern to peruse some arcane volume that he found mentioned in the main library on Realm, but couldn't locate there. Lealor reminded herself not to get too interested in dragon tomes when the real problem facing them both was finding a reliable way to return home. She knew both sets of parents would be frantic, trying to find them. If, she thought, they realized what had happened to them. "Did you happen to see any dragons in those mountains?"

"Well, no," Fafleen admitted.

"I bet you forgot all about our getting home, didn't you?" A nod was her answer.

"That's all right." Lealor reassured her friend. "Tomorrow I suppose you'll be returning to your books. I'll wander downstream and see if I have any better luck in finding someone with information."

"Up," the dragon said.

"Up?" Lealor repeated, puzzled.

"Upstream."

"Why not downstream?"

"Because there's a village of sorts upstream and nothing but solid trees in the other direction. I noticed when I flew in."

Lealor sincerely hoped Fafleen's flight had gone unnoticed by the villagers. She didn't want to cope with aroused and fearful neighbors who might decide on dragon hunting. Berdu hadn't made clear exactly why magic was dangerous or what caused the dragons' disappearance and she felt responsible for Fafleen. However, she didn't think it would be a good idea to tell her friend. Every so often Fafleen became all dragon, stubborn and bloodthirsty. If the dragon became angry and declared doom on the village, life would become very complicated very rapidly. So Lealor only nodded and kept her thoughts to herself.

Lealor used the provender bag to provide a meal. She never consciously realized she was using magic. To her, the bag was simply a gift from Grandmother Cibby. Fafleen liked eating too well to point out Lealor's inconsistency. After dinner, which the magic bag produced in abundance, Fafleen asked Lealor to come out and talk to her. It was awkward, with Pook and Lealor eating inside the cottage and the dragon guzzling down kippers, steakfruit, and chocolate cake outside the door. She was too large to fit inside. Lealor didn't like the situation much better when the dragon stayed outside the window and looked in. Her eye filled the whole window frame. It made Lealor distinctly uneasy to look into the pupil when Fafleen made a comment. So she cheerfully dragged a chair outside. It really was too nice an evening to spend inside anyway.

"Talk away. I'm listening," said Lealor.

"Well, you did wonderfully well all by yourself today."

Lealor grimaced. She had given all her old university texts to Fafleen, earning her undying gratitude. She recognized the psychology behind the statement and waited for the unpleasant part that she was sure would follow.

"So . . ." Fafleen took a deep breath.

"Don't exhale!" Lealor warned. The cottage, sturdy as it was, would have a hard time withstanding the dragon's exhalation from a distance of six feet. Lealor had visions of flying shingles and downed trees. Sometimes Fafleen forgot her own strength. Years before, Ebony explained calmly to a wide-eyed little girl that dragons were very powerful and had to learn to use their might in moderation. Her child had exhaled on a picnic one time and blown the food a half mile away. "And after all, dear," Ebony had hissed with some pride, "she is very young to be so powerful."

Fafleen's cheeks swelled as she held her breath and Lealor frantically signalled upward with her finger. Pook, ready to pull Lealor to the ground and shield her with his own body, relaxed as the dragon obligingly followed Lealor's directions.

A shower of green leaves and twigs rained down in response to Fafleen's action. Lealor gave a sigh of relief. She had been right in assuming her friend was still too excited over her find to think straight. "So," she said, to urge Fafleen to continue.

"So I'd like to stay there." She paused and slowed down when she noticed Lealor's raised eyebrow. "And just check in here once and a while. You could leave messages for me by my tree."

"Your tree?" Lealor tried to hide the amusement she felt by gesturing to the forest around them. The clearing in front of the cottage was so small that Fafleen's tail went snaking off into the brush. Within a few paces, twenty trees were near enough to touch.

"You're not teasing me, are you?" The dragon lowered her head until she was eye to eye with the girl.

The dragon's silver eye acted like a mirror. Lealor could see herself seated in the chair with the ever-vigilant Pook curled by her right side. "Not exactly. It's just not like you to be so vague. Those old books have you really excited."

"You don't understand, Lee. When our historians get an eyeful of the old book I found, it will delight them. It's like discovering the missing link would be for you humans."

Clearly, Fafleen read and absorbed all the books anyone gave her. Every time members of Lealor's family came back from Earth they brought books for Fafleen, once they saw how much she liked to read. Argen, especially, who loved books himself, brought her boxes of discards. The neighbors dropped off books for Argen after he told them he sent them to foreign countries. At first he was in big trouble with their parents, but Jarl finally saw the joke. What country could be more foreign to Earth than Realm?

"Well?"

"Well, what?" Lealor responded.

Fafleen raised her head and stamped. Lealor could hear the dishes rattle in the cottage.

"Can I?"

Lealor knew better than to say, "Can I what?" or worse yet, "May I." "Okay by me. How long do you plan this period to stretch?"

"Only a few days. I'll come back for snacks, if you don't mind."

Lealor could picture those snacks. Five or six bushels of steakfruit and enough baked goods to stock a small shop. "Sure."

"And you can leave any messages for me by my tree," the dragon's head pointed to the tree she slept in.

"Let's leave messages for each other under the door of the cottage. With so many trees around, I might forget which one."

"Very well." Fafleen tried to sound very adult and very responsible.

Lealor remembered how young she was for a dragon. "And if you should get lonely or anything, you know I'll always be glad to see you."

"Oh, I won't get lonely now. Not with all those books to read. And I haven't even taken the time to look at all of them. For all I know, hidden in the piles, there are several more really important finds."

"Well, remember to let me know if you decide to explore any more. It's always a good idea to let somebody know where you will be in case you get into trouble." Lealor took the dragon's nod to mean she agreed. "Tomorrow, I'll wander downstream—"

"Not downstream. Upstream. The village I saw is upstream."

"Right. Not down, up."

A soft snore from Pook made them both look at the bear.

"Tired him out, we did." Fafleen chuckled, but softly, so the bear could sleep on.

"Well, he's still recovering from that paw wound. I'll let him stay here. It's not good for him to walk too far and overdo. Then, too, if I meet any villagers, I really don't want to have to explain a bear.''

"Good night," the dragon said, waiting expectantly.

"Good night," Lealor answered, wondering what else Fafleen wanted.

"My teddy, please," Fafleen said, sounding exactly like a little girl in spite of being a good-sized dragon. Lealor had caused the teddy bear to disappear after Fafleen woke up. Evidently she still felt a little homesick.

"And if you don't mind, can you make Pinky permanent? Then I can take her with me to the cave.''

Lealor gave the dragon the pink teddy and watched the huge dragon settle herself awkwardly in the old oak.

Soon, soft snores from the bear and dragon told Lealor it was time for her to go to bed as well.

Later that night distant thunder woke Lealor. The cold wind told her a storm was coming. Pook ambled in and settled by the fire. "Just one more reason for Faffie to have a cave of her own," she murmured. Lealor frowned. "I guess it's all right to use magic in a case like this," she told herself. With a wave of her hand she cast a protective spell over the dragon and the tree. "Now at least she'll stay dry," she said softly as she pulled the covers up to her chin.

Outside, the wind herded silver clouds together until they turned black and raced across the face of the moon. Soon rain flooded down. The runoff gathered into rivulets and hurried to the swollen river which increased its pace to the sea.

Chapter
Six

THE sound of rushing water woke Lealor. Before she went to the bank of the river, she had a good idea of what she would find. The river was almost over its banks. "Well," she told Pook, who appeared behind her like magic, "I guess I picked a poor day to go adventuring. I need to ask Fafleen which side of the river the village is on. If it's across this"—here she gestured to the rushing water —"I'm not even going to try to visit."

Fafleen flew to check possible flooding before she would eat breakfast. "I'll earn my keep today," she told Lealor, "by making sure your exploring is safe." When she returned, she gave her permission for Lealor's expedition, but she added, with her mouth full of steakfruit, "You know, if you weren't so pigheaded, like all humans, I could fly you over anything you might want to see in half the time it's going to take you to trudge to that village."

Lealor winced. Never let it be said that dragons were tactful. In the stories she read, dragons were sneaky, sly, terribly wise, or didn't speak to humans at all. In the real world, however, her experience proved dragons to be forthright to a fault, impatient, sometimes foolish, and far too willing to give unasked-for opinions of the humans they knew. It was no use trying to convince a dragon that many, if not most, people were afraid of them. If Lealor really intended to live an ordinary life while she was here, starting out as the companion of a dragon, when the species was probably legendary in these parts, was not especially bright. So she clenched her teeth and smiled, as if she were not irked enough to give Fafleen a good whack with her broom.

It didn't help much that Pook had both paws over his mouth, for all the world as if he were trying to hide a grin.

"We've made out plans. Let's stick to them," she said. "After all, I don't want to keep you from those books. Just be sure you remember I'm here and check in with me from time to time."

"And that's another thing, Lealor. How long do you want to stay? I'm quite content, but I bet you're worrying about your folks. As the youngest egg—I mean, person—in your family, I bet your mother is pretty distraught."

"And what about yours?" Lealor shot back. "I've seen her lose her equanimity more than once over you and your brother!"

Fafleen giggled. "Yes, she goes off every so often like one of those rockets you humans keep shooting off back on Earth."

Lealor couldn't help returning Fafleen's grin as she pictured a dragon in orbit after a launch. "As for how long I want to stay, I guess several months, at least. It's not going to be easy to get the gate functioning."

"Are you sure you know how?"

"Well, yes, I'm sure I have the knowledge. The trouble is I've never actually done it. I always just watched."

"I understand," the dragon offered in a soothing tone.

"Grown-ups never let us dragonettes do anything difficult either."

Lealor had a momentary desire to argue that she was a grown-up, but she throttled it. She offered two pillowcases filled with food to Fafleen. "Now, you come back when that's gone."

"Oh, I'll be back. Don't worry. And this will be plenty." At Lealor's raised eyebrows, the dragon said airily, "I'll be living off the land, you know."

Lealor shuddered. She knew what that meant. The game in the area was going to be decimated on a regular basis. Berries and wild fruit didn't hold much interest for her friend.

Fafleen held her teddy bear between her sharp teeth and gripped a loaded pillowcase in each set of talons. "I'm off," she hissed through clenched teeth before rising straight up like a lightning bolt in reverse.

Lealor checked the cottage. There was food out for Pook. She didn't bother with water. With the river in full spate, she figured he could get all the fresh water he needed. When she left the clearing, he followed her. She commanded him to return, but he refused. Finally, she stopped and talked to him as if he were a person.

"I don't know how much of this you understand, but I'm going to try to reason with you. I don't want to seem weird—I mean, unusual—to the villagers. If I let you come with me until we meet some people, will you hide then so they don't see me with you?"

Pook nodded vigorously.

"You do understand me, don't you? Fafleen was right."

Pook nodded again.

"Very well. Remember, you promised."

Fafleen had told her the village was close to the river on the near side. Lealor decided to follow the river to find it. They had walked for some time before the bear growled, then faded into the brush beside the overgrown path she had been following.

"Pook, for heaven's sake, what got into you? First you insist on coming along, and now you've vanished."

A low growl told her Pook was still close by, although she couldn't see him. Then she heard it. A faint cry for help.

Lealor listened. "There it is again," she said, knowing Pook was close enough to hear her even if he was in hiding. At least he was keeping his promise, she thought as she hurried toward the sound. When she arrived at the bank of the river, she looked for the source. In the middle of a flooded area, she saw a small tree hung up on a piece of boulder which was visible because it disturbed the rapid flow of water that rushed by it. Clinging to the tree's branches like a wet kitten was a boy of eight or nine.

After studying the situation for a few moments, Lealor acted. She began by taking off her boots. When Pook saw that she was preparing to jump in, he growled.

"Pook, stop worrying. I'm a strong swimmer. It's not very far. That boy looks as if he's about ready to let go, and if he does, maybe I won't be able to save him."

Pook came out of the brush and stood beside her, nudging the magic provender bag which she always carried with her, tied to her belt.

"Go away, silly bear," Lealor said, trying to push Pook from his position between her and the water. "I've got to go and get him." The bear stood, solid as the rock which was holding the tree. He growled and nudged the bag again.

She sighed. Bears could be as stubborn as dragons or men. "Okay, boy. What is it? You must be trying to tell me something."

Pook nodded and put a paw on the bag, nearly knocking Lealor over in the process.

"You want me to use the bag?"

Another nod.

"What do you want me to ask for?" she wondered aloud. Pook scratched a long line in the dirt with his paw.

"A rope?"

Another nod.

She reached in the bag and brought out a long nylon rope, light, but strong. "And now, how are we going to use this?"

Pook nudged his head into the loops that the rope made.

"You mean you're going to swim out to the boy?"

Nod. Nod.

"Pook, you'll scare him to death. You're pretty impressive, you know."

"Help," the boy's voice, perceptibly weaker, called.

Pook growled impatiently.

"All right. All right. I hear you. Wait until I make a slip knot in this end of the rope." Her fingers worked busily as she talked. "Now I'll keep hold of this end. Are you sure you can get the loop over his body? Not his head, mind you. We don't want the poor child strangled before I can reel him to shore."

"Don't be afraid," she called to the boy, who watched with wide eyes. "I'm sending the bear out with a rope. Put it around you and I'll haul you to shore. Can you do that?"

The boy stared. He was petrified.

A loud crack came from the water. The tree had broken. Only the small net of branches to which the boy clung was upstream of the boulder. Pook sized up the problem instantly, and ran, carrying the looped rope around his neck. It was not easy for the bear to swim to the boy. He had to dodge floating bits and pieces of fallen trees and other debris without catching the rope in them. Swimming against the current tired Pook, but he had to come to the boulder from downstream so he could reach the child. When he finally got to the boy, he had trouble getting him to help place the rope around his body. He nudged and woofed encouragingly until the boy understood. The tired bear draped his body over the top of the boulder, and rested while he watched Lealor pull the boy to shore like some overgrown catfish. The child was too weak to scramble up the bank and Lealor had to pull him to safety herself as the bear watched. The remainder of the tree washed loose with a crack, and floated by, narrowly missing the bear, who was almost scraped from the rock.

"Come on, Pook," Lealor called. "Everything is all right at this end."

The bear, still recovering from the wound in his paw and the strenuous swim he had made to reach the child, had weakened considerably. He woofed with the effort it took to shove himself off the rock. He paddled as little as possible, trying to angle himself so the current would carry him to shore. He would have made it without trouble except for the huge log which bobbed loose from a pile where it had been snagged and rushed past, almost on top of him. The surge of water swamped him, dragging him under. His soaked coat weighed him down. He clawed his way to the surface. Only his will to survive kept his legs pumping. That and Lealor's frantic cries.

"Pook! Keep swimming! Come on, Pook!"

The bear was at the end of his strength. He made one final effort, and felt his hind paws touch bottom. Then his head drooped and everything went black.

"Oh, Pookie. You've got to be all right," Lealor said as she and the boy dragged the bear farther onshore. "Come on, wake up. Just wake up enough to help us get you all the way out of the water." She begged, and she tugged, and she pulled. The bear managed a few weak steps before collapsing on the grass.

"I'm pretty tired," the boy told Lealor. "I never rescued a bear before this," he explained.

"Oh, yes. What can I have been thinking of?" Lealor said. "We'll have to stay here for a while until my bear recovers. Why don't you just curl up here in the sun and take a little nap. I'll wake you when we're ready to go."

"I'm not going home," the boy said.

Lealor looked at him curiously. "We'll have time to talk about that later. You just sleep for now." She helped him find a comfortable position on the grass and waved a minor sleep spell over him to assure that he would rest. She could think of no way that did not entail magic to get them both to the cottage. And she had sworn off magic, so it was just as well, she thought. She was unaware that she had used magic to invoke the sleep spell.

She went over to the recumbent bear and curled up beside him. His fur was drying rapidly in the warm sun. He looked at her tiredly by raising one eyelid.

"Oh, Pook, you were a very brave bear. I'm so proud of you," Lealor told him, kissing him on the nose. Both his eyes flew open. "No, bear-of-mine," she told him, "I can't turn you into a handsome prince with a kiss. Go to sleep." And she patted him gently on the shoulder before snuggling close to him.

Some time later, she woke. The sun's position told her it was early afternoon. "All right, sleepyheads," she called gently, "it's time to wake up."

Pook groaned and raised his head. His exhaustion showed in the way he pulled himself to his paws. The boy, pale beneath his tan, was not in much better shape. Lealor felt the strain of all that pulling and tugging herself. She forced a smile before speaking. "Come on, you two. It isn't very far to the cottage. Then I can give you something to make a new bear and boy out of you."

"What cottage?" the boy asked, too young to consider politeness when he wanted the answer to a question.

"The old place in the woods over there," Lealor gestured, "that I've fixed up to live in."

"The old witch's place?" The boy's eyes were round and seemed as big as a dragon's in his tired face.

"I wouldn't know about that," Lealor told him. "There was no witch inside when I got there. It was just an abandoned place that no one wanted, so I moved in."

"Oh," the boy said, before moving on to his next question. "Are you a witch?"

Lealor didn't want to lie. Many people would call the magic

she knew witch's magic, so she evaded the question with one of her own. "Do I look old enough to be a witch?"

The boy still didn't look satisfied, so she continued, putting her hand to her nose. "And is my nose hooked with a wart on it?" She rubbed her nose with the tip of her finger. "I don't think so."

The boy laughed as Lealor had meant him to. He changed the subject with his next question. "Is that your bear?"

"Not exactly. He hurt his paw and I helped him get better. He's kind of adopted me. He's pretty protective."

"Oh." The boy thought about it for a moment then said, "Like a dog?"

"Yes, a little like that."

Pook growled, and the boy jumped.

"But a whole lot better," Lealor reassured them both. "He's an ever-so-nice bear who wouldn't hurt anyone who wasn't trying to hurt me."

"Did you train him to be a rescue bear?" was the boy's next question.

"No. He's just very smart." Lealor felt surprised as she realized how intelligently the animal had handled the boy's rescue and return to shore. Pook's own return to the bank showed he understood river currents and was able to plan and make use of them. Fafleen had certainly been correct in her assessment of the bear's brain power.

"Oh," the boy said again, frowning with thought.

It amused Lealor to see how he stopped to assimilate new information, then asked another question. Someday this boy would be rather wise himself. Realizing another query was forming in his mind, she asked one of her own first.

"I'm called Lealor and the bear's name is Pook. What's your name?"

For an answer, she received another question. "You don't know my parents, do you?"

"I don't believe so," Lealor answered. "I'm new around here."

The boy smiled. "That's good. I wouldn't want you to start thinking of taking me home 'cause I'm never goin' home."

Now it was Lealor's turn to say, "Oh." The boy looked like he was ready to run away. "Let's talk about that after we've had a little time to rest and get cleaned up." She gestured to her muddy clothes and boots. The boy and bear were muddy too.

The boy looked undecided about whether to accept her hospitality. Then Pook nodded several times, which made the boy laugh. "All right, Mrs. Lealor."

"I'm not married, boy."

"My name's Aldon, miss."

"Glad to meet you, Aldon," Lealor told him. "Are you coming with us?" she asked him as she turned and started back the way she had come.

"I guess I could come for a little while. I never met a real live bear before," he said. "And he won't eat me?" he asked.

"Not even a small nibble," Lealor promised, trusting that an intelligent bear would know little boys were not on the menu.

"Good," the boy said, the matter settled in his mind. He walked slowly up to Pook, unable to resist touching the bear, now that he knew it was safe.

Lealor watched, ready to act if the bear didn't like the touching, but Pook gently rubbed his head against the boy, which delighted him.

"Good bear," he said.

"Better call him by his name," Lealor told him. "You wouldn't like it if people just called you 'boy,' would you?"

"Guess not," Aldon said.

Lealor led the way back to the cottage, followed by Pook and Aldon, who had draped his arm around the bear's neck. Signs pointed to a friendship, Lealor thought when she glanced behind her to check on her companions. Aldon was a lot like she had been at his age, loving animals so much, he took them on trust. And as they had with Lealor, animals usually accepted his good will and would not hurt him.

She planned what she was going to say to Aldon to find out why he was running away from home. So much for her idea of seeming normal, she thought to herself. Aldon thought of her as a kind of bear tamer. All she needed now was for Fafleen to fly in with some kind of news. Or perhaps Berdu would pop in, literally, on her and her guest. No sense fretting over calamity until it happened, she told herself, opening the cottage door and waiting for Aldon and Pook to enter.

Chapter Seven

IT took eight buckets of water from the well to sluice Pook down. Aldon needed a bucket and Lealor used one on herself. When she pulled the tenth, and final, bucket up, she flexed her shoulders which felt as if they were asking for a divorce from her body. "Thank the Bright Ones that's over," she muttered.

In the cottage, Pook and Aldon were finishing off the last of the steakfruit from the bowl on the table. Lealor stood at the door, watching. Aldon would offer a fruit to Pook and then take one for himself. The boy left a row of stems neatly placed on the edge of the table.

"This fruit is really good. I've never had any before this," Aldon told her, wiping his mouth on the sleeve of a shirt Lealor had given him. It hung down enough to decently cover him.

She handed him his pants which a little sun magic had dried super fast. She didn't seem to be able to do without some magic, but she was trying to break her habit of using spells without noticing. Myst stayed invisible as Lealor had requested earlier so the dragon bracelet's look of disgust each time her wearer broke her vow to do without magic stayed her secret.

"Do you have any idea how far it is to the village upstream?" Lealor asked.

"It's only a candlemark or so," Aldon answered, having no idea that his questioner didn't know how long a candlemark might be.

The boy's curious eyes were taking note of everything in the cottage. Lealor didn't know if anything there might lead him to find out too much about her. She didn't want him to stay too long, in case Fafleen returned unexpectedly.

Lealor wanted to ask why he had run away from home, but she thought the question might disturb Aldon. So she asked instead, "Could you guide me to the village?"

"Why do you want to go there?" His voice showed he didn't think much of her choice of places to visit.

She knew better than to tell the boy she was looking for someone to help her, so she gave him an answer she hoped he would accept. "Well, for one thing, those people are my neighbors."

"Nothing ever happens there. It's just feed the chickens, help milk the cow, bring in firewood, day after day. I hate getting firewood worst of all."

From his tones, Lealor could hear the boy's unconscious imitation of his taskmaster.

"And you don't like cows, chickens, and warm fires?" she asked with a smile.

His look was answer enough, but his next words confirmed his opinion.

"'How can anyone have adventures in a place like Riverville?"

"Oh," Lealor said, understanding instantly. Her brothers still teased her about wanting to ride her tricycle to Hawaii when she was a four-year-old runaway. "Then it's pretty boring there, I guess."

"Nothing special ever happens. The most exciting thing is when my big sister comes home for the harvest festival."

"Well, if it's so dull in Riverville, I suppose it would be safe for me to visit, if, that is, I can find it."

"Oh, you'll be able to find it, all right."

"And you wouldn't want to be my guide?"

"I'd like to help, but if I go home, they'll make me stay."

Lealor gave no sign that he had just told her where he belonged. Instead she said, "Well, if it's so ordinary, anyone who brought a stranger to town would be a hero, wouldn't he?"

Aldon looked surprised, but after a moment's reflection, he said, "Yes. And maybe I could take you there."

"That's good. I was a little worried about finding it alone."

"Will your bear go with you?"

"Not this time. I don't expect I'll have any more adventures today. I'd just like to meet my neighbors and perhaps trade for some eggs."

"My mother has the freshest eggs in town. Our hens are the best layers of all. Everyone says so."

"Then do you suppose she'd trade some eggs for these berries that I picked?" Lealor uncovered two small tin pails filled with glistening berries.

"They look delicious," Aldon said.

"Would you like some?" Lealor asked, marveling at his capacity for food. He must have eaten seven or eight steak-fruits before she came in.

"Maybe just a few." He started eating the handful Lealor gave him. "I was awfully hungry."

"You left before breakfast?"

Aldon finished the last of the berries and wiped his hands on his newly cleaned pants. Lealor did not envy his mother the task of keeping him clean.

"I left while it was still dark."

"My goodness, that was brave of you."

"Not really. I often go out when the birds wake me up. My uncle is a hunter and he says no good comes of staying in bed until the sun rises."

Lealor hid a shudder; she could hear his redoubtable uncle saying the words. One of her greatest pleasures when she was on Earth was staying in bed after her alarm rang. "Do you want to be a hunter when you grow up? Is that why you get up with the birds?"

"Usually," he admitted, "I like to stay in bed until I have to do chores. If you're setting out on a day's adventure, you need to get an early start."

Again, his unconscious mimicry spoke volumes for his absent uncle. Lealor felt she would know him if she saw him. "I think we'd better start, don't you?" she asked, handing Aldon one of the buckets and taking the other herself.

Pook waddled over to the door, obviously planning to come with them.

"No, Pook. Not this time. You stay here and rest. I don't want you sick again. Remember how sore your foot was? You stay," she said firmly, hoping her stern voice would convince him she could manage without her self-appointed guardian.

For a moment, the bear looked as if he would defy her. He took a step forward and winced. His paw hurt.

"See?" Lealor said, resting her hand on his head. "Dear Pook, stay here and wait for me." She gave him the smile she reserved for her leprechaun friend, Rory. It never failed her.

In answer, Pook limped over to the fireplace and stretched out to make a living bear rug.

"He's really a big bear," Aldon said admiringly. "I bet my uncle—"

"You better warn your uncle that nobody is going to harm my bear," Lealor said, fiercely protective.

"Oh, no. Of course not. He wouldn't hurt a pet bear," Aldon assured her.

"I should hope not!" As she stamped out the door, Lealor's back showed her opinion of any hunter who would dare try.

Pook's eyes shone with an inner light. He absentmindedly rubbed his nose with one paw, looking very human as he did so. Then he stretched out in front of the banked fire and dozed off.

The passage of Lealor, Aldon, and Pook had cleared the old trail. At one time, many feet must have come this way, Lealor thought. In a few short minutes, she and Aldon passed the spot where she'd hauled him to the shore. She patted her magic bag, remembering the stout rope. Good old grandma, she thought, wondering how she would have managed without it.

Aldon went ahead of her from that point on. "If I'm your guide, I'd better go first," he told her. She could tell from his walk that he took his job seriously. In fact, she could almost see the hunter-uncle who probably taught him to travel through the woods.

She followed silently, wondering what kind of people lived in Riverville. She knew she could have asked Aldon questions and gotten some valuable insights on the villagers, but somehow it seemed sneaky, so she didn't.

She thought she caught a glimpse of Berdu in the underbrush beside the trail, but when she peered more closely, there was nothing. "What an imagination I've got," she muttered to herself.

"What did you say?" Aldon asked.

"Nothing important," Lealor told him. "How much farther is it?" Her legs were almost as tired as her arms. She was definitely out of shape for long forest walks following a river rescue. By the time she got home that night, she knew she'd be asking the magic bag for some liniment.

"It's just around that bend up ahead," Aldon pointed.

In a few more moments, they rounded the bend. Nestled in the curve of the river like a contented tabby, lay the village. Its peacefulness made it very attractive to Lealor, who missed civilization more than she realized.

Aldon led her straight to his home, one of the cottages on the outskirts of the little town. He opened the gate and let Lealor enter first.

A motherly figure bustled out the door and clasped a wriggling Aldon tightly to her. "Aldon Smithson, where have you been all day? We've looked everywhere for you. Your uncle said if you didn't turn up for supper, he'd start looking downriver for you in his boat, flood or no flood."

"Oh, mother," Aldon said, pulling himself loose from her embrace with difficulty.

Then Lealor's presence finally registered with Aldon's mother. "My bright stars," she said, "Aldon, you've brought us a visitor."

"I'm very pleased to meet you—all," Lealor said, looking at the two men and little girl who came out to see what was happening.

At this point, Aldon felt he was well on the way to being forgotten, so he introduced the members of his family. "My Uncle Gren, my father, my mother, and Jessa," he said, pointing them out for his guest.

The introductions really weren't necessary, except for politeness' sake. Dressed in green, Uncle Gren the hunter looked as if he were one of Robin Hood's merry men. Aldon looked exactly like his father, except his father was more muscular and clad in a leather apron such as all blacksmiths wear. Dame Smith reminded Lealor of the pictures of the Old Woman Who Lived in a Shoe in her nursery rhyme book. "And who might this be?" the blacksmith asked with a smile.

"This is Lealor—" Aldon paused at a look from his mother. "Miss Lealor," he corrected himself. "She lives downstream in the old witch's cottage and she and her bear pulled me out of the river and—''

''Hold on, youngster,'' his uncle said, in a voice Lealor recognized from Aldon's recital of his maxims. ''Start your tale at the beginning—and tell it slowly,'' he cautioned.

So Aldon told how he met Lealor. He didn't realize how dangerous his situation had been. The looks on the faces of the adults who heard him showed they appreciated the danger he had been in. His mother gave him another hug when he finished and his father clapped him on the shoulder. From the way Aldon's eyes lighted up, this was a rare accolade. His uncle tousled his hair. The brief ritual of touching him reassured his family that he was alive and well.

''What are we all doing out here?'' Dame Smith said, obviously flustered by the unexpected company. ''Come in, come in,'' she said, gesturing vigorously toward the door. ''Surely you're tired after your long walk.'' She led the way inside.

This cottage was larger than Lealor's. It had an upstairs loft and a side door led to a blacksmith's work area and forge. The members of the Smith family had earned their name. No wonder Aldon hated getting firewood worst of all. In busy seasons, filling the immense woodboxes would be almost a full-time task.

Dame Smith seated Lealor at the long table that dominated the room. ''Now, it's not long until supper, so I won't spoil your appetites. A cool drink and a bite of cookie wouldn't hurt a flying buzzer,'' she said as she filled a mug from a stoneware jar wrapped in wet cloth that stood on the windowsill. The cool fruity drink tasted delicious to Lealor. Everyone had a mug with her, even the little girl, Jessa.

During the conversation that accompanied the cool drinks, the story of the rescue retold by Aldon with graphic gestures and many childish exaggerations, earned Lealor the gratitude of her hosts. Aldon explained that Lealor wanted to trade for some eggs. His mother was adamant that she was giving Lealor a basket of eggs and some of her sweetfruit jam to go with the home-made bread she had baked that morning. Then Lealor insisted she couldn't carry those buckets of berries home and would have to leave them for the children's breakfasts. Uncle Gren, who hadn't taken his eyes off Lealor since he first saw her, said he would walk her home when she was ready to go. Lealor worried about his offer because she didn't want a confrontation with her bear. Pook looked really formidable, and since they thought she was an ordinary person, they wouldn't know Myst and Lealor's own magic was all the protection she would probably need.

Somewhere during these neighborly exchanges, Jessa had a coughing fit. Dame Smith fed her some sweet herb syrup, which didn't seem to do much good. Lealor reached into her magic bag, tied to her belt, and took out several kinds of herbs. She selected two small bunches and told Jessa's mother how to prepare them. "If you give her a spoon of this before she goes to bed, she should have a good night's sleep," Lealor said.

"I'm so glad you're an herbwoman," Dame Smith said. "Our local healer, Fialla, is ill herself. No one in Riverville knows what to do for her. Would it be too much of an imposition if I asked you to stop and see her before you leave today?"

"I can't promise to do much but look. I may not have what I need in my bag," Lealor said. "I'd be glad to try."

As they walked through the village, Dame Smith introduced her to everyone they met. Lealor had enough invitations for dinners to keep her dining out for several weeks. Lealor thanked everyone, but said she needed to settle in before she could start socializing. Everyone understood. They were getting ready for the winter. In another few days, the harvest would be in full swing. Everyone she met invited her to the harvest festival. Dame Smith never intruded on anyone's invitation, but she filled Lealor in on each person they met.

Several of the women who wanted her as a guest had young, marriageable sons. The herbwoman, Fialla, was old, Dame Smith explained. If Lealor married into a Riverville family, her talents would be a blessing to the village.

Dame Smith's information was never malicious, but it was honest. By the time Lealor reached Fialla's cottage, she had a good idea of what the village was really like.

Fialla, however, was a total surprise.

When Lealor entered her cottage, she smelled the herbal scents of all the good plants that were drying in the racks along one wall and in the bundles overhead that hung from the rafters. The whitewashed walls made the interior of the room bright.

In spite of Fialla's age, she was an imposing figure. Her fine, pale hair wisped around her face, which was round and wrinkled as one of the apples from the barrels in the root cellars people dug to store fruits and vegetables throughout the winters. Because she was six feet tall, she bowed her head when she passed under her rafters.

Dame Smith introduced the two women, then pleaded work at home as an excuse to leave. Fialla and Lealor watched her go. When the door closed behind her, the old woman turned to Lealor and smiled. "Welcome to the world of Widdershins. I suppose you're from the gate," she said.

Chapter
Eight

"**Y**OU know about the gate?" Lealor asked in astonishment, admitting by her question that she also knew about the gates.

"Oh, yes, I know about it." Fialla sat in her rocking chair. Lealor relaxed on the bench beside the fire, which burned bright and hot although only a small amount of wood rested on the grate. Minor fire magic, she thought. Fialla is more than a simple village healer.

"I'm glad to know you have not forgotten us," Fialla continued, her gnarled hands grasping the arms of the chair. "It's been a long time since last we had a gatemistress on Widdershins."

"How long?" Lealor asked.

"Seven generations of my family have lived and died since the destruction of the gate," Fialla said with a sigh. "And people in my family have long lifelines," she added as an afterthought.

"What happened?" Lealor did not ask the question from simple curiosity. If she understood what kind of forces distorted the powers of the gate, she might better be able to return it to its original state.

"A new group of priests arose in the temples, almost overnight. Soon they controlled all the big centers of worship. The temples were rebuilt, and the Lady had only a niche in the corner instead of the main altar. The god that they replaced her with is cruel and avaricious, judging from the tithes his priests demand from the people. Under the Lady, gifts given helped the needy and ill. Now, the greedy priests tell the people that the new god demands money and goods. The Lady never needed gold or silver. This god takes his share —some think more than his share—of everything bought and sold. Priests stay in every village of over a hundred people. When so many live in one location, it is their privilege to build an impressive place of worship to honor the god. Then the priests will gladly take over the matter of the tithes for those towns fortunate enough to have one." Fialla rocked sadly for a moment. Lealor, used to dealing with older people, waited patiently, knowing there must be more to the story.

Fialla's eyes twinkled. "Funny, there haven't been over ninety-five people in Riverville for generations."

"Since about the time that the priesthood told the people about that rule, right?" Lealor's grin showed her understanding.

"We couldn't have a temple so near to an abandoned gate, could we?"

"Abandoned?"

"Yes. Over the years, forgotten by the villagers. We thought it was safer so."

"We?" Lealor probed gently.

"Village elders and the Keepers."

Lealor brightened. "Keepers, here? What a relief. I thought I'd be all alone."

"You are . . . almost," Fialla told her with a sigh. "I am the last Keeper trained in the village, but I'm not really a Keeper. Over the years we were so busy hiding the gate to keep it from total destruction like the others on Widdershins that information became forgotten or never taught. By the time my ancestors realized how much, it was too late."

"So the priesthood destroyed everything?"

"Everything they could find."

"They have a lot to answer for," Lealor said, clenching her fists.

"They alone could not have come to power. If the magic users would have banded together, they could have withstood the priests. What weakened the magic wielders was their fighting among themselves. Only the Keepers used magic sparingly, and only they were willing to share what they knew without thought of gain. The priesthood was able to convince the general populace that all magic users were evil."

"I know," Lealor said. "Only a few bad experiences with magic users sets ordinary people against all use of magic."

"The magic users and the folks who didn't use magic fought a tremendous battle west of here in the mountains. The magic users begged the dragon king to join them and fight the priests, but he refused. His great magical powers and those of his subjects would have made a great difference. One legend claims destruction. Another says he was transformed. No one knows for sure what really took place over there." Fialla waved in the direction of the mountains.

"What happened to the dragon king's subjects?"

"They disappeared."

"How sad."

"Not as sad as if they'd stayed," Fialla said, shutting her eyes as if that would close out the grim pictures that formed in her mind.

"What else did the priests do?" Lealor leaned forward in her effort to hear.

"They began persecuting the weren."

"The weren?" Lealor wasn't sure what weren were, but she remembered Berdu's mentioning them.

"A race of shape-shifters. Most weren't really magic users. The werefolk simply had the ability to change their shape. The priest convinced the people to kill any they could catch. They preached that all magic was evil. And people believed them. They forgot about what good neighbors the weren had been and all the times magic users had helped, and not harmed them." Fialla shook her head. "For a while, many weren died, then suddenly—almost overnight, according to my granny—no one saw any more. They didn't come in to the villages to trade, and they abandoned their homes in the forest. I don't see how they all died, but whether they took wing and flew away like the dragons, I couldn't say." Fialla, who had stopped rocking as she told her tale, began rocking again.

While the old woman talked, Lealor had listened too intently to notice how tired she was. The healer was so pale that it was hard to see when she became even more ashen. Finally Lealor noticed.

"I'm sorry," she apologized. "I didn't mean to tire you when you're ill."

"Nonsense. If you're here to mend the gate, most people will welcome you with open arms. Folklore remembers the gates and their Keepers as good and the times as a golden age. It's only the priesthood that want all new things stamped out. My mother said we made almost no progress in any field after the gates were closed. The one here remained protected somehow. All it will take is several powerful magic users to remove the spells laid upon it, and it should work."

"The magic users didn't bespell the gate, did they?"

Fialla shook her head.

"Then who did?"

"The priesthood. They couldn't make the gates work for them and in their anger, they did their best to destroy them, telling the people they were evil."

"Hold on a moment. The priesthood? I thought they were against magic."

"Oh, they are. Except for themselves that is."

"You mean they forbid others to use the power and then use it themselves?"

"I'm afraid so. By the way, let me warn you. Don't ever do anything that could be construed as magic use. It will earn you punishment as a witch."

Lealor laughed. "No one is afraid of magic anymore. Arcane lore is part of almost all of the gate worlds where science hasn't taken hold."

"Heed me, child. It will not be a laughing matter if the priesthood gets you in its clutches."

"What about you?" Lealor gestured to the fire, which burned merrily in the fireplace without any added wood.

"Minor fire magic requires almost no power. It is safe. Even I might be in danger if anyone noticed my abilities. So I'm very careful what I do. I use herbs in my healing. Fialla the old herbwoman, the healer, is how I'm known by the villagers. It would be a very different thing to be Fialla the witchwoman."

"Then magic is all right if no one knows you're using it?"

"To a degree, if a great many small spells take place in any one area, they leave a trace that a witch-finder priest might notice. It's best to leave magic alone unless great need drives you, child."

"All right. I'll be careful," Lealor promised. "Can I do anything for you? The villagers seem worried."

"Most of my problem is old age. There is no cure for that. I fear I've left it too long to choose a successor."

"Did you have no child to follow after you?"

"My husband and daughter died of a plague years ago."

"Oh, I'm sorry," Lealor said. "I didn't mean to remind you of sad things."

"After all these years, I feel resigned. I have looked for years for someone with the talent to become a healer. I think

I can train the Smith's little Jessa. All I can do is hold on until she is old enough to learn. Already I have taught her some of the simpler herbs. She can identify them and knows what they cure, but she is too young to actually help any patients. And then,'' Fialla smiled, ''there are the . . . other . . . things a healer must know.'' Her head nodded toward the fire. ''Some knowledge is too dangerous for a little one to have.''

''You're in pain, aren't you?'' Lealor said gently, noticing how slowly and stiffly Fialla moved. ''Back at my cottage, I think I may have something that will help you—''

A discreet knock on the door interrupted her.

''Come in,'' Fialla called.

''I came to get Lealor for supper,'' Aldon said. He placed a covered basket on the table. ''Mother sent your supper and some fresh bread and sweetfruit jam.'' Wide-eyed, he looked around the room. Usually his mother brought food to Fialla herself, but with unexpected company, his mother needed every minute to prepare what his father called a respectable feast on short notice. ''Can Lealor come now?'' he asked.

''Yes, Aldon, she may come,'' Fialla said as she rose from the rocker.

''I'll try to get back here tomorrow,'' Lealor told the healer.

''Thank you. Thank you both,'' Fialla said, uncovering the heavy basket Dame Smith had sent. ''Please tell your mother I am much in her debt. I shall not forget her kindness.''

''I will,'' Aldon promised as he and Lealor went out the door.

The dinner was superb. Although Lealor did not want to admit it, the closeness of the family reminded her of her own. She stifled a twinge of homesickness as she walked through the woods with her guide.

''Is something the matter?'' Gren asked, stopping to bend his head to look into her eyes.

Lealor originally had no intentions of allowing anyone to walk her home, but considering the eggs, bread, sweetfruit jam, and leftovers Aldon's mother had hospitably heaped on her guest, Lealor had little choice but to accept the offer of Aldon's uncle. So she smiled up at him and wondered what was wrong with her. Here she was with a personable young man who obviously liked her, and she couldn't manage a single romantic ripple. Even the huge moon shining down on them from a sky filled with stars didn't make a dent.

"No, nothing," Lealor answered. "I was thinking that this evening is cool." Before Gren could take that as an invitation to offer his cloak or put his arm around her, she hurried on to another topic. "How much longer will it be until winter?"

"Ah, that's a good question to distract my attention." Gren chuckled softly.

"I really would like to know the answer."

"We might have as much as a month before the first snow. However, if things go as usual, we could have it any time. The weather in these parts is notoriously sneaky. One day will be bright with warmth in the sunny air and cool breezes in the shade. The next morning you can awake to several feet of snow piled in front of your door."

"And once we have a snowfall, how long will it last?"

"We're lucky there. It will probably stay on the ground for about three months, then one morning you'll awake and find icicles dripping on everything. Within a few weeks, spring will be here again."

"That's unusual. Most of the time where I come from, winter is long and drawn out. It snows and thaws, then snows and thaws so you can never tell exactly when spring arrives. Sometimes the weather fools the plants too. Then the little green shoots get their noses nipped when it freezes again."

"Some say it used to be like that here in the old days, but that some wizard named Keeper put a spell on the whole area and changed the weather forever."

"A wizard named Keeper?" Lealor wondered if Gren hated magic users.

"Wizards as a rule are a bad lot. Legends say that Keeper lived in the area where your cottage is."

Lealor laughed. "Then I guess it's safe for me. Even if Keeper returned, he'd probably not harm me."

"Seeing as it's been hundreds of years since anybody's heard from him, that big fight the magic users had with the priesthood probably destroyed him and the priesthood's armies over in the mountains."

"You hunt over a wide area, don't you? Have you ever found anything magical over there?"

"Sometimes I've had a wan chancy feeling while I've been hunting, as if something or someone is watching me, but I've never found anything magical. I wouldn't know what to do with it if I had," he said gruffly, "and you had better not be looking for any magical places or things either. You could stir up more trouble than any magic you found would be worth. We've been fortunate in Riverville so far."

Lealor looked at him with a question in her eyes.

"I mean, we've not got a temple there. We're situated near the river and could easily become a larger place if we wanted to. Anybody who wants to live in a bustling, thriving town may move to one. The elders of Riverville aren't foolish enough to want the priesthood setting up shop among us."

"What about the taxes—I mean tithes?"

"Oh, the elders send them to the priests every year. And if the potatoes are small, and the fruit a little wormy, well, what else can you expect of a poor village like Riverville? Then too, we don't always count very well. What civilized priest wants to make a two- or three-day journey over notoriously bad roads, to see how to help the poor villagers?" He grinned at his companion. "Sad, isn't it?"

"Oh, very," Lealor managed through her laughter. "You poor, poor people."

"Well, we're not nearly so poor as we'd be if we had a temple saddled on our backs, and you may take my word for that." Gren's voice turned grim. "I'm the tax deliverer for the village. I have to go in to the duke's castle to hand it over. The priest always gives me the shivers if he crosses my path. You may be sure I plan my visit so I'm never there when there's an obligatory service. I'm in and out of there quicker than a furkin taking a piece of cheese out of a trap."

"In your oldest hunting suit, I presume?"

"Threadbare," he said solemnly.

"It's not far now," Lealor told him, hoping to keep the conversation going.

"How do you know?" Gren marveled at her woodcraft. Most village girls knew little, and cared less, for the forest. Lealor had said she was certain she could find her way home alone, and she had proved it several times during their walk.

"The berry bushes. They ring the cottage. They're especially thick right behind it. There are no others between it and Riverville. I noticed today when I followed Aldon. I didn't know then I'd have a guide home."

"Sensible," Gren approved. He wondered how she would react to a crisis. Probably like most women and girls he knew, she'd panic.

"Here we are," Lealor announced triumphantly as she walked into the clearing before the cottage. In her joy to be home, she swung around without watching her step, tripped, and would have fallen if not for Gren's strong handclasp. She looked up at him, silvered by moonlight for a second before the moon went behind a cloud. She felt, more than saw, the huge ursine shape that reared up from the brush beside the path.

Gren pulled her behind him as he turned to face the roaring bear that towered over them both. "Lady bless," he murmured while struggling to pull his axe from its sheath at his waist.

The cloud obligingly scuttled away from the face of the

moon, giving Lealor and her escort their first good look at the angry bear.

"Is this your pet?" Gren asked quietly, never taking his eyes from the monster, who must have been foraging for berries before they disturbed it.

"I'm afraid that's not Pook," Lealor told him, trying to sound much braver than she felt at the moment.

Chapter Nine

G REN swallowed, pushing Lealor firmly behind him. "When I raise my axe to strike, I want you to run for the cottage and shut the door."

"And stay there, too, I suppose," said Lealor.

"Get ready," Gren said.

"No." Lealor's reply was soft, but determined. "I'm not budging. Give me a moment to see if I can soothe the bear."

"Woman, are you moon-daft? Look at the size of that thing."

"I've got a way with animals. Let me at least try," Lealor said. She could feel the bear hesitating. She was sure she could control it if she had a chance.

"I'll count to ten. If you haven't convinced it to go by then, I'll attack . . . and you run! Agreed?"

"That's not much time—" Lealor began.

"Then I'll attack now." Gren raised his axe.

"All right, all right. Put down your axe."

"Moon-daft," Gren murmured. "Crazy as a necklace bird . . ." He slowly lowered his weapon.

Lealor paid no attention to him. Every ounce of her concentration centered on the bear. She projected friendliness, warmth, harmlessness. The bear did not respond. "Seven, eight," she heard Gren say.

The two humans were so intent on the bear, they missed seeing Pook as he entered the clearing. One look told him the situation. He heard the man say, "Nine." Why was the man counting instead of protecting Lealor? Pook charged.

The wild bear turned her head toward Pook as he reared to his full height between Lealor and her. Pook's fangs gleamed silver in the moonlight. He showed no signs of giving her any consideration because she was female. Pook knew the she-bear recognized that this was his territory, and he had no intention of sharing. She dropped to all fours, turned, and exited the clearing.

"Ten," Gren said weakly. He counted again, Pook, the she-bear, and her mate. Surely, there couldn't be three bears this gigantic in the same area. How had he missed seeing traces of their presence? Perhaps it was time to settle down in Riverville. Lealor would make a fine wife, he decided.

"This is Pook," Lealor told her human defender as she walked between Pook's paws and received a gentle bearhug from him before he backed off and dropped to the ground.

The astounded Gren managed to say, "Glad to meet you, Pook," before he realized he was talking to a half-tamed bear as if it were human.

Pook grunted. Then he turned and walked into the cottage.

"I can't say I'm sorry that's over," Lealor told Gren with a smile.

"Are you all right, lass?" Gren hoped the moonlight hid his pea-green complexion from his companion.

"Of course. I still think if I'd had more time I could have

handled that bear. I bet in spring there will be a cub or two around here.'' She gave Gren a stern look. ''Any bears around here are off-limits.''

''Naturally, if I see any dragons shall I put them on my don't-shoot list?''

''Well, now that you mention it, yes.''

''Lass, you're moon-daft for certain. If it weren't for the fact no one's seen dragons in these parts for years, I do believe you'd try to make friends with them.''

''Why not?''

''Why not!'' Gren exploded, throwing his hands in the air in a gesture of surrender. ''To be so beautiful and not have the sense of a child,'' he said conversationally to the moon, which had returned to unclouded brightness.

''Piffle! Such a fuss over nothing.'' Lealor looked exactly like her grandmother as she repeated one of her favorite sayings.

''Lass, you may do fine here through the winter—although I'm coming to check on you from time to time—but in spring, you'd best plan to come to my sister's in the village.''

''And why, pray tell?'' Lealor stood, arms akimbo, the perfect picture of feminine obduracy.

''The she-bear and her cubs-to-come, for one. And that bear, Pook,'' Gren said, gesturing theatrically toward the cottage door where an interested Pook stood watching.

''Oh, come in and stop arguing, for Lady's sake.'' Lealor pushed her way past Pook.

Gren, however, was unable to enter the cottage because of the bear's bulk. ''How?'' Gren asked.

''Pook, move over,'' Lealor commanded.

Pook looked at her and stood his ground.

''Pook, did you hear me?''

''He hears you all right. He's just not about to move to let me in. Make a pet of a bear and he gets notions,'' Gren said, trying to push past Pook to no avail. Pook faced the hunter and yawned, showing his sharp teeth and huge fangs.

"Impressive, at that," Gren murmured, placing the basket on the ground and stepping back.

Then Lealor tried to get through the door. Pook wouldn't move for her, either. In fact, he seemed to fill the doorway completely. "Pook," Lealor warned.

The bear stood in the doorway like a stone statue, and as easy to dislodge as one, too.

"He seems quite happy with me out and you in," Gren remarked with a smile. The situation was not without its humorous side and Gren had a well-developed sense of the ridiculous.

"Oh, drat," Lealor finally said. "Look, Gren, I'm tired. It's been a long day. And you still have to walk home. I'll see you tomorrow if you're in the village. I plan to bring some things to Fialla."

"Very well," said a somewhat amused Gren, noticing how pretty Lealor looked when she was provoked. "I'll go." Then he turned to the bear. "You win—this time," he told the bear before he left.

So Lealor stood in the doorway and returned Gren's wave as he walked from the clearing to return to Riverville. As soon as he was out of sight in the moon-dappled shadows, she turned her attention to Pook, who ambled over to the fireplace and sprawled in front of it, innocence shining from every hair in his fine pelt. "You bad bear! Shame on you! What if Gren had insisted I return to Riverville with him because you wouldn't obey me?"

Pook growled.

"And how would you have stopped him?"

Pook yawned, showing his teeth and fangs.

"You're as stubborn as any man I've ever met—and that's no compliment," Lealor told him as she felt his amusement. She took off her boots, and bent to rub her sore feet. "I've walked a million miles today. I'm certainly tired enough. Tomorrow, I'll get some things ready for Fialla. I recognize quite a few of the plants here. It's harvest time for herbs. I'll try to select mine and some to replenish her stores as well." Lealor sat on the edge of her bed. "I'll just stretch out for a minute and rest," she said as she pulled the covers to the foot of the bed. "How good this feels!" Within minutes she was fast asleep.

Pook rose and padded over to Lealor. He nudged her with his nose. A ladylike snore was his answer. He moved to the foot of the bed and awkwardly took the covers in his mouth. He managed to cover her before he returned to his place before the fire.

The next morning Lealor ignored her aches and pains. She breakfasted with Pook, packed some interesting small jars and boxes into a basket, and set off for Riverville. Several times she stopped along the trail to gather herbs she recognized. By the time she reached Fialla's, she had a load of things to share.

"Come in, come in," Fialla said. "I was expecting you."

"Good morning," Lealor greeted the healer. "I've gathered a few of the herbs I need and some extras for you. I'm surprised at how many different kinds flourish so near the path."

"I've limited my gathering to the sources nearest the village," Fialla explained. "Don't forget that the Keepers were herbalists. A strong stand of any herb usually spreads if it's not harvested into extinction. Most people won't go downstream on this side because of the legends. Think it's haunted, they do."

Lealor joined Fialla in her chuckle. "Some of the spots felt warded against animals."

"You could well be right, child. A sun ward is almost invisible, but will last forever—or until some magic user deliberately destroys it. The last of the magic folk had better things to do with their time before they disappeared, and I made use of those herbs for years without any trouble." Fialla had been bundling the herbs Lealor divided as she spoke. She placed hers in baskets which hung from pegs on the side walls of her cottage.

Lealor replaced her bundles carefully in her basket. "I'll dry these when I get home." She reached into a corner of her basket and brought out a salve. "If you try this, it will help you."

Fialla took it and sniffed it inquiringly. "What herbs go into this?" she asked.

"Some that don't grow here. At least I haven't seen them yet," Lealor told her. "Part of the ingredients are special and don't exist here, so I've put a small duplicating spell on the box."

"Thank you. The spell is very well done—for an herb-woman."

The two healers smiled at one another in the understanding that two masters of a craft share.

A knock on the door announced Aldon's arrival. "Those old leaves cured Jessa's cough overnight," he said. "Now some people would like you to look at them . . ." He glanced at Fialla. "Mother says if Lealor can help those folks, you can husband your strength. Nobody there has anything seriously wrong with them."

Lealor spent the rest of the morning dosing the villagers and their animals. She felt much more secure with the animals than the people, but her veterinary training helped her handle all her patients. The main difference between the two kinds was that animals couldn't tell her what was wrong. Her special abilities came in handy. She could sense the pain her patients felt and that made a true diagnosis possible. She sighed with relief when the last woman left with cream for her cow's udder. She had given the woman a generous container full, sure that some of it would find its way to the woman's hands when she used it and saw how well it worked.

Over the next few weeks she made a practice of going to Riverville every two or three days. She really didn't want patients trouping out to the cottage if she could avoid it. For one thing, she was never quite sure what Pook might do since his unsociable behavior the night Gren walked her home. Second, it was just as well if no one saw Fafleen on her infrequent visits to pick up more steakfruit and pastries. Her visits dwindled in proportion to the hundreds of books she was finding secreted in the cave.

The weather continued to be perfect with bright, crisp days of cloudless skies which turned to cool nights, star-spangled as a rule. No matter how long Lealor studied the skies, she was unable to recognize a single constellation. After the first few weeks, she quit trying. At night she felt most lonely. She was glad when Berdu dropped in. Steakfruit remained his favorite refreshment, but he developed a real fondness for root beer. Lealor hoped her sparse use of the magic provender bag wouldn't cause trouble later. She had taken Fialla's warning very seriously after she had given it some thought.

The day of the harvest festival dawned, bright as a newly minted Realmcoin. Lealor felt ready for some fun. She had spent hours studying the few magic books she had brought with her. She finally decided what to do to reestablish the gate. Unfortunately, she needed at least three others able to wield the powers to effect a repair. The Keepers who disconnected the gate had done so thoroughly. The priests had not damaged any truly important part of the gate because they did not understand how it actually worked. Only someone Keeper-trained would be able to handle the energies necessary to make the gate function again. Today at the harvest festival she planned to ask Fialla how to find others qualified to help her restore the gate. No matter what the answer was, however, she planned to have a good time.

"Lealor!" Gren called out as he entered the clearing in front of the cottage.

It was only the second time he had visited. Pook took an extremely dim view of Lealor's having the hunter around. She decided that perhaps the bear sensed Gren was a hunter. That would account for his animosity toward him.

"Just wait there, Gren. I'll be right out." She remembered the past few weeks as she poured a generous helping of steakfruit into a bowl and left it on the table. Pook often foraged on his own, but Berdu would miss the fruit if he stopped in. The fact that she was not there would not deter him. Root beer filled the crock she kept cooling in the small stream nearby. He would find it, she was sure. The children also knew the whereabouts of the root beer. Aldon and Jessa came once or twice a week. Their mother would only let them come when Lealor invited them. She would have been appalled to realize the children shamelessly asked to visit.

After Gren tracked the she-bear across the river and into the mountains, there was nothing in the area to fear except Pook himself. Lealor had an excellent reputation among the villagers. If she said Pook was safe, then Dame Smith believed her. The children used the bear as a backrest when they got tired and a pony when they wanted a ride. He listened to Jessa sing songs and Aldon tell stories of what he would do when he grew up. He became, in fact, the perfect sitter for the children who loved him. Gren knew that Pook waited on the path outside the village whenever Lealor was visiting. So long as Lealor had some protection, he kept his distance from the cottage. Gren repeated his call once he reached the door.

"I'm almost ready," Lealor said, pulling a warm shawl off the hook where she kept her outdoor clothes. "Now you do understand I won't be home tonight, don't you, Pook?"

Pook, sprawled in front of the fire like a furry teenager, raised one eye to show he was listening, not bear-napping.

"Lady bless us. Surely you don't expect that stupid bear to understand you."

Pook growled softly, startling Gren.

"Don't be so growlly. Gren didn't really mean it. You're quite the smartest bear I've ever known," Lealor assured Pook with a kiss on the top of his head.

The two humans set out for Riverville, followed at a distance by the bear. Neither Gren nor Lealor said a word about the bear until they were close to the village. Lealor turned and called softly. "Pook, I know you're there. Everything's fine. You go home now."

Gren strained his ears and just managed to hear the bear moving off in the bushes. "You know, that's amazing. I didn't realize he was behind us until you spoke to him. How do you do it?"

"I just know Pook, that's all. He's even more stubborn than most men I know."

Their first stop was the blacksmith's house. Lealor gave each of the children a piece of candy.

"Now don't let that spoil your noon meal," she warned.

"Oh, we won't," Aldon said, turning to his sister for confirmation. She nodded in shy agreement, her mouth being too full of candy for her to answer.

"You spoil them dreadfully, you do," Dame Smith said.

"May we go over to the meadow?" Aldon asked.

"If you promise to take good care of your sister, son."

Aldon grinned, seized Jessa's hand, and pulled her out the door. He didn't want to wait around for someone to find a chore for him to do.

"Gren, can you help me for a moment?" The blacksmith's voice boomed from the forge.

"If you'll excuse me, lassies," Gren said, bowing low before he exited the room.

"That man! He'll be the death of me," Dame Smith said, laughing until the tears came to her eyes. Then she explained to Lealor. "He's the very image of that foppish courtier that took Nelda back to the duke's court last winter when Jessa was so ill. Our Nelda is a favorite of the duke's wife," she told Lealor with pride.

"One of these days Uncle Gren will get himself into trouble with those impersonations. You mark my words, mother."

Lealor turned to look at the pretty girl who just climbed down from the loft.

"This is my other daughter, Nelda. Aldon's probably told you all about her. She works at the castle."

Nelda smiled at Lealor. "Oh, dear. If Aldon has told you about me, you've heard truly dreadful things, I bet."

"Only nice ones about his big sister."

All three women laughed at this, for Nelda was barely five feet tall. Even Dame Smith, whose diminutive size was noticeable, was taller than her daughter.

"Nelda, why don't you take Lealor over to the meadow? There's all sorts of holiday booths set up for the fair."

"If you're sure you don't need anything, mother . . ."

"Why don't you stay and help if you want to?" Turning to the older woman, Lealor said, "I can pitch in too, if you want me."

"No, things are well in hand. You young ones go along and I'll follow later." Dame Smith crossed to the fire and stirred the pot that bubbled there, filling the room with the aroma of one of her justly famous stews.

"Come on, then," Nelda urged, taking Lealor's hand and pulling her through the door as if they were little girls again. "Hurry, before mother changes her mind." Lealor went willingly. Evidently, Aldon had learned the vanish-before-they-find-something-for-you-to-do trick from his older sister. Just as they passed Fialla's door, one of Nelda's friends hailed her.

"Excuse me," Lealor said politely. "I need to see the healer. I'll meet you in the meadow."

Nelda nodded in agreement and waved to her friend. Lealor knocked on Fialla's door.

"Who is it?" Fialla called, immediately following it with "come in," without waiting to see the person she had invited inside.

"It's only me," Lealor answered, belatedly aware that she really hadn't responded to the question asked.

"Lady's blessing on you, Only Me," the healer teased. The medication Lealor gave her had restored much of her mobility. Today she sounded as cheery as the first bird to return in spring.

"I can see you're in what my granny calls 'fine fettle,' " Lealor told her.

"Indeed, I haven't felt so well in months. I'm even planning to hobble over to the meadow to see the fair." The old healer looked over to the corner where her walking stick rested.

"Hurray for you!" Lealor said, and meant it. "I have some good news and some bad news."

"This sounds like one of the jokes the children tell," Fialla said, playing along by asking, "what's the good news?"

"I've found out how to restore the gate."

"Wonderful! And the bad?"

"I'll need three others who can use the power to help me."

"Oh my stars and whiskers," she said, rubbing her soft and hairless chin. "You do have a problem."

"With you and I to make two, we only need two more."

Fialla's face grew serious. "Child, I do not have the power."

"But—but—but, the fire magic and the healing . . ."

"That is not the same as the power to work a gate. Not everyone has it, you know."

"Do you know of anyone else?"

"Give me some time. Perhaps today I'll see someone I can use as a messenger. It's been years since I needed to speak to anyone with that kind of power. Those with magic power have to stay well hidden."

"I know. How long do you think it will take to find someone?"

"I really couldn't say. Perhaps by next summer . . ."

For a moment Lealor felt a pang of homesickness so strong she felt tears well into her eyes. Then she mastered herself. She had wanted adventure, hadn't she? Didn't Grandma Cibby often say to be careful what you asked for because you might get it? And what difference would a few more months make? So she smiled. "Very well. I'll try to be patient. You will let me know how the search is going, won't you?"

"Of course, child. Now run along. I'll be over later."

When Lealor went outside, she found Gren waiting for her. The sunlight sparkled in his short golden beard. He looked exactly like one of Robin Hood's men to Lealor.

"Are you ready to go, lass?" Gren asked, offering her his arm.

"I am, kind sir," Lealor said. She curtsied and let him escort her to the meadow.

They walked past the stalls where animals were for sale. "No bears here for you to rescue." Gren made a pretense of being vastly relieved.

"Oh, you!" Lealor made a face at her companion as if she were Jessa's age.

They stopped before a battered tent. Lealor held her breath. She scented evil magic within. That was impossible on Widdershins. Myst didn't tighten on her arm. That was strange. Lealor looked at her bare wrist where the dragon talisman curled, but she saw nothing. Well, she'd told Myst to keep out of things, more or less, and she was getting what she wanted.

Gren strolled on for a step or two and then turned back to Lealor. "Surely you don't want to have your fortune told by that charlatan," he said. "He's an absolute fake."

"I believe you," Lealor responded. "No one can really tell the future—at least, not on demand and certainly not for money."

Two giggling girls had joined them at the front of the tent. A talking bird chained to a post announced from time to time, "Lorsham, Master of the Future, tells all. Lorsham! Lorsham!"

Lealor stood before it with a disapproving twist to her mouth. "Balderdash!" she muttered.

Gren took her hand, preparing to move on.

"Healer, do you not believe in the powers of the Far South?" One of the girls, a blonde with braids crowning her head, gazed up at Lealor, trusting her to tell the truth.

"We just wanted to hear him for fun," her dark-eyed friend put in, looking at Gren shyly.

"Why, Lealor here, can probably tell you the future herself," Gren spoke spontaneously, without thought.

"Yes, I can," Lealor said, amused to see the shocked look on Gren's face. Then she passed her arms theatrically through the air and said in a solemn voice, "I can see through the mists of time, two girls passing into this tent and being told lies. When they come out, they will be poorer than when they went in."

The girls and Gren laughed, understanding her joke at once. Lealor, however, had a blank look on her face. Her voice died to a whisper. "You, Talin," she addressed the darker of the two girls, "will marry a rich merchant." Lealor's face froze. Then she blinked. "What?" she asked.

Talin watched Lealor with awed eyes. She was dumbstruck.

"And me?" The blonde shook her saucy curls. "What can you tell me?"

Gren shot a look at Lealor and wondered what was the matter with her. "You girls are silly. No one can prophesy. It would be magic and you know that's evil," he told them. "Go along now."

The girls hurried off as Lorsham, the fortune teller, came out of his tent. Lealor took an instant dislike to him. She felt that same heart-stopping cold within that she experienced when she saw a snake. Wasn't she a trained animal doctor? She wished she didn't have this prejudice against snakes, but she did. Her eyes focused on the long finger with dirty nail that shook under her nose.

"—And I'll thank you, young lady, if you'll kindly go somewhere else and stop disrupting my trade," the scrawny man in the threadbare robe covered with stars finished what had evidently been a longer tirade. She had missed most of it, trying to hide her reaction to him.

"We are sorry," Gren apologized. Lealor was white as a snow flower. What had upset her so?

Lealor was still trying to place the man. He reminded her of someone . . . That was it! His lank, greasy hair and long nose reminded her of the Pardoner in the *Canterbury Tales*. That man had been a hypocrite and liar, too. She allowed Gren to pull her away. For a full dozen paces, they said nothing.

Finally Gren broke the silence. "And what exactly was that all about?"

"What was what about?" Lealor's puzzlement showed on her face.

"That foolishness about marrying a rich merchant."

"She will," Lealor said with confidence as his words reminded her of what she had told the girls earlier.

"And how in this world or any other would you know that?" Gren was skeptical.

"I—I just know, that's all." Lealor knew she had made a major error in showing her talent for prophecy. Here, where magic was forbidden—except to the priesthood, she reminded herself—her words could bring her harm.

"Then why didn't you tell the other girl something?"

"Because she will die in childbirth." Lealor's voice left no room for doubt.

"You have the gift to tell the future?" Gren's normal baritone sounded as if he had borrowed his voice from someone else.

"More of a curse. It seldom happens to me, but when it does, it is true." Lealor turned her unhappy face to his.

With an effort, Gren shook off the icicles that ran up his spine. "Well, let's think no more on it. Today is our day to enjoy the harvest festival fair." His quick consoling hug took her mind from the incident because it so surprised her. Not many men would hug a woman they believed to be a witch.

Later, Gren won the archery contest he entered. Then he insisted Lealor have the tiny silver arrow that was the prize.

"Ah, pretty lassie," a voice cried out, "will you not be giving the man some thanks for the gift?"

Lealor stifled the pang the words gave her. She missed the leprechaun Rory. The man teasing her spoke just like her friend. She wanted—no, she needed to go home. A chill wind blew by her. Or was she just fey? She shook off the feeling with action. The crowd laughed as Lealor gave Gren a quick kiss of gratitude.

As the afternoon wore on, she looked for a long time at the wares the merchants had for sale. One clever carving of a man with a wolf's muzzle so intrigued her that Gren bought it for her. A jeweler showed her cape pins decorated with strange stones as well as necklaces and rings. She knew better than to admire anything much. Gren would probably insist on buying it for her and she did not want him to feel proprietary. She would have scandalized everyone concerned if she had bought anything for Gren, so she satisfied her urge to spend by buying a toy soldier for Aldon and a rag doll for Jessa. She popped them into her provender bag to leave her hands free to eat the tartlets Gren bought them.

"These are delicious," she told him, licking a spot of filling from her lips. "Back home, we'd call these pasties." She watched Gren finish the last of his tartlet without spilling a drop on his mustache or short beard.

Gren swallowed the last of the treat and said, "In these parts, pastries are big. They have a bottom crust and an upper one. In between there might be any kind of fruit or some of my sister's meat, vegetables, and gravy."

Lealor didn't bother telling him she'd said *pasty*, not *pastry*. What he described to her she called a pie. "Where did all the people come from?" she asked. She knew most of the folks from the village and many strangers were looking at the wares for sale in the stalls from which gaily colored streamers of cloth flew. The local women were outfitted in their best. Even the men had put on festive attire. Some children who ran from stall to stall stopped and began watching with wide-eyed delight as a puppet show began from the back of a wagon fixed as a stage.

She and Gren stopped to watch as he said, "Actually, most of these merchants come from Draconsgate."

Seeing her puzzled look, he added, "It's the duke's city."

"That explains the sellers. Where did all the buyers come from? Riverville isn't this big, is it?"

"Not officially, but there are many families who live to the north and east of here. They never miss the chance to celebrate harvest in town."

"I can't see, Uncle Gren," Jessa complained, appearing from nowhere.

"Better?" Gren asked after he placed Jessa on his shoulder.

"Much, thank you," Jessa said, already giggling at the actions of the puppets.

Lealor saw Aldon climb on a hastily erected fence beside the wagon before she directed her attention to the stage, too.

Both the children and nearby adults watched, completely absorbed in the antics of the characters as they thwacked at each other in mock battles. Lealor kept an eye out for Aldon, because the makeshift fence didn't look any too sturdy. He would sit on the top rail, she thought to herself.

Within the fence, a mettlesome horse shied away from the loud laughter of the audience. Then the dealer entered the enclosure. When Lealor saw the horse's ears flatten, she knew trouble brewed for the man. As the dealer approached the animal, it backed away, eyes rolling. The man cursed under his breath and grabbed for the rope halter. The horse reared, then wheeled, kicking the fence where Aldon sat.

Lealor didn't waste a minute. She pushed through the crowd, some of whom had not even noticed the boy's fall. Lealor ducked into the enclosure, where the man stood motionless. "Gren," she called. "Keep that horse away from here."

"Right, lass," he said.

Quick as she was, Lorsham, the fortune teller, got there first. His hands looked dirtier than ever against Aldon's almost white hair.

"I will care for him," he said.

The owner of the horse had led him away, freeing Gren. He knelt beside his nephew. He ignored the man's offer. "Can you help him, lass?"

"Let me see," she said. When Lealor looked at the boy's pale face, she knew he had a serious injury. She reached for his hand, feeling for a pulse. The weak beat was erratic. She sensed the pain in the child's head. Her fingers gently felt his skull. An indentation marked the spot where the hoof had struck.

The crowd made way for the old healer. Fialla came forward and knelt beside the boy. She and Lealor exchanged a look. This injury was not a simple matter for herbcraft to cure. Fialla shook her head. "The boy will die, child," she told Lealor.

"No," Lealor said fiercely. "He will not die." She ignored the tightening of the invisible Myst. In her determination, she rested her hands gently on Aldon's head and used her powers to move the bone outward so it no longer pressed upon the brain of the child. She raised her pale face to the old herbwoman and nodded.

"Someone help move the boy to my home," Fialla said.

Gren carried Aldon out of the meadow while another villager cleared a path.

The fortune teller watched them go. The look in his eyes boded no good for anyone concerned.

Chapter
Ten

LEALOR sat in a chair by Aldon's bedside. Fialla hovered nearby.

"Well, child?" Fialla asked.

"He will be well," Lealor said, pale and strained. It took energy to heal a major injury like Aldon's.

"I'm glad for that," Gren said. He noticed Lealor's pallor. "Are you sure that you're all right, lass?"

"Just tired." Lealor summoned a smile, warm as a candle's glow on a dark night.

Dame Smith, her husband not far behind her, burst into the room. "Aldon!" she cried out as she saw the ashen-faced form on the cot.

Aldon's father asked a wordless question of Fialla. His wife was on her knees beside the cot, holding Aldon's hand in hers.

"He'll be fine after a bit," Fialla told him. Lealor nodded her confirmation.

"Lady bless him—and you," Dame Smith said to the healers.

"It will be best if he spends the night with me," Fialla said. "If he wakes, I'll dose him with an herb tea for the headache he will have. For now, he needs his rest."

"Thank you, lass," the blacksmith said. "And you, too, Fialla." He and his wife left the cottage together.

Lealor sighed. She had lost all taste for the evening's festivities. She only wanted to go to bed and sleep for a moon's turn.

"Ah, lass," Gren said, "you have worn yourself out. Come to my sister's and rest a while."

"It's going to take her longer than that, Gren," Fialla said as if Lealor were not present. "She needs several days of rest."

"It was healcraft, wasn't it?" he asked the old herbwoman.

Fialla only nodded. "Come, child, rest here."

"That's your bed, Fialla." Lealor's voice showed her exhaustion. "I want to go home," she said like a little girl. She found she didn't mean the cottage in the woods, she meant home on Realm.

"Will you not stay with us?" Gren's hand rested lightly on her shoulder.

"Home, please," Lealor said.

"Very well. Drink this." Fialla handed her a cup in which a cloudy liquid swirled.

"Wasn't this drink for Aldon?" Lealor asked, drinking as she was bid.

"I can make more." Fialla smiled at Gren, who hovered nearby like a mother greenwing protecting her nest. "It's only a restorative to help her make the trip home."

"Have you set your mind on this?"

Lealor nodded, too tired to waste strength in talking.

"If you will walk her home now, it would be a kindness. The restorative is powerful, but will only last an hour or two.

She needs to be safe at home before it wears off," Fialla said.

"All right," Gren agreed.

Lealor rose from the chair and approached Aldon. She placed her hand on his forehead. All was well. "Lady bless, Bright Ones protect," she recited, too tired to notice how surprised both Fialla and Gren were by the pale-green aura that surrounded her and her patient.

She straightened. "Let's go now."

"Are you sure, lass?"

"Of course," Lealor almost snapped.

Without another word, Gren led her out of the cottage and down the street. He picked up her bundle from his sister's. Lealor left the soldier and doll with Nelda, who was getting ready for the dance that night. Lealor accepted her profuse thanks graciously and hurried off with Gren. She could feel the flush of the herb's power within her, and she realized it wasn't her own will that kept her going. She felt she'd made herself very vulnerable. If Lorsham's bird was a magical creature, perhaps it could report to its master. Who was Lorsham? Nobody good, she knew already.

Gren took her arm and walked close beside her on the path. He had to, for the trail between the cottage and town was still largely overgrown. Lealor preferred it that way.

In spite of the many questions that seethed within Gren's head, he kept his silence, recognizing Lealor's exhaustion. How had she managed to heal Aldon? He heard Fialla say Aldon would die. He remembered the determination in Lealor's voice as she insisted Aldon would live. As he reviewed the scene mentally, he recalled the form of Lorsham, hanging over Aldon and the two healers like some bird of ill omen. The fortune teller had watched the two women carefully, as if he needed to see exactly what they would do. Gren couldn't remember seeing Lorsham before at a festival fair. Fialla didn't act as if she knew him either. Why would a stranger who had no actual wares to sell visit a backwoods fair? Could the priests have sent him as a spy? Riverville had so far escaped having a temple. Could the priests be suspicious? Gren decided to talk to the elders before he took the next tax payments to the duke.

They reached a wide place next to the river. It was only a short distance from the cottage. Lealor smiled at him. To Gren she was almost unimaginably beautiful in the pale moonlight.

"I can make it from here." She slipped her arm out of his and stood alone.

"Are you sure, lass? I'd feel much happier if I could see you safely within."

"I'm a little old to be tucked up like a child." She looked into his concerned face. "I'll be all right. I promise."

And somehow, he knew she would be.

"Besides," she teased, "I don't know what Pook would do if he caught you in the cottage, tucking me in."

"Yes, there is that." Gren's rueful smile showed he was imagining the scene. "Very well."

She took his hand. "Gren," she said.

"Yes, lass?"

"Thank you." Her voice was sincere.

He marvelled that she could honestly thank him after what she had done for Aldon. "My family and I owe more thanks to you than you do to me."

"How could I not help Aldon when I had the power to do so?"

"Good night," he told her, turning abruptly and starting back the way they had come.

"Good night, Gren," he heard her call softly after him.

He had taken twenty or more paces on the pathway home before it occurred to him that perhaps he should check on her, without her knowledge. He would worry if he wasn't sure she made it into the cottage. If Pook caught him, he'd yell for help if the bear wouldn't accept his explanation. He turned, ready to go back. Then he saw the huge shadow of a dragon pass over the face of the moon. He watched as the dragon flew lower and lower. It landed in the clearing he and Lealor stood in only minutes earlier and headed for the cottage. He started to run. Lealor needed him.

Then Pook appeared on the path in front of him.

"Let me pass! There's a dragon . . ."

Pook did not seem disturbed by the news.

He tried to pass. He had no time to waste. Pook blocked his every attempt to go to Lealor. He finally stopped and really looked at the bear. "Can you understand me?" he asked, feeling like a fool as soon as the words left his mouth.

Pook nodded yes.

"Is that dragon a"—he paused, searching for a word, any word, that would express a relationship between a human and a dragon—"friend or associate of Lealor's?"

Another nod yes.

"She doesn't need me to protect her?"

Another yes.

Gren took a deep breath and tried to calm his racing heart. "Very well. Good night to you, then." Gren turned and retraced his footsteps silently.

Pook did the same.

As Gren walked the path to Riverville, he realized he had fallen in love with Lealor, brave, talented, desirable. What exactly was Lealor? A special bond existed between Fialla and Lealor. The bear was as intelligent as a human. Perhaps he was a weren. Gren had seen many strange things in the western mountains, but he had noted them and passed on. He was a hunter, pure and simple. He had never, though, seen a dragon, a thing from legends, before this night. And she was its friend. Was she a dragon, herself? Another shapeshifter—or, since this was the very stuff of folk tales, a weren? He told himself she couldn't be. And yet . . . no, he'd know somehow. He was only a simple hunter, a very good hunter. He knew when it was time to give up on a hunt.

On the outskirts of Riverville he met Lorsham, floundering along the almost invisible pathway to Lealor's cottage. "Good evening to you," he said, wondering what the man, obviously no woodsman, was doing away from the fair site.

Lorsham peered into Gren's face. "Oh, it's you. And where would your meddling companion be? I thought you two would be at the dance."

"I was just out for a breath of air." Gren wasn't going to tell this man anything. Daylight didn't make Lorsham impressive and now the moonlight made him look almost sinister. Perhaps it wasn't only womanly vapors that made Lealor wary of this man.

"Alone?"

The tone of Lorsham's voice made the question an insult.

"Yes, alone."

"Abandoned by the Fire Hair, eh?"

Gren nodded.

"Where'd you meet her, boy?"

Gren clenched his teeth. It would never do to hit so old a man, but how he wanted to! "She came in on a wagon with her family, from east of here somewhere. They pulled out at sundown. She didn't give me any directions how to find her again, either."

"Troublesome sort, she was. You're better off without the likes of her. If you should find her again, I'd like to know where she comes from. No one in town knows anything about her."

Gren said the first true words he had spoken to Lorsham when he said, "I don't imagine I'll be seeing her again before the snows." He nodded politely to the man, thinking to himself that the villagers took care of their own.

The next morning Gren arose early, as usual, and packed for an extended hunting trip. Many times he wintered where he was if the hunting was good. The well-provisioned family stood ready for winter without any more help. In a few days the snow would come and he would be miles away from town, too far to change his mind and come home easily.

After Gren left, his bewildered brother-in-law said, "But —but I thought he'd planned to spend this winter here with us."

"Poor boy, she must have refused him last night," his sister told her husband privately.

Gren crossed the river and headed west. He didn't plan to find any answers there, but he did need time to think, and he always thought better in the wilderness.

As he walked, he reviewed the happenings of the day before. He was only a simple hunter, he thought. A simple hunter who had fallen in love—with a witch.

Chapter
Eleven

LEALOR spent two days at the cottage, resting. She wanted to see how Aldon was progressing, so on the third day she walked into Riverville. Fialla answered her knock on the door with a cheerful, "Come in."

Lealor looked at the cot where she had left Aldon. It was empty. She turned white as a ghost flower. "Aldon—" she began.

"Don't worry. He's been at home since yesterday afternoon," the old healer told her. "He felt far too frisky to stay in bed another day. Since his headache left him after the first few candlemarks, I turned him over to his parents. They know how to keep an eye on him." She stood, looking out of the door. Then she motioned to her guest. "Come and see for yourself."

Lealor looked where Fialla pointed. A small group of children running down the street stopped to play a circle game.

Aldon stood in the center waiting to break out. He stayed until the proper time in the song and then ran, reaching the freedom outside the circle. "A complete recovery, I'd say."

"And so do I. You have a great deal more healcraft than I do, child, but you may have made yourself an enemy."

"An enemy? Why would anyone be angry with me?" Lealor turned her astounded face to Fialla.

"You did nothing wrong. I'm afraid that Lorsham found the injury when he touched the boy's head. A serious wound like that usually causes death, but the boy survived."

"I couldn't let Aldon die, Fialla."

"Of course you couldn't, but I wish that Lorsham had not had the opportunity to find out how dangerous a wound it was."

"I didn't think about him." Lealor frowned, remembering the man. "Abominable cheat! Taking the money from those gullible girls. And how dare he call himself a fortune teller? Isn't that against the priests' law? Prophecy is a magical gift."

Fialla busied herself making them a cup of tea while she answered. "True, but the priests' law reaches no farther than the temples, and many back-country places do not bother to give lip service to them and their god. The simple people remember the Lady, although many city folks worship the fashionable god of the priests."

"I have talked about him with Gren, but I still don't know his name. Who is this god?"

"It is best not to name him. A chance remains that use of his name might call the attention of his not-so-humble priesthood." Fialla handed her a cup of tea.

Lealor sat at the table, cradling the cup in her hands. The outside air had a decided nip in it so the warmth from the tea was doubly appreciated.

"Are you planning to stay in the cottage over the winter? You're most welcome to stay here with me if you wish."

"I'd rather be at the cottage." Lealor realized how ungrateful her refusal sounded, so she continued. "Actually, I not only have the bear Pook to take care of, but I have another friend."

"Aldon has been full of your doings since you first came, but he has never mentioned anyone else." Fialla stirred a second spoon of sweetherb into her tea.

"My friend Fafleen came with me through the gate. We didn't mean to come. Something—or rather someone—tampered with the gate while we were in transition and we came here, rather than my planned destination."

"Who is so mighty that he can meddle with a gate when it is working?"

"I only know of two people, or beings, who would dare. One is a man of great evil called the Shadowlord, and the other is a young Bright One called Baloo. Baloo, I suspect, is responsible for our being here."

"I have heard tales of the Bright Ones, passed down in my family for generations. I never heard of this Lord of Shadows. Is he from the old legends too?"

Lealor shivered. "No, I only wish he were a legend. He lives, somewhere, and plots evil. On Realm, my father and mother fought him, but he escaped. On Achaea, he planned destruction again. I was his prisoner, but my parents and their friends rescued me." The tea wobbled slightly in her cup. No, the Shadowlord was very real. For a moment, she wanted to tell Fialla of Myst, and her early rejection of the talisman bracelet and all the sorrow that came from the decision made when she was only a child.

"Then you are here to find this Shadowlord and punish him?"

"No, as I told you, I came here on the whim of an infant Bright One. My family always searches for the Shadowlord, but he stays well hidden. Many worlds have gates. The Keepers can only watch and hope they find him before he spawns more evil." Lealor smiled ruefully. "Spawns more evil. How foolish and melodramatic that sounds, but it is the truth."

"What does he do that is so wicked?" Fialla sipped her tea while she waited for the answer to her question.

"On Realm he gathered horrible creatures from imaginary worlds to fight for him. They were to form his army, but my parents, dragons, and heroes my father called from Other-whens battled them and caused him to flee. On Achaea, he convinced the scientists of Atlan to help him. He planned to forge a universal gate to all times and all places. To do this he needed the power of Achaeasun. Baloo, the infant Bright One cradled in Achaea's sun, awakened early and would have died without my mother's healing." Lealor's eyes clouded as she remembered her childish attempts to destroy the Sha-dowlord's machines. He had looked at her in dragon form and changed her back into a child with one wave of his hand. Then he had forbidden her to change shape on pain of being forever that animal or creature she changed into. . . .

"And?" Fialla leaned forward, intent on Lealor's story.

"And what?" Lealor came back to the present with a rush.

"And what happened next?"

"Sorry. I forget that everyone doesn't know about the Shadowlord. The gate he formed was unstable, nearly causing Achaeasun to nova. When the gate itself exploded, the force of the blast destroyed the Isle of Atlan on all the time lines where it existed. Mishandled gate power can backlash on all concerned without the proper wards."

"And no one knows where this Lord of Shadows is now?"

"No, and it's been almost twenty years since he escaped the last time."

"I can understand why you might ignore a person like Lorsham after having experiences with a man like your Sha-dowlord."

"Fialla, that's just it. I can't convince anyone, but when I was a child and looked at him, I swear he was all sparkly and shiny inside. His body looked like an old man, but he wasn't. He wasn't," she insisted. Her fingers went white about the cup.

"I believe you, child. What do you think he is, then, if he's not a man?"

Lealor shook her head. "I'm not sure. My parents asked me that question, too. Then I didn't know. For years I had such nightmares about my experience with him that no one willingly asked me anything to remind me. Now that I'm older, I think . . . no, what I think is impossible."

"Few things are impossible. Do you believe him to be a demon?"

"No. Something much more incredible than that." Lealor looked at Fialla and suddenly knew that the old herbwoman would not laugh at her. She took a deep breath and said, "I think he's a Bright One."

"Why would a creature of such power work with gates? Legends say the Bright Ones were never flesh. Their pure energy could manifest anywhere and any time they chose." Fialla poured her guest another cup of tea.

"What if he didn't know he was a Bright One?"

"If they truly rock the Bright Ones in star cradles as the old lullaby says, how could he not know, child?"

Lealor opened her mouth as if willing herself to speak would produce the truth. Then she sighed. "I don't know."

"Sufficient unto the day," Fialla said.

"You're right about that, at any rate."

"If we move the furniture about, we could make enough room for another bed for your friend," Fialla offered.

"My friend wouldn't fit in this cottage."

"Is your companion an ogre or giant, then?" Fialla's face showed a lively interest, but no fear.

"Fafleen is a dragon."

"Ah, that explains your unwillingness to have unexpected visitors. Does she lurk in the woods or turn invisible when someone besides you is present?"

"How she would hate the idea that she would 'lurk' so someone wouldn't see her! She is a very proud young dragoness. Because she's so young, I wouldn't expect her to become invisible for very long periods. And invisibility is a magical aspect." Lealor took another sip of her tea. "I really am trying to avoid magic as much as possible."

"That is wise. Taming a bear is something people can believe, but taming a dragon . . ."

"I didn't tame her." Lealor almost choked on her tea imagining how indignant Fafleen would be if anyone suggested that dragons needed to be tamed. "On Realm, where we come from, dragons are personages, highly civilized beings, and much more intelligent than the fortunate humans they befriend." Lealor smiled at the look on Fialla's face. She added, "At least according to Fafleen."

"What did you do with her when Gren came to the cottage?"

"Oh, she has interests of her own. She discovered a cave filled with old volumes of forgotten dragon lore. For one so young, she's quite a scholar."

"The Cave of the Dragon King," Fialla breathed.

"Then you know of it?"

"Indeed. The old legends say the king of the dragons loved learning. Some humans gained great rewards by bringing him books."

"Fafleen must be just like him. Since she found the cave, she only flies by to check on me. She feels she must protect me from harm." Lealor set her cup down with an audible thump. "It's ridiculous. I'm a perfectly capable adult," Lealor began. She flushed, realizing that was something an adult did not have to announce.

"Don't you feel a responsibility toward her also?"

"Yes, but—"

"Friends care."

Lealor did not try to answer. Fialla was right. Her fingers went to her wrist and touched Myst gently. After a moment she said, "I have another reason for wanting to be by myself for a while."

"Gren?"

"Am I so transparent?"

"This is a small place. Everyone noticed."

Lealor made a face. "I hate the idea of people spying on me."

"There is little news in Riverville. The actions of one of our most eligible bachelors interested many. You have no need to worry. The day after the festival Gren left at sunup. Aldon told me his uncle would spend the winter trapping."

"I thought he was staying in town this winter."

"So did Aldon."

"Oh, dear."

"If you plan to come in, you need to do it soon. I feel winter in my bones."

"No, I'll stay at the cottage."

"If you are sure that is what you want to do, I'll care for the villagers. We will only send for you if we have need."

"I want to see Aldon before I go home to hibernate with Pook."

"If you have need, send Pook to me with a message."

"Don't worry. I have all types of food. The villagers insisted on gifting me after I healed them. I'm very healthy. Pook actually shows no signs of sleeping the winter through. At least not so far," she added as she stood. "He's all the protection any mortal should need."

"Lady bless," Fialla said, giving her a hug.

"Blessings be," Lealor added before leaving.

The Smiths were hospitable as always, but after seeing for herself that Aldon had recovered, Lealor left the village for home.

During the time she was in Riverville the sky had become overcast. Halfway to the cottage, she met Pook, who paced back and forth on a short stretch of the path.

"Are you waiting for me?" Lealor touched Pook lightly on the head.

He nudged her gently with his nose before setting off at a

rapid pace. He looked back at her once, as if urging her to hurry.

"Pook, wait. I don't intend to run."

The bear woofed and waited until she came closer before moving onward at a rapid pace.

"Oh, silly bear. Why are we rushing so?" However, she increased her stride as a chill wind blew from the west, bringing the first flakes of snow.

Lealor liked snow and would have stood to watch, but Pook hurried her onward.

Neither of them noticed the black bird that watched them with beady eyes and swooped after them for a time until the wind almost blew it from the skies. With an almost snakelike hiss of triumph, it headed east, pushed by the snowstorm's winds.

Chapter Twelve

LONG before Lealor and Pook reached the clearing in front of the cottage, snow covered the ground. The wind increased until Lealor had to bend forward to keep going. When Pook saw, he got between her and the wind. It made it easier for her to move steadily. They plunged into the band of trees that sheltered the cottage and immediately, Lealor felt the difference in the force of the gale and the temperature. Although she used magic herself, the warding spell was so carefully interwoven with the nature of the forest, she never realized before that magic protected the cottage. For a moment, she worried that the craft of that warding would shout *magic user* and cause her problems, then common sense came to her rescue. If no one had noticed in all these years, this year would probably be no different. The snow, which whirled like a dervish outside the protected area, landed lightly on tree, bush, and ground. The snowflakes gently dusted the roof of the cottage. The sight reminded

Lealor of holidays. If someone not sensitive to magic came, he might well think the haven around the building was natural. Lealor opened the front door and entered the comfort of her warm cottage. She struggled out of her boots and gloves, congratulating herself for having the forethought to prepare for colder weather "just in case" as her mother often told her.

She stood gazing out the warded window. Only a little cold seeped into the room; however, she knew she needed to pull the shutters closed before going to bed. She had blankets and didn't mind a little chill, but if anyone came and her window was wide open in winter, it would take more explaining than she was willing to do.

She pulled off her boots and left them by the fire. Then she shrugged out of her coat and padded over to hang it on its peg. Pook pawed her slippers from under her bed.

"Hint, hint, huh?" she teased, laughing as Pook put a paw over his nose. His eight-inch claws made the half of his muzzle uncovered by the furry paw look like a walrus mustache.

She untied the provender bag from her belt and moved to the table. "Magical or not, tonight we're having a good old-fashioned hot meal."

Pook lumbered to the table and stood at his place, waiting while she set out huge bowls of hot vegetable soup. She got a loaf of bread from the warming oven attached to the fireplace, and added a dish of butter. Pook picked up his bowl and drained it in one gulp.

"Pook, don't bolt your food," Lealor said, handing the bear a door stopper of buttered bread which he ate in three bites. She shook her head. "I suppose you want more?" She said this as she returned his bowl to the bag to be refilled. This time he lapped decorously at his dinner, the edge of his hunger dulled.

By the time she finished her soup and bread, it was quite dark outside. "Oh, fiddle," she muttered, knowing it was time to close the shutters. She lit the big lamp that hung from a beam in the center of the room. It started burning at her touch in spite of hanging for years, unused. "More undetectable magic," she murmured to herself. Next, she redressed and went out, Pook trailing along with her. In seconds she removed the pegs holding the shutters against the walls of the cottage and repegged them in the closed position. Pook stretched to his full height and sniffed the air. Like all bears, his vision was poor, but his sense of smell was superb. Satisfied that no danger lurked, he followed Lealor into the cottage.

She quickly readied herself for bed. The magical flame sprite that would keep the fire burning during the night danced and leaped over the wood, creating heat and a dim light that lulled Pook and Lealor to the edge of sleep.

"I know Fafleen hates the cold, so I don't have to worry that she's out in this storm. Ice dragons thrive in it, but Fafleen, like most dragons, wants to be warm and toasty in winter weather. I wonder what's become of Berdu . . ." she murmured, just before she drifted off.

The next morning, snow ruled the world as far as Lealor could see. Most of the trees had lost their leaves and stood, stark and bare like living icicles, against the slate sky. A solid pall of clouds covered the sun. From them, snow drifted down, quietly covering everything. Lealor carried out bunches of cut grass for the deer and swept a bare spot to hold sprinkled seeds for the birds. She remembered Aldon looking like an ambulatory haystack as he carried piles to the shed behind the cottage. Jessa had been proud as she collected apronfuls of seeds from the wild plants that hemmed the path. The rest of the day Lealor prepared herbal remedies and studied the books she had brought with her. She wondered how Fafleen was coming along on her translation, but she didn't worry about her. It was best if no one saw her. A blue dragon would stand out vividly against the snow. Fafleen might stay away all winter, for she had plenty of supplies and was very self-sufficient. She and Lealor had discussed this possibility earlier.

Almost a month passed before there was any change in Lealor's routine. Early one morning a messenger from Riverville broke a path through the fallen snow.

Lealor opened the door and saw Hugh, one of the farmers that lived outside the village. "What brings you out in drifts like this?" she asked, gesturing for him to come inside.

"Fialla sent me with a message. The duke's little son is ill and no one can cure him. Nelda told the duchess about you, healer, and now the duke summons you to his court. The messenger awaits in the village."

"Well, sit down by the fire and warm up while I get ready."

Hugh doffed his cap and went to stand near the hearth. He narrowly missed stepping on Pook, who sprawled before the fire in his usual place.

The bear rose with a roar of outrage that even frightened Lealor. Hugh turned as white as the snow outside and backed carefully to a spot just inside the door. No amount of urging on Lealor's part could induce him to move farther into the cabin, although Pook moved to one corner and sat, keeping an eye on their visitor.

Hugh watched the bear and Pook watched Hugh. Lealor thought they looked ridiculous, glaring at one another, but she gave up trying to make them act civilized. All she could do was hurry so the awkward situation would last no longer than necessary. Bears and men, she decided privately, were the only two things as stubborn as dragons.

Pook growled softly as she collected what she thought she might need to help the boy. She talked to Pook as if he were another person. She always talked to animals this way, and even if Hugh thought she was crazy, she wasn't going away without trying to make the bear understand. She explained to Pook about the note she was leaving for Fafleen, just in case she should decide to come to visit. She tried to impress on the bear that she would be quite safe, but his growl showed he didn't believe her. When she was ready to go, he blocked her path to the door.

"Pook," she said, aware that Hugh never took his eyes from the bear, "you must move or you'll be sorry."

The look on Hugh's face said as plainly as words that he wanted to see how Lealor controlled an eight-hundred-pound bear.

Lealor was wondering about it herself.

"Pook, I intend to go. If you don't let me pass, I'll—I'll hit you on the nose!" she said, quite pleased with herself for thinking of something that might work and was not magical.

Pook woofed once, then turned his back on her and settled down by the fire. Lealor had a distinct impression that if he could have talked, he would have said, "Don't say I didn't warn you!" Once the way was clear, Hugh and Lealor wasted no time in starting out for Riverville.

The walk to the village was difficult, for once out of the cottage area, the snow was almost thigh deep. Hugh had broken a trail so her walk was not as arduous as it might have been. Once in the village, she stopped to see Fialla, and Aldon's family. The messenger from the castle tried to hurry her, so after Lealor spoke to her friends, she wasted no time in climbing aboard the sleigh the duke had sent. The messenger had fed the rested horses, making the trip to the castle as rapid as anyone might wish, considering the snow.

A change of horses and a relief driver awaited them at the halfway point. Snuggled in furs like a princess in a Russian fairy tale, Lealor slept in the sleigh. The next morning at sunup, they entered the castle courtyard. Lealor felt sorry for the horses, even though they had changed teams a second time at a crossroads inn. They had given her time to eat and walk around briefly, before loading her up again and rushing onward. She felt so tired, she didn't remember much about the stop except it was a relief from the cold.

The servants woke her and helped her out of the sleigh before they hurried her inside the castle. The somewhat dazed Lealor stood in the huge entrance hall until Nelda, the Smiths' daughter, came briskly down the stairway. Before Nelda smothered Lealor in a hug, Lealor had time to notice that Nelda's clothes were a good deal finer than anything she had worn to the festival.

"Oh, healer, I'm so glad you came. Little Reynal is so ill. We've tried everything," she continued, as they climbed the stairs.

While the hall below seemed warm, the halls they passed through felt distinctly chilly to Lealor. The grand tapestries on the walls impressed her although she knew they were there more to keep out the cold than to awe visiting healers. Nelda ushered her into a tower room, nodding to the guard outside the door. They entered a small chamber crowded with toys and people.

"The boy is dying," the black-robed priest told the duke.

Lealor looked at the priest's cold face, specter pale. The poor child, she thought. Tended by someone who looked like he lived on curdled milk, what chance had he to recover? And the smell! A scent of black magic filled the room. Was it, she wondered, meant to kill or to cure the boy? She took small breaths, intent on inhaling as little as possible of the noxious vapors in the room.

"That's the priest, Credolt," Nelda whispered in Lealor's ear.

"Very well," said the tall man with the silver hair and jeweled sword. Lealor guessed him to be the duke, not from his dress, but from his bearing.

"Perhaps if you made another offering at the temple . . ." Credolt said, attempting a smile which only made Lealor dislike him more.

"No," the duke told him firmly. "You may leave," he added as Nelda and Lealor's presence finally registered.

The fire smoked fitfully when the door opened for Credolt and his three companions to leave. The duke waited until only Nelda, Lealor, and one other man were in the room.

"And your opinion, Dr. Small?" The duke muted his powerful voice, although the room seemed more spacious somehow without Credolt and company.

To give him credit, the doctor did not want to talk about the child's condition with the boy on the bed before him, but he was bound to answer his superior. He turned from the bed to face the duke and shook his head slightly from side to side. His sigh said more than words could have conveyed.

"Very well," the duke repeated. "You may leave." He waited until the door closed behind him. He smiled politely at Lealor, but he spoke to Nelda. "And this is . . . ?" he asked.

"The healer, sir. Lealor," Nelda said with a curtsy.

Lealor inclined her head respectfully. She had never curtsied to anyone in her life and she did not intend to begin now.

"You are young, Healer Lealor."

Lealor nodded, standing quietly while every instinct said to go to the boy.

"You have heard the prognosis of the priest and the doctor?"

"Yes."

"And you are still willing to try to save my boy's life?"

"If I can, sir."

"Is there anything that I need to do before you begin?"

"Yes." Lealor's tone was grim as she moved to the side of the bed. "Have someone take out all these toys for now. Clear this room of this smoke. Is there somewhere we can move Reynal while we clean?" She hurriedly put a stasis spell on the boy so his condition would not worsen.

"We've prepared a room for you next door," Nelda said.

"We can move Reynal there. You go, too. You've had no rest since the trip. I had a meal sent up for you," Nelda said as the duke lifted his son carefully and carried him from the room. The child's ash-blond hair and pale face seen against the rich brown of the duke's jacket gave Lealor a pang.

"I'll see to this." Nelda piled toys into the arms of the two women who appeared at the door like magic.

"Make sure you open the windows and air this room well, before we come in again." Lealor looked at the smoking fire. "And if there's no way to get that fireplace to draw correctly, we'll have to find another room."

"I'll take care of everything, healer," Nelda said, her manner showing her approval of Lealor's orders.

Lealor entered her room with a feeling of relief. Anything was better than that smoky, magic-filled room next door. She saw the duke sitting on his son's bed, holding his hand. Reynal looked better to her already, but he was a gravely ill child.

"My lord, can you tell me what measures have failed to help Reynal recover?" Lealor placed her hand on the boy's forehead. He radiated heat. The special healer's gift the goddesses of Achaea gave her as a child told her all she needed to know about the extent of his illness.

"We've tried everything. Prayers in the temple, sacrifices to the god, potions, pills, leeches—"

"You allowed them to put leeches on the boy?" Lealor's fists clenched.

"Why, yes. Nothing else seemed to work so Credolt talked with Dr. Small and convinced him to apply the leeches. You don't approve?"

"Have you ever seen what a bleeding wound does to a warrior on a battlefield?"

"Yes," the duke answered, considering her words.

"And isn't stopping the blood the first thing to be done in case of a bleeding wound?"

"Yes," the duke said, already seeing her point.

The door opened.

"Then why didn't your own good sense tell you that taking blood from a sick child was a bad thing to do?" Lealor entirely forgot to whom she spoke, she was so angry.

The woman who entered the room answered for the duke. "You must remember how ill Reynal is. We were ready to try anything."

"My dear," the duke said, rising to take his wife's hand.

Nelda bustled in. "The room is ready. It's cleared and aired. I had new logs laid on the fire, and it's drawing fine, now." Noticing the duchess, she smiled. "My lady, this is Lealor, the healer who saved my brother's life."

"We've been talking," the duchess said.

Nelda glanced at the tray on the table. "Why, you haven't eaten a thing!"

"All I'd like is a hot cup of tea for now," Lealor told her. "What's more important is getting this young man changed into clean clothes and in a freshly made bed."

"You take time for your tea, healer, and I'll help Nelda with Reynal," the duchess said.

Lealor smiled. Evidently, Reynal's parents had been shoved to the side by all those quacks who were trying to cure him. Lealor thought it was most important for people who really cared about a sick person to help him. She would be glad for any assistance they would give her.

The duchess left with Nelda, following the duke, who carried Reynal. A maid appeared almost at once. Lealor sat wearily in a chair and allowed the girl to pull off her boots. She took the cup of tea the maid handed her and she wiggled her toes in the thick socks she wore for the trip. The maid brought her soft slippers for her feet. Lealor spit out her first sip of the hot tea. Every sense warned her of danger.

"Is the tea too hot?" the maid asked.

"Where did this come from? Was it made for me?"

"Oh, no. I took it from the special foods prepared for the young duke."

"Reynal eats only these—special foods?" Lealor scrubbed her lips with the back of her hand. Something special was in the boy's food, no doubt of that.

"Is something wrong? Don't you like the tea? I can make fresh. There's a pot of hot water on the tray." The little maid was anxious to please, but Lealor did not entirely trust her.

"Just bring me a cup of plain hot water," Lealor commanded. Once she had it, she reached into her provender bag for some tea laced with a special restorative herb. The bag delivered flawlessly. To take the maid's mind from what she had seen, she said, "I've clean stockings in my bag." Lealor sat, watching the girl retrieve them. She was content to save her energy for healing Reynal. She needed this brief time to recharge her own spirit for the fight ahead of her. She sipped her tea and allowed the girl to change her socks.

"How fine a wool this is, healer. What kind of stockings are these?"

"Orlon," Lealor answered without thinking.

"Or-lon? What kind of animal gives that wool? I've never seen an orlon."

Lealor was so tired she felt silly. She stifled a giggle. "Wild orlons are very rare, even where I come from," she said. She sipped her tea thoughtfully after she dismissed the maid. She knew she had a battle before her. She preferred resting before taking on a responsibility like this, but the boy needed help now, not when it was physically convenient for her. She rose and went to her charge. Nelda had the room aired and Reynal in bed. This time the duchess sat on the bed, stroking the boy's head. The duke stood beside her, watching.

"It's almost time for Reynal's medicine. Do you want me to give it to him?" Nelda asked, holding a vial in her hand.

"By no means," Lealor told her. She took the vial and sniffed cautiously. Nothing she had ever heard of before, but her magical sense told her it would not aid in the child's recovery. She reached into her provender bag. It was as well that her grandmother had modified it especially for her, or it would have produced only food. She remembered her father telling about the time he had with his when he wanted it to produce a coin for a boat ride. She fished out a bottle of liquid antibiotic. She didn't know if using the bag would leave a magical residue or not, but now, she needed all the help she could get to start the healing process, so she risked being detected by some priestly snooper.

The duchess held Reynal's head elevated so Lealor could spoon in the medicine which smelled like fruit.

"He'll sleep now," Lealor told the anxious parents. "I'll stay with him tonight. Please see that no one but Nelda comes in here until tomorrow."

The duke nodded his agreement. He and his wife had decided they trusted this flame-haired healer in spite of her youth. She was far from the aged granny they had expected. Both the duke and the duchess kissed the boy before leaving.

"Well, that's one improvement, at any rate," Nelda said.

"What?" Lealor asked, busy settling herself comfortably beside her patient.

"Letting his parents minister to him. Credolt and the rest of those men thought they should stay away." Nelda's sniff said as plainly as words her opinion of that policy.

"Nelda, I want you personally to prepare every bite that Reynal and I eat. Can you do it unobtrusively, so no one notices and makes a big fuss?"

"Why don't I keep bringing the special food up here, and then you can share yours with Reynal?" Nelda didn't need telling what Lealor was guarding against. "Do you want me to take turns sitting with him tonight?"

"No. For tonight, I'll sit." Lealor took Reynal's right hand in hers and placed her other hand on his neck. His pulse was stronger already.

"I'll bring you a meal later," Nelda said as she slipped out the door.

The rough panes let in a little dim light. Lealor wondered where the day had fled, but realized it was only late afternoon.

The dark grey outside the windows was only the harbinger of night. Leaden clouds dropped snow which the wind blew against the pane unrelentingly. Lealor smiled at the sleeping boy. She started pouring her strength into his body to help him fight the illness. Later Nelda came in to attend to the fire. Lealor slept bent over her patient, also sound asleep. A soft green light glowed from her and the boy.

"The Lady's blessing!" Nelda breathed in awe. She hurried off to tell her mistress Reynal was in very good hands indeed.

Chapter
Thirteen

FOR Lealor, the next three days remained a hazy period in her memory. She sponged, dosed, and literally forced energy into Reynal. Her periods away from him were brief necessities. By the end of the time, she was pale and thin, but her much improved patient remained weak. Over the course of the next week he stayed awake longer and longer. Lealor remained close, just in case, but by the second week after her arrival, she was confident of the boy's recovery.

His parents showed their appreciation by showering her with gifts, since she refused the gold the duke offered. She took her meals with Reynal as a means of missing the formal dinners in the banquet hall; however, she did consent to ride the dappled grey mare the duke gave her as a present. Her herbal skills became open knowledge when word of the young duke's recovery became public. Castle servitors asked help for their ailments and for those of their relatives and friends.

Since the duke requested that Lealor stay with them until spring, in case Reynal had a relapse, she was quite willing to give aid where she could. She carefully refrained from practicing on the members of the court. They could afford the fees of the doctors in the town. While it was sensible to avoid stirring up enmity by taking paying customers away from the local medical practitioners, she felt as if animals should be her real patients and she only helped the poor because her care was better than none. Most of what she did was simple healing of sores, boils, cuts, coughs, and other minor ailments. She passed along a great deal of basic health information in the process.

Reynal studied part of every day with his tutor. This gave Lealor some free time for herself. She spent much of it in the stables, helping in the care of the animals. Some days were too icy or cold to risk injury to her horse, which she named Little Bit. Caring for the animals gave her a quiet pleasure that the constant company of the courtiers did not.

One afternoon as she came into the courtyard outside the kitchen, she saw a boy chopping wood for the fires. Lealor often walked through the kitchen on her way to the stables, so she recognized him as one of the cook's youngest helpers. The boys who helped the cooks were culinary go-fers, going for this or that at the cook's will. Lealor remembered how Aldon hated bringing wood for the forge. She wondered what he would think of the huge kitchen fires that never all went out. At least one fire burned heartily all night, in case some visitor or other awoke and wanted hot food. She didn't have a drop of noble blood and when she saw how hard ordinary folk had to labor to keep the nobles in the castle happy, she felt satisfied by her common antecedents.

Her stride took her across the courtyard to a back door of the stable. Just as she pulled it open, she heard a strange *thunk* followed by a yell. When she turned to look, she saw the boy swaying dizzily, propping himself on the ax. On his left legging a red stain grew exponentially. Lealor didn't need to see the wound to know the ax had hit an artery. The boy's life was seconds from ending. She sprinted across and ripped the cloth of the legging from the injury. He was in such a shocked condition that he was not even embarrassed. Lealor unhesitatingly put her hand over the gushing wound and began to heal. She probed deep with her mind, willing the flesh to close and begin to mend.

The cook waddled out the kitchen door and called, "Taydolf, you scatterwit! Didn't I tell you to hurry with that wood?" He continued scolding as he crossed the courtyard. By the time he finished speaking he stood next to the injured lad, and his voice changed considerably. "What on Widdershins happened? I sent the boy on a simple errand to get wood, and now he lies in a pool of blood."

"He hit himself with the ax," Lealor explained, turning her head briefly toward the cook while inwardly she commanded, "heal."

"Oh, healer, it's you. Lucky for him that you were near. It must have been a fearsome wound." The cook wiped his hands on his apron over and over.

"I've repaired the damage. It isn't as bad as it looks," Lealor lied, not wanting the true extent of her powers to become known. "Let me have your apron to cover him. It's freezing out here."

"Who would have thought the lad would have had so much blood in him?" The cook shook his head and held out his apron. "He's such a little lad."

"Sending him out here to chop wood at his age wasn't a very wise idea," Lealor said with a grim look in her eyes. She always carried a few bandages and some healing herbs since news of her healing talents spread. For once, it was turning out to be an excellent habit. She reached into her coat pocket for a roll of cloth and bandaged while she listened.

"I didn't send him to chop it, just to bring in a few armfuls. Old Tom is the wood chopper. He never should have left the ax out by the pile."

"Yes, besides being unsafe, it rusts the metal and ruins the edge," said Lealor, who had chopped quite a bit of wood since she arrived on Widdershins. She brushed the boy's orangy hair out of his face and smiled at him. Too shocked to speak, he rested quietly, content to let the healer take care of him. The cook was thoughtless, but not cruel. "Make it clear when you send the small boys out that they are not to chop wood. If there is none ready, they must tell someone, not try to use the ax themselves. This boy might have been permanently maimed, trying to bring you wood." She frowned as she considered the situation. The cook looked so concerned that she added, "But the boy will recover. This time we were lucky. He'll need a week or so of rest before he resumes his full duties." She looked down at the boy, awkwardly covered by the apron. "Send someone out with a blanket to take him to his bed, will you?"

Drundle, one of the serving men, arrived with a blanket. In moments, he wrapped the boy and carried him inside. It never occurred to Lealor to wonder who sent him. The priest, Credolt, who viewed the healing through an upstairs window, felt disturbed by the faint green glow he had seen.

"I wonder," he murmured to himself, "if there is any advantage in sending this upstart healer to the temple. In only a few more weeks we will need the spring sacrifice. She is both young and lovely. By the time we hold a trial, sacrifice time will be very near. I'll write a letter to my superior, Priest Lustven." His eyes gleamed with satisfaction.

Within four days, the spring thaw started. Everyone told Lealor that it would snow hard at least once more before spring really arrived, but the worst of the winter was over. The duke decided to take a fortnight's trip to inspect the northern defenses. Before he left, he specifically asked Lealor to stay until his return.

"Healer, usually I try to take my son with me when I make the rounds of the frontier posts. It's good for him to get away from court and learn a little about real life. The men like seeing him, too. When the day comes for him to take over, he will know the job and the men.'' He noticed Lealor's frown. ''Now, I can see a much improved Reynal, but he's not well enough to come along with the chance of the weather's turning. If I wait much longer, the trip will be one long slog through the mud. The nomads don't normally raid until high summer, but I want to make sure all is in readiness,'' he explained to Lealor.

''I'll be glad to keep an eye on his health while you're gone,'' Lealor said, looking the duke straight in the eye as she said it.

The duke knew exactly what might threaten his son's health and his grim nod of agreement showed it. The astute duke remembered well how Credolt's ministrations had affected his son. He always protected his people from the depredations of the priesthood as well as he was able. Doing this had earned him the enmity of the priesthood, Credolt in particular. However, the duke never thought the priests would seek revenge by endangering a child. He learned a great deal about the temple religion during his son's illness. He planned to redouble his vigilance over the priests in his domains and rear his son in his image.

During the next few days after the duke left, much coming and going kept the roads full. Everyone felt tired of being solitary. The merchants were moving all the goods they could before the roads thawed totally. The weather cooperated wonderfully, cold enough at night to freeze the roads, but with a hint of warmth and bright sunshine during the day to herald the coming season.

In the winter, few messages came from Mancy, the capital where the King lived. With the approach of spring, a series of mail pouches arrived. Lustven seemed delighted with Credolt's candidate for the spring sacrifice. Every spring it was more difficult to find a suitable candidate for the ceremony.

Having someone without a family to bewail her doom would be a welcome change from the usual political maneuvering that went on in Mancy every year when sacrifice time came again. The witch hunter would arrive within three days with a suitable conveyance to bring the witch who healed to face her trial at the temple in Mancy.

Credolt put down the letter. He rubbed his hands together as he considered the timing. With the duke gone, there was no one strong enough to oppose the arrest of Lealor. She would be in the capital before the duke returned home if his luck held. If the main thaw obliged, it would be weeks before the duke could arrive in Mancy to attest to Lealor's innocence. No one condemned for witchcraft had ever escaped the justice of the priests after the trial. For once, his lips managed a true smile, but while his face changed for the better, his eyes remained as cold as the snow atop Mount Neverthaw.

On the day the witch hunter arrived, Lealor got an early warning from Nelda, who had a series of informants which would have better suited the master of a spy network.

"Lealor, the witch wagon has come," Nelda told her friend with a worried look in her eyes.

"What's a witch wagon?" asked Lealor, who wondered why she should care as she picked up the beanbag she and Reynal had been tossing before the tutor came for the boy's chess lesson.

"When the priesthood has evidence of witchcraft, the witch wagon comes out to transport the accused person to the temple in Mancy. We've heard tales in Riverville about how cruel the witch hunters are. It's one of the reasons the elders refuse to let the town grow large enough to require a permanent priest. Who knows what he might send in his reports to the temple?"

"Oh," Lealor said lamely. She felt she couldn't just stand by silently while obvious injustice happened. "Do you know who they are accusing?"

"Usually my sources know, but this time there is no word."

They looked at Reynal playing chess with his tutor. The boy almost glowed with health. A newcomer to court would never know how ill he had been so short a time before.

"He's much better," Nelda said approvingly.

"When the spring sunshine came, the last of the pallor disappeared," Lealor said as she put the last of her medicines in her magic bag.

"You talk as if most of the credit didn't belong to you."

"My healing powers are a gift."

"I have seen the Lady's green glow when you healed," Nelda said, not sure if she should mention the fact or not.

"A green glow?" Lealor felt surprised. On Realm and Earth she never glowed.

"Well, on Widdershins, those with true healing power from the Lady cast a green halo around them when they heal. It helps us tell if we're in the presence of honest magic."

"What do you see if the magic is evil?" Lealor asked out of curiosity.

"Oh, nothing. The old lore tells us that no evil magician or healer can cast a green glow, for that comes only by the will of the Lady."

"Then no one who is innocent should fear the witch hunters." Lealor smiled. One less problem to tackle. In a few days she should be able to return to her cottage. She wondered what news Fialla had for her. If no one could help her activate the gate, she was ready to let Fafleen try to take them home.

"Yes, but the trials do not have to be honest. In the past the accused have not wanted a chance to protest their convictions. No one can speak to the accused—"

"Why ever not?"

"The priests wish to protect people from the evil magic of the witches." Nelda pursed her lips briefly, then continued. "So we do not know why people refuse to defend themselves.

At least that is what the priests tell us. They say the witches' guilt keeps them silent.''

"Not exactly unbiased witnesses, are they?" Lealor could practically smell the corruption of the priesthood. Somebody should do something about them. The god they worshipped truly deserved better priests. Once a group of unscrupulous men got into the priesthood, they could manipulate events to their own interest. Even nonbelievers wouldn't want to fight against a god—just in case they should be wrong and he decided to act against them. Suddenly, she wanted to return to her cottage in the woods where she had friends.

A knock on the door announced the messenger of the duchess.

"Come in," Lealor invited.

"Come to the audience hall at once, healer." Leydon, the messenger, spoke solemnly.

"Very well. Let me take time to change clothes so I'll be presentable."

"I said come at once. With no delays."

"What on Widdershins is wrong with you, Leydon?" Nelda asked. "Lealor will be there right away. Don't worry."

Leydon bowed and left without saying anything more.

"Very strange." Nelda frowned. "It's not like the duchess at all. Leydon and I have always been friends. He looks like he swallowed a pucker fruit."

"Oh, anyone can have an off day," Lealor said before she waved to Reynal and went to her room to wash her hands and face as quickly as she could.

For some reason the atmosphere weighed on Lealor as she entered the audience hall. Credolt stood next to a pair of men dressed all in black. A third black-clad man had his back turned away from Lealor. He was whispering to the priest. All color in the room seemed dimmed. The duchess sat in the duke's chair. She wore a worried look on her face.

"Healer," she began.

"Seize her," a voice said. It was the man with his back toward Lealor.

Lealor's eyes widened. She recognized the speaker before he turned to face her. It was Lorsham, the nasty fortune teller from the fair.

"Surely, witch hunter, you will give her leave to collect her possessions—" the duchess said, half rising from her chair, as if she sensed she needed all the authority she could get.

"No," Credolt said, gesturing to her to remain seated. "Search the witch's room quickly. If we allowed her to return to it, she might work evil magic or escape."

Behind Credolt, the door opened fractionally and remained open long enough for the secret listener to hear the priest speak. The door closed silently. Lealor doubted anyone else noticed it. All her senses were alert. She frantically tried to remember what she left in her room that might incriminate her. Worse yet, was there anything from Fialla that might catch her in this priestly net?

"Priest Credolt, if she must go to Mancy to stand trial, may she not go in a carriage? She did cure my son."

"No, never, not permitted. The witch wagon is specially warded to protect innocent bystanders from any evil spells." Credolt enjoyed flaunting his power, but he could see that the duchess, who had always been open to his suggestions, was changing her opinion of him. He therefore pretended to relent. "However, you may put clean straw in the wagon to cushion her and keep her warm in the cold. See to it," he commanded a servant.

The duchess looked ready to countermand the priest's order, but Lealor spoke. She did not want anyone here to get in trouble. After all, Myst would protect her from real danger, she told herself.

"That's all right. If I might have my cape . . ."

"No," Lorsham said. "The cape might be magical!" His

smile paid Lealor in full for her interference at the fair. She should have a cold, miserable trip to the dungeons of the temple. This thought caused him to smile.

Bright Ones, Lealor thought, noting the wintery grimace that the witch hunter used as a smile. He makes Credolt look positively benign.

"Then she shall have mine," the duchess said, motioning to a servant, who hurried to get it.

Everyone stood still. No one said anything, although the duchess looked as if she would like to speak privately to Lealor.

Credolt took the cape and examined it carefully before handing it gingerly to Lealor. He acted as if she had some noxious disease he was afraid of catching.

"Can you not wait a few days until my husband returns?"

Credolt's heart beat fast. The last thing he wanted was to face the duke for control of Lealor. The witch hunter came to his aid.

"No, that is not possible. We leave immediately for Mancy."

With a nod to his two burly subordinates, he bowed to the duchess, turned, and exited the audience hall.

The two men took Lealor in charge and hurried her from the room. She could barely keep up with the strides of her captors, but as she took her last glimpses of the castle, she noticed Nelda on the top landing of the stairs, making the gesture Aldon had taught her that meant friends were helping.

Chapter
Fourteen

LEALOR was thankful for the cloak the duchess had given her when she felt the sharp bite of the wind in the courtyard. One of the stableboys was carrying a last load of golden straw to put in the iron-barred wagon. She looked at the pitiful few wisps of old straw on the ground. No luxuries for witches around here, she thought flippantly. She smiled at the boy as he exited the wagon.

He nodded to her shyly. "It's all ready, healer," he said.

The guard on Lealor's left released her long enough to strike the boy. "Not healer. Witch. Has she laid some spell on you?"

"Oh, no sir." The boy scurried off before the guard could correct him again.

Lealor silently gritted her teeth. She liked Olwen. They had worked together curing a lame horse. She taught him some of the herbs and remedies to use in healing horses. He was a quick learner, too. She couldn't blame him for hurrying away from the brutal guardsmen assigned to her. On Widdershins, witches couldn't afford popularity. It was too dangerous for other people.

With a shove and a curse, the men helped Lealor into the wagon. They closed the iron door and locked it. When Lealor heard it clang, she shivered. For the first time she felt cut off from her friends.

She looked around her prison. Crude but sturdy planks formed the witch wagon. One closed-in corner behind the driver's seat contained a chamber pot. From this, she deduced no rest stops were allowed her. Thank Bright Ones her provender bag looked worthless, and more important, harmless. She wondered if they would bother feeding her on the trip. While she wanted to see more of Widdershins, she had not planned to make a trip all the way to the capital city. She watched Lorsham enter a closed black carriage which probably contained all the comforts they denied her. With no warning, the driver of the witch wagon whipped the horses and Lealor's journey started with a jolt that would have left her on the floor had she not been holding on to the bars of her cage. She felt sorry for the horses who had done nothing to deserve the unfair treatment they were getting. The stablemaster had given the witch hunter two of the nastiest nags in the stable. Lealor remembered the boys complaining of bites and kicks when they tried to groom them.

Within a few miles, she had reason to be extremely thankful for the new straw. When she grew tired of standing, she tried sitting. The straw protected her body from the full effects of the constant jolts of the wagon. The horses kept a steady and rapid pace. If they showed signs of slowing, the driver whipped them. Lealor watched the scenery with interest. The rolling lands of the duke gradually flattened into a monotonous prairie, dotted here and there with small stands of trees. Lealor guessed from their size that they were probably fruit trees. The breeze was slightly uncomfortable, but the sun beaming down on them kept her from being really cold.

At sunset, however, they showed no sign of stopping. The terrain changed again. Many tall trees formed unbroken forest on both sides of the road. They shaded the wagon from the last rays of the setting sun. Lealor felt tired and sore before they finally drew into an inn yard. The town around it was small and bleak. Lealor waited quietly for her captors to speak to her. To her surprise, no one said a thing to her. Lorsham did stop to give her a triumphant look as the servants led the horses into the barn, but he told her nothing of her future or the trip. After he entered the inn, the servants gave her surreptitious looks and a wide berth. They completed their tasks and hurried inside.

The driver had parked the witch wagon outside, next to the barn. The night was going to be cold, Lealor could tell, because she already felt chilled. She decided they had forgotten her when the nastiest of her guards brought her a battered tin cup containing water.

Lealor would not give him the satisfaction of asking anything. She already knew the news would not be good. She held the cup of ice-cold water in her hands and watched the man carefully.

"Well, why 'nt cha askin' me where supper is?"

For a moment, Lealor considered spitting in his face, but decided it would be below her. Even if her captors were brutal villains, she did not have to sink to their level. So she replied, "If you want me to know, I suppose you'll tell me."

A grudging spark of admiration lit the eyes of the man. "Ya got spunk, witchwoman. Too bad, wasting all that courage."

Lealor asked, "Why?" before she remembered he would use anything she said to mock her.

"The trial." He shook his head. "I can think 'a lots 'a things ya'd be good for besides priest's meat." He leered, leaving her in no doubt as to what use he had in mind.

"Priest's meat?" Lealor had not heard the term before, but it didn't sound good to her. She knew anything he told her would not be comforting, but some scrap of information might prove useful.

"Wouldn't want ta spoil the surprises awaitin' ya in the temple dungeons, Fire Hair." He laughed.

Shivers ran up Lealor's spine at the sound, but she faced him quietly. Pleading with someone like him was useless.

He stared at her so long she felt really uneasy. She trusted that Lorsham kept the keys to the witch wagon on his person. For that mercy, she was glad. Finally, he turned and left her alone.

"Oh, dear," Lealor sighed. She reached into her provender bag and brought out a sandwich. In for a penny, in for a pound, she thought, and blinked her eyes at the cold water in her cup which obligingly turned to hot tea with three spoons of sugar, just the way she liked it.

She heard a mouselike scratching sound, so small she could barely hear it. She looked at the straw carefully. "Come out mousekin. I'll not harm you." She placed a piece of her sandwich near the straw and waited. To her surprise, a small hand reached up from outside and grabbed the bite of sandwich.

"What in the world—Show yourself," she commanded.

"Please. You said you wouldn't hurt me," the boy said, rising to his full height which brought his eyes on a level with the floor of the witch wagon.

"Of course I won't hurt you." Lealor was getting exasperated with the whole witchy business. Since promoted to witch status, people acted like she was going to turn them all into toads or something nauseating.

"Yes. You promised. I didn't know witches kept their promises."

Lealor didn't bother denying she was a witch. What would these people say if they knew her powers were gifts from some goddesses when she was a child and that both her mother and her great-grandmother really were witches? She sighed. "No, I won't harm you. I promise." She saw his eyes on her sandwich. They looked like hungry eyes to her. "Would you like a sandwich?"

"A sand-wich?" he asked.

For a moment she thought, slow-witted boy, but then she realized that sandwiches were an Earthly invention. "Two pieces of bread like mine with meat inside," she explained.

He nodded shyly. She reached into her bag and pulled out a double-decker ham and cheese on rye with tomatoes and lettuce thrown in for good measure. The boy needed the calories.

He had to hold the sandwich in both hands. It was too big for him to get it into his mouth, so he nibbled it like a mouse. His eyes lit up when he got his first bite. He took several bites, but stopped before he finished it.

"Did I make it too big?" Lealor asked with a smile. She was right. The boy seemed half starved.

"Oh, no. It's very good, but I need to save some of it for later."

Lealor raised her eyebrows in inquiry.

"I ate more than my share, but my mother and little sister will still be glad to get this." He patted the little pouch he wore on his frayed belt.

"Hard times at home?"

The boy nodded.

She reached into her pocket and pulled out the only coin she owned. Aldon had given her a half-bit piece for luck when she left for the duke's castle. Lealor figured it wasn't lucky for her, and Aldon would never know she had given it away. Perhaps a small spell would make it lucky for this boy and his family. She waved a hand over it. A faint green glow lit the dark briefly, then dimmed. Now it would duplicate itself every time someone spent it.

She handed it to the wide-eyed boy. He took it without hesitation. Clearly he knew the story of the green glow. "This must be a secret. You understand?"

"Yes." He clutched the small coin in his hand as if it were pure gold.

"Now, put it in your pouch."

He obediently dropped it in.

"Every time you spend that coin, it will reduplicate itself, so you will never be without money. You must be careful. If you spend a great deal of that coin around here, someone might ask how you got the money and find out you have a magic coin. No one must know."

"They might think I stole it, too," he said.

"Right." Something bothered him. Lealor could tell. "What's the matter?"

"Please, Miss Witch, may I tell my mother?"

"Of course. Boys should never have secrets from their mothers." For a moment Lealor wished she could see hers, but she shrugged off the childish desire.

The boy was feeling more comfortable with her. "Your hair certainly is red," he said.

"Yes, it is," Lealor admitted.

"You came from the duke's castle?"

"Yes."

"I have something I'm supposed to give you."

Lealor's mouth dropped open momentarily. "What can you possibly have for me?"

"Some man had a message from Nelda for you." He rummaged in his pockets looking for it, while Lealor fidgeted. "I came because I'm brave and he gave me a whole penny piece." He fished out the crumpled note and handed it to her.

A yellow rectangle of light opened out from the inn. Someone was coming.

"Quickly! Run and hide. Remember to spend your money very carefully!"

Her only answer was another scrabble—gone into the bushes like the mousekin she had thought him to be at first.

The second guard stomped out, rattled the gate to the wagon and checked the lock. "Fool's errand," he grumbled, ignoring Lealor. "Told him nobody ever escaped the witch wagon. Made of iron, isn't it? Witches can't work magic surrounded by iron."

Lealor looked at him solemnly, but inside, her body felt light. Her magic did work, in spite of the witch wagon. She could still free herself, if she wished. She considered whether to melt the bars to slag, explode the wagon, or simply make it disappear. Then she realized why no one ever escaped the wagons. They were innocent victims without a shred of real power. She gritted her teeth. Well, she'd stay a prisoner until she knew the whole, sorry story—and then, they'd find out what happened to priests who messed with people who really did have power!

She had given up trying to do without magic, but she still thought it a good idea to hide Myst. She took a minute to talk to her bracelet, something she had been neglecting to do regularly, she reminded herself. It was easy to forget about the crystalline talisman, since she stayed invisible and had not tightened on Lealor's wrist in warning when the witch wagon came for her.

Without wasting any more time, she cast a tiny concealment spell and took out the crumpled paper.

"Dear Friend," the message began. "I've taken the liberty of moving some of your things out of your room. They are already on their way to your home. I'll see your friends hear about what has happened to you. I'm sure the duke will act when he gets back. Try not to worry. Lady protect. N."

The note cheered Lealor. She knew she could not save it, so she reluctantly blew on it, reducing it to ashes. A chill breeze nipped around the edge of the barn and scattered the ashes to the ground. Lealor curled up in the front of the witch wagon, pulling the straw over her. The large cloak covered her completely, once she drew her legs up. She turned the satin lining to the outside and snuggled into the rich fur, blessing the fierce vervel who died to keep her warm.

Even with the straw piled, the hard floor made sleeping difficult. Three more days to the capital, Lealor told herself, remembering Reynal's geography lessons. She fell asleep, not aware that the temperature around the wagon was a full twenty degrees warmer than the air in the remainder of the yard. The bright moonlight of the chill night made invisible the green aura that surrounded Lealor. Two silver tears rested on her cheeks.

Chapter
Fifteen

THE three days seemed long to Lealor. The constant jouncing of the witch wagon bruised her in places she had never been aware of before. The odd thundering sound of the wheels on the unpaved roads became an irritation. The sick joke of the ice water for her only meal also palled.

As they traveled nearer to Mancy, the little towns became more numerous. At each, priests subjected Lealor to public scrutiny. While a few gawkers filled with hate jeered at her, a number of the townspeople remained quiet, casting her secret looks of sympathy. These attitudes told Lealor that most of the population remained unimpressed with the priesthood. Sadness hung in the air. She detected an inverse ratio. The larger the temples, the unhappier the populace.

In spite of having a nourishing meal every night, she was hungry. Part of the softening up process made the accused witches physically miserable when they arrived at the temple. From the hate calls of the rude, she learned the name of the god the priests worshipped. Sardoom. Roughly translated it meant He Who Rules the Skies. Jumped-up impostors needed overblown names. The Lady, who was entitled to the name She Who Rules the Night, would never countenance being called by so grandiose a title.

Lealor was so aggravated by the time the wagon actually pulled into Mancy, she healed minor problems and cast a gentle good-luck spell on the poor who were jostled by the wagon as it pushed its way down the streets. The black coach containing Lorsham had hurried before them, eager for the comforts of civilization, Lealor bet. That meant only the guards might notice her magic. They showed muscle, not mind. They named her *witch*, so she might as well deserve it. If Lorsham were representative of the priestly clan, no amount of innocence saved anyone accused.

She hadn't expected the temple to be in the poor section of town they traveled through. When she thought about it, she knew why the witch wagon was taking so long to arrive at its destination. They paraded her through Mancy as a kind of object lesson. See the wicked witch we are protecting you from and thank the priests. If she looks innocent to you, fear the priests and give them no trouble. Sardoom's priests were capable of truly nasty scheming. Lealor ran her hand over her bracelet. Myst still clutched her wrist, although she remained invisible.

Finally, the witch wagon rattled through better sections of town. Imposing ranks of large stone buildings formed the last two blocks before they reached the Temple of Sardoom. The wagon wheels rolled easily across the level marble squares of pavement in the temple courtyard. Sardoom welcomed ostentatious display, judging by the temple grounds. No one spared expense in creating the temple environs.

The wagon rolled to a halt beside a small door on the side

of a huge slab of pink marble. Incongruous, Lealor thought, watching curiously. She had never seen a jail or dungeon so pretty. She didn't enjoy the scenery for long.

A fresh set of guards wearing priestly vestments ushered her unceremoniously out of the wagon. All humanity vanished from their eyes as they looked at her. A cold psychic aura surrounded her and the priests. They said nothing to her, but pointed the way she must travel along halls which inclined ever downward. She passed rows of closed doors with peep-hole grates at eye level and food slits, also closed, a foot above the ground. She wanted the reassurance of Myst's presence, but the dragon bracelet did nothing. She did not dare to rub her wrist for fear of drawing attention to the talisman. She grudgingly admitted to the impressiveness of the trip to her cell, but she refused to admit her fright, even to herself.

The leading priest opened a cell on the left and stood aside, a bony finger pointing within. Lealor entered. The door closed slowly with a faint creak. The light from the corridor dwindled, then vanished as a hollow boom reverberated followed by the sound of the key in the lock. Lealor was alone in the darkness and silence.

"Is anyone in here with me?" she asked softly.

Her words echoed in the dark.

"Very well," she muttered before casting a warding spell against any priestly snooping. To her surprise, it worked. "My magic is unaffected by the priests' spells," she said aloud. She turned, ready to open the door. She gestured. The door remained closed. "Correction, Myst," she told her bracelet. "Some of my magic still works." Lealor lit mage fire so she could see her prison. Beside the door, two holders for torches stood empty, ready to light the small room if anyone cared enough to bring torches. A pallet lay in one corner, none too clean. It looked as if it might almost fit the iron bed frame that stood against the far wall. A bucket stood in one corner beside an open drain in the floor. "All the comforts of home," she mused.

She cleaned the pallet and replaced it on the bed frame with a wave of her hand. She sat heavily, surprised at how good it felt to sit without the sound of rolling wheels and the jounce of the witch wagon banging against her. She pulled a bowl of warm water and washcloth out of her provender bag. After she cleaned herself, she combed her hair and braided it, defiantly using the bag to provide a rubber band for the end. She didn't have any idea how long she might be imprisoned, so she reached into the bag for a cup of hot, sugared tea, a roast beef sandwich, and a bowl of navy bean soup. After eating, she whisked everything back into the bag and stretched out on the pallet. She ached all over. She snuggled into the cloak and drifted off to sleep almost as soon as she pulled the cloak over her. Her last thought was that the duchess had given her the nicest present she had ever had.

Myst materialized briefly and flew around the cell, checking it thoroughly. It seemed safe enough. She returned her physical form to Lealor's wrist, and resumed invisibility, but her spirit arrowed through the ether, searching for her father. She needed Wyrd's advice.

Back at the cottage, Pook had almost worn a path in the floor pacing back and forth. Something told him Lealor was in danger, but he wasn't sure what to do about it. His keen hearing told him someone had entered the clearing. He padded to the door of the cottage and waited for the visitor. An old woman came up the path. When she saw him, she smiled. Her bright eyes looked at him and then she nodded and entered the cottage, passing him without any show of fear.

"Changer's greeting," she said.

Pook woofed companionably and settled beside the fire.

"I have news for Fafleen. Will you convince her to come here so we can plan what to do?"

Pook nodded and made a whining sound that Fialla correctly interpreted as a request for more information.

"The priests arrested Lealor for witchcraft and took her to the temple prison in Mancy."

Pook growled.

"I don't like it, either. The local priest waited until the duke was away, then brought in a witch finder. He locked Lealor in the witch wagon and whisked her out of the dukedom so quickly I'm sure the priest feared the duke's intervention. Lealor told me about Fafleen. I'll stay here and wait while you go into the mountains and find her. She must fly to rescue Lealor, if she can get to Mancy before it's too late."

With no sign he understood, Pook rose and left the room. Fialla watched as he headed west. She put the kettle on the fire, noting that Lealor used a fire sprite to keep it lit. The cottage was well-warded, for no sign of magic showed outside. It must have been Aldon's cure that alerted Lorsham. Then she sat to wait.

Pook crossed the river and headed into the mountains. He followed an almost invisible path that led west. He flinched when Berdu appeared before him, but he did not stop traveling.

"Wait, you fool bear," Berdu gasped. He trotted just behind Pook whose distance-eating lope never slackened. "I need to give you something."

Pook stopped and turned back toward a red-faced Berdu. He tipped his head to the side in inquiry.

In between puffs, the little man carried on a monolog. "How's an animal like you going to convince Fafleen to return?" He shook his head. "No sense. Nonsense. No sense," Berdu muttered to himself while searching in his pockets for something. At last he drew out a piece of birch bark. He took a moment to smooth the bark. Then he used his long second fingernail to inscribe a symbol on the bark. "There. That should fetch her." He handed the message to Pook. "Just give her that. See you remember, now!" With these words, he disappeared. Pook wasted no time in returning to his original course with the bark clutched in his teeth.

Three days later through the grey mist that precedes dawn, Fafleen flew into the clearing before the cottage, dropping the disgruntled bear she had carried in her talons.

"I'm here," she announced unnecessarily, since she filled the clearing and only a blind man could have missed seeing her.

Fialla stood in the cottage door. "I am glad to make your acquaintance, Fafleen. I am Fialla," the old herbwoman introduced herself.

Fafleen wasted no time on courtesy. "I got your message. How did you learn the symbol for *danger* in dragon script? Few humans have the patience or intelligence to learn our language." Fafleen didn't wait for an answer, but continued talking rapidly. "How did this happen?" Fafleen fumed. "I leave Lealor alone for a few weeks, and the next thing I know, she's in trouble."

"Lealor went to heal the duke's son. She was successful, but the priest accused her of witchcraft and sent for a witch hunter. She originally met the witch hunter here at the fair. They didn't get along. He posed as a fortune teller."

Fafleen interjected a snort. "That explains it."

"Nelda, a village girl who works for the duke, sent Lealor's things to the village. I've taken charge of them."

"If witch hunters are active, I'd suggest you hide anything you have that might incriminate you," Fafleen advised as if Fialla lacked the sense to know how dangerous any connection to Lealor might prove.

"I did." Fialla gave her a wintery smile. She could see exactly what Lealor meant about the dragon's attitude toward humans. Somehow the old parchments never mentioned how snobbish dragons could be.

"What do you suggest we do now?" Fafleen saw nothing incongruous in her asking a mere human for instructions.

"It will be necessary for you to rescue your friend."

Fafleen's nostrils expanded, the equivalent of a martyred look for a dragon. "I knew that," she hissed softly. "Have you any suggestions as to how?"

"I can draw you a map of the way to Mancy. I have already prepared an amulet to allow you to fly safe from the priests' traps."

"What traps?" Fafleen banged her tail in irritation. It took too long for humans to share information.

"When the priests banished the dragons, they set magical spells to guard the kingdom from them. If the dragons had not left, they would be no threat to the kingdom now, for the spells the priests set so long ago still exist."

"You know a great deal of magic for a simple herbalist."

"I am old. My family is dead. I study the old books that remain for me to guard. It is safe to share what pitiful magics remain to me. One who comes from the gate must be trustworthy. Your powers seem to augment my own." She smiled. "Also I have been careful so that the priests know nothing of me and my—abilities."

The dragon paid scant attention to Fialla's explanation. Saving Lealor held most of Fafleen's interest. "What should I do in Mancy?"

"Before I can tell you that, I must see what is happening to Lealor." Fialla took a bowl from within her cape and entered the cottage where she filled it with water.

Pook, who had watched the exchange, entered the cottage too. Fafleen was too large to join them, so she laid her huge head outside the door with her eye positioned to watch what happened within.

The old woman poured hot water over a pinch of herbs and added a vial of some oily substance. The mixture reminded the dragon of an egg-coloring kit Seren had given her brother except that the swirls of color arranged themselves to form a picture. Fialla put her finger to her lips and looked both Pook and Fafleen in the eye to make sure they understood before she muttered words in some outlandish tongue neither the bear nor the dragon had heard before. With the completion of the spell, the picture came to life and the three could also hear as if they were present in the room where Lealor was being tried.

Sleepy as she was from her early rising, Lealor sensed a different magic in the courtroom. She glanced around, but could see no source. The priests were all listening to a long roster of so-called charges that Lorsham read aloud.

"And that she did, willfully and with full knowledge, heal within the city of Mancy from the very witch wagon itself," Lorsham concluded, fiercely rolling up the scroll from which he had read.

Several of the priests looked at Lealor as if doubting that she could heal from within the guarded witch wagon. Lealor smiled at them quietly, awaiting her turn to speak.

"What say you?" the high priest of Sardoom asked, not of the accused, but of the assembled priests. They looked at one another and each nodded. "Guilty." The first priest in line began, "Therefore we pronounce—"

The high priest raised his hand and the voice fell silent. "Mardal, you may have a few minutes to speak to the witch."

From the shifting bodies and odd looks on the faces of the other priests, Lealor could tell how unusual a proceeding this was. Originally, she had expected a chance to speak in her own behalf. She did not want any of her friends or acquaintances to try to speak for her. In this priest-ridden society, who knew what might happen to them? She found out about the rules as her case continued. Now she knew that in the temple court the accused was always guilty and so, granted no chance to speak.

Mardal, an old greybeard, tottered over to her and beckoned for her to follow. He moved slowly, tapping with his staff. Lealor followed, glad she had used a spell to lighten the chains they had loaded her with. Except for being awkward, the fetters intended to force her to the humiliation of asking the guards to support her or to make her fall to her knees, were of no importance. Once in the small antechamber, Mardal sat on a bench along the wall. Lealor got her first close look at her advocate.

The guards positioned her before the priest. He nodded his dismissal and they left.

Mardal's silvery eyes gazed unseeingly at her.

"Why, you're blind," Lealor burst out.

"Yes. Sardoom took my sight."

"How horrible!"

"Ah. No, child. The god in his mercy took it gradually, allowing me to get used to the darkness."

Lealor realized she was in the presence of one of the god's real followers. The lines in Mardal's face spoke of resignation and peace, not the hellishness and avarice engrained in the faces of the other priests. "I'm sorry," she said, seeing nothing unusual in her compassion for suffering.

Mardal inclined his head. "I grieve also. That you should be a witch with so fair a voice is sad. Had you chosen to train that voice in Sardoom's service you would sing for him."

Lealor made a face, happy momentarily for Mardal's affliction. At least he couldn't see how disgusted the idea made her. "Did they make no attempt to save your sight?"

"I prayed to the god, but my superiors told me if it was the will of Sardoom I would see. If not, I would serve in darkness."

Lealor snorted. "Would you like your vision restored?"

"I am ill. The healers tell me I shall not see another harvest season. Which is true, in any case." Mardal chuckled at his little joke. He fell silent for a moment. "I should like to see the flowers in my garden and the birds that have sung so sweetly for me since the god took my sight."

Here sat a truly good priest. Lealor thought that Sardoom must be a poor god—if he existed. Her guards had taken her to the alter of Sardoom so Lealor could be awed by the might of their god, but all she had seen was an outsize gilded statue. She felt none of the presence she felt on Achaea when she had seen the gods there during her childhood. And Mardal believed in this sham! In a spontaneous excess of pity, she reached out and lightly touched Mardal's eyes.

Green light flared. Lealor's own eyes closed against the brightness. When she opened them, Mardal looked at her from eyes which saw again.

"Child," he gasped.

"Now you can see your garden," Lealor told him with a smile.

"You are a witch!"

"No. I am a healer. There is a difference. My powers were given to me when I was a child." She could tell Mardal felt very disturbed about his cure. "Sardoom," she called, feeling like a hypocrite, "if it was not your will that your faithful servant Mardal see, revoke the healing." She paused, waiting. Since she didn't believe Sardoom existed, she didn't expect anything to happen and it didn't.

"Sardoom, I thank you for your gift." Mardal's hand shook as he wiped a tear from his cheek.

Again, nothing occurred. Lealor relaxed. It was always risky betting against the gods on a strange world. If Sardoom had existed, he might have chosen to blast her to smithereens. A shaft of light came through the small window set high in the outer wall. It illumined Mardal.

"My child, my superior commanded me to tell you something."

Lealor lifted her eyebrows.

"If you claim to be a simple healer, your sentence will be death by the flames, for your powers go far beyond healing."

Lealor swallowed. Even with Myst to save her, the prospect didn't appeal.

Mardal raised an admonitory finger. "If you should choose, you might volunteer to be of service and so escape burning."

"What kind of service?" Lealor's experiences with the priesthood had left her suspicious of anything they planned.

"Many years ago we fought a war against ungodly magic wielders."

Lealor nodded. She knew about that.

"There still remained among us truly magical beings, the weren and the dragons."

"So I've heard."

"In Sardoom's name, we priests banished the dragons—for a price."

"What price?"

"Every year a great dragon comes to the sacrificial rock on the coast and takes from us a maiden." Mardal's face showed his grief. He seemed incapable of continuing.

"Nobody wants to be the sacrifice, right?"

Mardal nodded.

"Go on." Lealor's words dropped, cold as ice crystals into the silence in the chamber.

"No death by fire, if you volunteer to go to the dragon willingly."

"So that's what that guard meant by priest's meat," Lealor muttered too softly for Mardal to hear. She took a deep breath before answering. "I have no choice but to agree." Privately, Lealor thought it would be easier for Myst to handle a dragon than a crowd of maniacal priests and deluded citizens. She had only one question to ask of the kindhearted priest. "When?"

Mardal looked at his hands which he folded in his lap. "Tomorrow morning at sunrise," he said.

Chapter
Sixteen

FAFLEEN raised her head and snorted a gout of fire into the air. "Tomorrow!" she hissed.

"The sacrifice always occurs at dawn on the first day of spring. I did not plan on the priests' cunning. They gave her a choice of which death she prefers." Fialla spoke as she rummaged in her cloak pockets. "Now where did I put . . . ah . . . here it is." With these words she drew out a small silver box.

"What do you have there?" Fafleen put her eye to the doorway again like a gigantic peeping Tom.

Fialla took a parchment packet from another pocket in the cloak and went to the blocked opening. "If you'll move back a bit, I'll come out," she said calmly.

The dragon moved away, dropped her head, and waited. Pook followed Fialla from the cottage. Intent on the problem of rescuing Lealor, they didn't notice when Berdu materialized at the edge of the clearing. He moved himself to a good vantage point and slowly faded from sight without any of them realizing he was listening.

Fialla opened the parchment. The dragon and the bear saw it was a map as she spread it on the ground in front of Fafleen. "This is where we are now," Fialla told them, placing a small stone on the map. "This circle"—her finger touched it lightly—"is where you must go. You cannot reach her within her temple cell. To the east of Mancy lies Spellcape. The sacrificial rock is on this spur of land that juts out into the water. The great dragon will come out of the east."

Fafleen extended a claw and delicately, for a dragon, scratched a line on the map. "And this is the distance I must fly?"

"Yes, but you will also have need of this." Fialla proffered the silver box.

"What's in here?" Fafleen took the box in her talons. She cocked her head like an inquisitive robin and shook it gently.

"During the war between the magic users and the priests, the ordinary citizens were always afraid the dragons would side with those with the power. The priesthood placed bane wards over the countryside to protect the people."

"Fine thing. The priests using magic when they warred against those with the power. How—human." Fafleen couldn't resist a chance to draw attention to human hypocrisy.

"The priests have ever used magic. They only forbid its use to any who are not priests." Fialla's grim smile showed she understood the irony in the situation.

Pook growled softly at Fialla's words. His keen nose detected Berdu, but since the little creature had helped with the message to Fafleen, the bear saw no need to expose him.

Fialla continued speaking. "Within this box is a powerful charm against dragon bane wards. Carrying this, you can fly overland without harm or hindrance."

"I wish I had flown around more so I'd know the area. If I had, I could just pop over there." Fafleen's talon touched the location of Spellcape. "Now, I'll have to fly the whole way. It's going to be close, but I think I can make it by tomorrow morning." Fafleen's second claw retracted in the dragon sign for luck.

Fialla held out a pouch she took from her belt. "Do you want to carry the box in your talons, or shall I put it in the pouch and tie it to your leg?"

Fafleen clutched the box tightly. It almost fell from her talons when she stretched her wings in a brief warm-up. "All right. I guess I'd better have you truss me up like a carrier pigeon. I won't have any time to waste looking for the box if I should drop it. Why humans don't make things a reasonable size, I don't know."

Fialla hid a smile from the dragon as she placed the silver charm box in the pouch and tied it carefully to the dragon's leg. She refrained from telling Fafleen that anything a dragon considered reasonable in size would be so huge she couldn't have carried it to the cottage.

"If I start now and fly all night, with time out for a tiny snack to keep up my strength, I should just make it," Fafleen said.

Pook woofed. He had seen the dragon eat. Her tiny snack would be a whole cow or deer. He waddled over to Fafleen and reared to his full ten-foot height. The dragon towered over him by another ten feet. She paid no attention to him. He roared.

"Yes, Pook. What do you want?"

Fialla watched quietly. The bear's size was impressive, but standing before the dragon made him seem like a small boy asking his mother for something he wanted desperately and feared he would not get.

Pook waved his paws for attention and roared again.

Fafleen hissed her disdain. "How am I supposed to know what this berserk bear wants?"

"He wants you to take him with you."

Pook dropped down to all fours and nodded to Fialla.

Fafleen flexed her wings. "You weigh a ton, bear."

Pook growled.

"All right. I'll try. If I feel you're slowing me down, I'll drop you off somewhere in the woods, though."

Pook nodded.

Fafleen grabbed him, rather ungently, Fialla thought, and spread her wings. With the first wingbeat they rose into the air. The takeoff wobbled badly, but the small clearing hindered the dragon. By the time her sixth wingbeat pulled them high above the forest, she had compensated for Pook's weight and size. She flew rapidly for a few minutes before she remembered the length of her flight and slowed. How should she confront the evil dragon that would accept Lealor for a sacrifice? She shifted ideas around in her head until she felt dizzy. Then she simply told herself she would wait and wing it, never realizing how funny her thoughts would seem if anyone heard them.

While Fafleen's takeoff appeared casual, she had used her photographic memory to imprint the map in her mind. She had planned how far she must fly by sunset to achieve her estimated time of arrival. Pook hung, most ungracefully, clutched in her talons. His thick pelt protected him from their sharpness, but hanging for hours above the ground was uncomfortable, Fafleen knew. She wondered what part he planned to play in Lealor's rescue. After several hours of flight, the dragon began to notice the not inconsiderable weight of the bear. She flew on, mentally gauging the distance she covered. An hour before sunset, she could see that carrying Pook slowed her. She watched until she saw a broad meadow surrounded by trees. No human habitation marred the landscape, so she decided to set Pook down.

Pook growled as Fafleen lost altitude, but the dragon ignored him. She settled to the ground and released her hold on the bear.

He immediately rose on his hind legs and roared.

"Forget it, bear. I'm sorry, but I'm starting to feel tired.

Fialla's charm does work. I can fly through the warded areas, but it takes a lot more effort than I ever thought it would. The closer I get to Mancy the more wards I will meet. Carrying you is just too much. Both of us on the way won't equal one of us there tomorrow at dawn. It will be a close thing, now.''

Pook dropped to the ground and growled.

"No sense arguing. This is where you get off," Fafleen said. "Bye, Pook. I'll tell Lealor you meant to come."

And with these words, Fafleen stretched her mighty wings and ascended, leaving an angry bear behind her on the ground.

Pook wasted no time roaring after she disappeared in the distance. He started walking after her although he knew it was futile. Darkness fell as he labored onward. His fastest pace put him so far behind the dragon that he growled to himself. He stopped at several streams to drink, but he took no time for food. He would be too late to take part in Lealor's rescue, but he would be near and perhaps he could still be of some assistance. He waddled down a steep slope, the shortest distance across the area being a straight line. One of the rocks to which he trusted his weight slipped, wrenching the paw that Lealor had helped heal. From that time on, Pook limped. After a while his paw swelled. It became harder and harder to put weight on it. Finally, Pook sat down under the bright moon and complained as bears do with a woo-oh sound. His part in Lealor's rescue was over.

Then he felt a strange ruffling in his mind. He thought he heard a voice say, "Poor bear. I help." For a moment, everything went black. His nose felt the cold, but his fur kept his body warm. When the blackness ceased and he could see again, he was on the point of land next to the pole which was outfitted with the manacles to hold the sacrifice. His paw no longer ached. He looked up at the moon and bowed his head. The strange feeling in his mind retreated, but he felt his thanks appreciated.

He began to look for a good place to wait for dawn.

* * *

Lealor, too, awaited the dawn. She had a rough idea of time from the meals the priests served her. After the last one, she found herself pacing the floor. A movement in the far corner caught her eye. It did not surprise her. She had placed the meals the priests brought her on the floor for the mice. They didn't find the food inedible. She used the provender bag to provide her meals. Something about the movement in the corner was different. She went over to see and for a moment, she froze in horror. She couldn't help it. She hated snakes. The horrid thing had probably eaten those nice little mice. And worst of all, there wasn't a stick in the room to keep it away!

She sat on her bunk and drew her feet off the floor. She watched as a three-foot snake drew itself out of the hole. When the entire creature was within the room, it drew itself up and inflated before Lealor's fascinated gaze. In a matter of seconds Berdu stood before her.

"Berdu!" Lealor cried, her happy face ample reward for any visitor.

"Shhh!" Berdu placed a finger to his lips. "I can't stay. Powerful magic . . . powerful magic . . ." He muttered to himself as if he had forgotten Lealor entirely. "So weak, so weak . . ."

"Berdu—"

Berdu's eyes lit up. He raised a finger. "That's it!"

"What is?" Lealor asked, relieved he had come to the point at last.

"Steakfruit!" he announced triumphantly.

"Steakfruit?" Lealor hoped Berdu wasn't part of any rescue operation. He'd probably get everybody concerned killed.

"Do you have any steakfruit?"

"Well, I still have the provender bag . . ."

"Excellent. Let me have it."

Lealor untied it from her belt and passed it to him.

"Good," he said, and tipped the bag into his mouth which, snakelike, seemed to be able to hold a bushel at a time.

Lealor watched as he gobbled the fruit straight from the bag. He didn't even seem to chew. He ate just like Fafleen, she thought.

"What did you come to tell me?" Lealor asked as he finally lowered the bag and passed it back to her.

"Not to worry," Berdu said with a reassuring smile, but all Lealor could think of was his pointed teeth—not human.

"Not to worry!" Lealor's words almost exploded. "That's a ridiculous message! Here I am waiting for dawn so I can be fed to some overgrown Saurian—"

"Tsk, tsk, mortal."

Berdu reminded her of Rory. How Lealor wished he were here. He wouldn't just stand there eating as if that were the most important thing in the whole world.

Berdu interrupted her thoughts as if he knew what she was thinking. "That old herbwoman friend of yours has sent Fafleen and that tame bear to rescue you." He paused to think. "If, that is, the dragon can fly fast enough and she doesn't forget and drop the bear."

"How did Fialla manage to find out what happened to me?"

"Water witching. Saw it in a bowl, she did. Uses bits and pieces of the old powers . . . magic . . . evil magic . . . dangerous . . . No magic," he warned, looking around fearfully. "Be ready tomorrow at dawn." With these words, he became thinner and thinner, and vanished like quicksilver into the mouse hole he had used as an entrance.

"Berdu! Wait! I want to know more!" The snake's tail vanished even as she spoke. "Myst! Did you hear that?" Lealor asked. The bracelet lay like dead metal on her wrist, refusing to tighten or move. When would Myst get over the sulking fit? "Be ready? What in the world can he mean by that?" she muttered to herself as she paced up and down her cell. She had no way of knowing Myst had sent her essence to visit her father to ask for guidance.

Lealor couldn't convince herself to try sleeping. Sleep seemed too close to death for her to want anything to do with it. To Lealor, dawn seemed far away and all too close at the same time.

Fafleen stopped only long enough to bolt a farmer's sheep whole. She had no time for a decent meal, but if she did not eat, she might lack the strength to fight the dragon at dawn.

Well, she thought to herself, at least that's settled. First I fight the dragon and then I free Lealor and fly away with her. One part of her mind thought, "A piece of cake." At the same time, she remembered her mother's words, "If your eyes are bigger than your stomach, you may end up with a tummyache, daughter." Fafleen hissed. Those human sayings her family had a tendency to use could be quite disconcerting!

She would have sold her scales for a chance to rest. Air freighting that bear had been a mistake. What business did a dragon have carting around a friend of a friend, anyway? Her wings ached with the effort. She had never before flown so far and so fast. Her breath became a series of short hisses. She felt the tremor in her wings as she forced them up and down. Finally, she began looking for a place to land. She had to rest or she would arrive at the rock too weak to do anything except hiss—if she had that much breath left. The road below had widened. A good sign. She must be approaching the capital. She saw a flat field a distance away from the road. Excellent, she told herself. She could take time for twenty winks and still arrive at dawn. She settled wearily to the ground, trying to ignore the hunger pangs. A growing dragon needed a great deal of food. She felt like a hero for snacking on that sheep instead of decimating the farmer's flock. He didn't know how fortunate he was, she decided, carefully tucking her tail under her body so the tip stayed warm. Cold tail, bad cold, the dragon saying went.

At least she could report to her mother that she had followed good hygienic practices while on this adventure. She sat, meaning to rest only a few moments, but shortly, her eyes closed and a gently snore seared the grasses before her as her head sank to the ground. She slept.

Fialla, always a light sleeper, awoke. She had returned home after the dragon and bear left for Mancy. Someone was in the room with her!

She nodded at the fire, which flared up, lighting the room. A little man stood beside her table, looking into her magic bowl.

"And who are you?" she asked as she rose from her bed.

"Blood and bones, woman! Ask something important! Can't you feel that the young dragon is in trouble?"

"Are you sure?"

"If I was sure, don't you think I'd be doing something about it? Use this to see where she is!"

Fialla filled the bowl with the correct ingredients and snapped her fingers. All the candles in the room bloomed with light. She looked into the bowl and saw Fafleen sound asleep.

"Let me see where she is, mortal woman," Berdu said.

"Can you do anything to help?" Fialla asked.

"How am I to know? Me against that dragon. Oh, dear. No good ever comes of meddling . . . no good . . . those wards are so painful . . . meddle, meddle."

Fialla watched as the little man faded to a misty outline and then disappeared!

Chapter
Seventeen

BERDU materialized behind Fafleen. "You're getting ancient, Berdu," he murmured to himself. "At one time you made pinpoint landings half the world away. To be young and magical—that's real treasure." As he spoke, he walked around to stand before the dragon. "Oh, my scales and talons," he whispered. "She doesn't know me. If I yell to wake her up, she may singe me like a roast rainbird." He paused, deep in thought. Then he took three steps forward so he was directly in front of Fafleen's nose. He drew back his foot as if he intended to make the point after a touchdown. At the same time he brought his foot forward he screamed, "Wake up, youngling." He dematerialized just as his toe connected with the dragon's nose. Fafleen didn't even take time to consider the little man in her strange dream. The grey mist hung over the field, waiting for the sun to burn it away. In the east, a lighter band of sky half hidden by clouds indicated where the sun would rise shortly. She propelled herself into the air and flew as she had never flown before.

Pook hid on a ledge facing the sea, away from the crowd of people and priests that accompanied the sacrifice to the appointed place. He took a chance and reared up enough to see over the lip of rock that hid him from the people. He scanned the sky. Where was Fafleen? He knew his eyesight was bad, but surely he should be able to see a dragon coming!

He dropped down from the awkward position and looked eastward. The edge of the sun's disc rose above the sea. In the brightening day he could just make out a speck that grew larger even as he watched. He heard a priest say, "The dragon comes."

The great red dragon was as big as a pad on his paws when Pook decided he could wait no longer for Fafleen. The sea was deep at the bottom of the cliff. If he could free Lealor and push her into the sea, they might still escape. The dolphins served the weren. They would help Lealor get to the sailboat they were to bring him. As prince, he had proved his were ability by staying in bear shape for a full year. He was eager to return home and to help Lealor. He hoped she knew how to swim. It would certainly simplify matters if she could. If not, he would have to manage. On land, they had no chance of surviving.

Back at Fialla's, Berdu hopped in anguish, holding one foot. "Well, woman," he said between hops, "can you see what's happening?"

"The dragon rose in the air and flew like an arrow. I don't know if she reached Lealor in time." Berdu's bravery surprised Fialla, so she only smiled a little at the weird figure he cut jumping up and down on one foot.

"Well, look!" Berdu commanded with a screech of exasperation.

"Someone spilled all my herbs while trying to use my bowl," Fialla said gently.

A shamefaced Berdu replied, "Don't you have any spare herbs that will do?"

"No. The spilled herbs will not work for farseeing. It takes hours to set the spell without the special ingredient," Fialla explained. "I have no more of it, either."

"Special ingredient? What is it?"

"Powdered dragon's scale. I doubt I can ever get any more."

"Have you a file?" Berdu peered at her from under his bushy eyebrows.

"Yes, but—"

"Then get it, woman! The dawn is breaking!"

The puzzled old lady gave him her file. He rubbed it over his long second fingernail. "Try this," he told her, tapping the fine powder from his nail from the palm of his hand into hers.

"But—" Fialla believed it would never work, but she decided to humor her guest.

"Button your lip, and just do it!" Berdu hobbled next to Fialla to watch her set the spell on a fresh bowl of water with the powder from his nail filing in it. "Got to stop meddling in human affairs," he murmured to himself.

For one brief instant, they saw Lealor at the stake and a red dragon in the distance, flying over the waves. They did not see Fafleen. Then the colors ran together and everything disappeared.

"Bring it back, woman! I wish to see!"

"I can do no more. It is in the hands of the Lady," Fialla said. She rubbed her tired eyes.

The animation Berdu had displayed dwindled. "Gone . . . all gone . . . all my power . . . all gone . . . gone . . ." As he spoke, he became paler and paler and finally with a *pop* he disappeared, leaving a puzzled Fialla to rock and worry all alone.

Pook climbed over the ledge, stood on his hind legs, and roared the terrible challenge of an angry bear. The priests and their guards, who had backed away to a respectful distance, turned and hurried farther down the hill.

Once the priests stood at the bottom of the hill with the people, the high priest turned to the captain of the honor guard. "Command your men to shoot the bear!"

"What if an arrow should hit the girl?"

"Fool! Can't you see that the bear is between us and the sacrifice? Have your men fire, I tell you!"

The archers were awaiting the command, having nocked their arrows when they heard the high priest. The captain said, "Fire, but don't hit the girl."

The high priest had shrieked his command, so Pook and Lealor heard him over the growing murmurs of the incredulous crowd. The wood on the stake that held the chains was old. Pook's great strength allowed him to paw the chains free as the first flight of arrows flew around them.

"What now?" Lealor did not see how she and Pook could escape. The crowd and the guards cut off any chance of getting down from the promontory. The red dragon flamed the air as he got ready to dive.

Pook looked over his shoulder at the dragon. He saw the archers ready to shoot again. He wasted no time in pushing Lealor to the edge of the cliff and over. He jumped, glad to be out of the hail of arrows. He ignored the two wounds he had gained shielding Lealor. Below, a pod of dolphins had taken charge of her, chains and all. They gathered around her in the water, buoying her up until she understood they would give her a ride if she would grab hold of one of them. Pook commanded them to take the girl to the boat that awaited him. Not daring to change into his human form where the priests might see, he paddled after them. Already the dolphins and Lealor were far enough from shore that the bowmen posed no threat. It would take some time for the priests to organize ships to search for Lealor. He looked up in time to see the red dragon diving directly at Lealor and her escorts. Pook stopped trying to paddle after them and sank beneath the waves.

Fafleen was easily a mile from the scene when Lealor and Pook hit the water. She had the excellent vision of a bird of prey and could see the red dragon diving. "Oh, my scales and talons. I hope I can do this." She used her dragonly ability to travel and popped into view right under the nose of the red dragon, uttering a von Fafnir war cry that would have pleased her granddragon if he had heard it.

The look on the red dragon's face was ludicrous. A pale blue female with silver eyes, half his size, threatened him. In his surprise, he vanished.

Fafleen gritted her teeth. She felt as a human might if someone hung up a telephone in her ear. How dare that red devil disappear from before her eyes! Two could play that game. Her brother delighted in teasing her, then disappearing with some item she wanted. He had never been able to escape her wrath. This big bully should know what it meant to tamper with one of her friends! She wanted to find dragons to help her translate the old books she had found, too. With no more thought than that, she disappeared as well. The confrontation between the dragons caused consternation in the priests and populace. The question on everyone's mind was whether the dragon thought that the treaty had been broken. He might reappear and flame everyone on the headland! As that thought occurred to people, they started to leave. The high priest wanted to be well away from the place in case the dragon felt cheated of his prey. How had the blue dragon been able to fly over the land? Considering the problems posed by the dragons, one redheaded witch seemed very unimportant. Now that the dragons were gone, it was too late to retrieve the witch. The high priest dispersed the remaining crowd and returned with the other priests to the temple, making plans to renew the dragon bane wards and offer sacrifices to Sardoom.

The cold sea water revived Lealor's wits. The farther the dolphins took her, the stronger her powers became. She wondered exactly what the priests did to turn the sacrifices into mental flyweights. It had to be a spell over the headland, for she had deliberately refrained from eating anything the priests sent her for food, fearing some mind-altering herb.

She murmured a spell of unbinding and her chains fell from her. She released her hold on the dolphin she rode long enough to kick off her shoes which the sea water had ruined anyway. A second dolphin waited until she was ready, then nudged her. She understood this dolphin would give her a ride next. By the time the sun set she felt exhausted. She also felt like a prune, as if the water had wrinkled her into her eighties long before her time. The dolphins, like steeds, took turns bearing her onward all day. She had no idea where they were taking her, but anywhere was better than where she had come from, she decided.

The waters gradually grew warmer as they made their way southward. A bleeding dolphin joined the pod. Lealor gestured until the others let her use a healing spell. The dolphins surrounded the newcomer, leaving Lealor to tread water, tired as she was. Finally two of the pod helped the dolphin. They swam faster than the group that returned to continue giving Lealor a ride. Soon they were so far ahead she lost track of them.

At moonrise she looked over the silvered sea and saw a sailboat coming toward her. When Lealor's dolphins brought her to the side, the young skipper leaned over and smiled. "Your sailboat awaits, milady."

Lealor thanked the dolphins and turned to climb into the boat. Her tiredness made her awkward. To her horror she found she could not pull herself up. The man took her hands and one of the dolphins flustered her greatly by giving her a needed boost from the rear.

"Upsadaisy," he said as she landed ungracefully over the side.

The young man turned to adjust the sails, giving her a moment to catch her breath and regain her composure. Although there was almost no breeze, the sailboat whizzed through the water. Lealor recognized that they traveled by the power of magic. The more she thought about her rescue, the more questions she had. By the time the skipper of the boat turned to her, she had a half dozen of the most important ones ready for him.

"Why do I think I recognize you from somewhere?" she asked, feeling foolish, for surely she wouldn't forget so attractive a man.

"Question time already?"

It annoyed Lealor that her question amused him. While grateful for her rescue, she felt tired and hungry and hardly able to cope. Her patience had evaporated along with most of the water that was in her clothes. Even her thoughts were cross. *It wouldn't be in good form to demand he feed me, but how I'd like to eat!* Could she ask him to return so she could look for Pook? A hollow feeling inside her told her the bear might well be dead, but she wanted to know for sure. Never before had she become so attached to an animal.

As if he heard her mental conversation with herself, he passed her a flagon of some sweet drink. After she swallowed a few mouthfuls, she felt amazingly restored. When he turned to get some food, Lealor saw two fresh wounds along his back.

"Strange," she thought. "How does a man get marks like that? I'd swear they were made by arrows . . ."

He returned to her with a basket of fruit. She looked into his eyes. The moonlight changed the colors of everything, but she was ready to swear his eyes were brown, like his dark hair. "Pook?" she whispered softly.

He made the same sound the bear had when not pleased. It was Pook! No matter what he said, she recognized him now, moon glamored or not. "Pook!"

The happiness in her voice would have made a stone sing. He nodded. "No, not Pook," he told her. "My name's Rand."

"Let me put some salve on your back," she said, reaching into her provender bag. Her fingers groped, but the bag remained empty. "Oh, what a time for the charm to give out!"

"Don't worry. The salt water stung, but it cleansed the wounds. I do have some healing ointment here somewhere," he said, rummaging under one of the boxlike seats. "Here it is!"

Lealor took the ointment from him. "Turn around," she commanded. "This may hurt," she warned.

"Just like old times," he joked.

"Shape-shifter?"

"Weren," he corrected. "I'm glad you don't mind. Many women would have a fit, here alone on the sea with a weren. Then, I guess a girl who has dragons for friends is pretty shockproof."

"All the members of my family have dragons for friends. And besides, Fafleen is really quite nice when you get used to her."

"She didn't improve much on closer acquaintance with me," he said, remembering his trip while clutched in her talons.

"If you're flying Air Fafleen, it's better to ride on her back. Her talons are sharp."

"My fur protected me."

Fed, and somewhat revitalized by the sweet drink, Lealor wanted some answers. "Might I ask where you're taking me?"

"Home," he answered.

"And where might that be?" Lealor hoped her remark didn't sound sarcastic, but she felt too tired to be polite.

"Fire Mountain Island," Rand looked at her and continued, "the place where the weren live since we left Magilan. We trade to the east and south of the island, but most of us long for news of our old home. I spent a year in wereshape to learn what is happening there. I couldn't turn back into a man until I had completed my time. It's a rite of passage with the members of my family."

Only one piece of information registered with Lealor. "An island with an active volcano on it?" The weren could certainly pick winners, she thought. First they were forced out of Magilan by the priests and their people, and now they lived on an island that could blow its top at any minute.

"We monitor the volcano closely. Our wisewomen can often predict the future. We'd have plenty of warning before an eruption," he told her as if he knew what she was thinking.

"How will I return to my cottage?"

"You should stay away from there for a time. It might not be safe to return too soon. You must have come through that old gate with the dragon. Perhaps our wisewomen can help you return through the gate if that is your wish."

The food and drink on Lealor's empty stomach were making her sleepy. She smiled at Rand, blinking her eyes like a child who wants to stay up even though it's past her bedtime. "I'd like that."

"Then sleep now. Tomorrow at dawn we'll be home!"

"Home," Lealor thought. "What a lovely word. I promise I'll try to appreciate it more—if I ever return." Her eyes closed. She never felt the brief kiss Rand gave her before he covered her lightly so she wouldn't get chilled.

Through the night he watched so no harm could come to her. The dolphins returned and rejoiced with the prince who was coming home at last.

Chapter
Eighteen

L EALOR awoke as Rand lowered the sails. A city
    sprawled at the foot of a high peak. Halfway up the
    side a fairy-tale castle glistened in the clear morning
air. The harbor curved along the crescent of a bay. No wonder
Rand loved his home. She couldn't believe she had slept
through the bustle of the busy docks. "Why didn't you wake
me?" she asked as he tossed the mooring line to an old man.

"There was nothing you could do until we landed," he
said, waving his thanks to the man who tied up the sailboat.

"Isn't it kind of dangerous to have a small craft like this
moored in such a busy place with all these bigger vessels?"

"Don't worry. This is the royal mooring. No one will so
much as chip the paint on the rail," he said, helping her onto
the dock.

"Won't you get in trouble—" she began.

"So many questions for such an early hour in the day."

He waved at the man who brought a horse to the end of the dock. "Come on," he urged, pulling Lealor along with him.

"Here's Talisman, Your Hi—" the man said with a bob of the head.

Rand interrupted him in mid-word. "Rand, Jonn." Then he turned to Lealor. "This is Jonn, the best friend and servant one could have."

Lealor smiled shyly. Everything was moving so fast! She watched Rand clap Jonn on the shoulder as a token of his thanks.

"Can you ride?" Rand asked.

"Of course!" Lealor was most indignant. She had already made friends with the horse. Her father had proudly said that if a beast had four legs, Lealor could ride it. She had ridden wild unicorns as a child. She had no qualms about this beauty.

"May I?" Rand gestured to Jonn's mount, waiting behind him.

"Of course, Your—"

Rand's finger silenced him. "Let's go," he told Lealor.

As they rode through the city, the early morning sun gilded the pastel houses that lined the streets. Rand led the way higher and higher. Finally they climbed so high that Lealor knew their destination was the castle. The road widened, so they rode side by side. Lealor, filled with questions, hardly knew what to ask first.

"Do you live in the castle?"

"Yes. It's a nice old place. Hundreds of retainers live there to serve the royal family."

"Who are the king and queen?"

"The king is Erik and his queen's name is Alian. They have three children."

"What do you do?" Lealor eyed the brilliant flowers that seemed to spring naturally from every patch of ground beside the road. Some, she was sure, were species she had never seen on Earth or Realm.

"Me? Mostly errands and things for King Erik and Queen Alian."

"Things like checking up on Magilan?"

"Sometimes. The kingdom of Magilan is northwest of here. I've traveled on the merchant ships to the south west where the wildings are and to the south east to trade with the desert dwellers. The dragons lire far to the northeast of our island. I've even visited the Witches' Wood on Aerie Island several weeks' journey south of here."

"Widdershins is a lot bigger than I thought. I've never heard of any of the places you mentioned."

"No reason why you should. No Widdershins kingdom has people with your fiery hair."

Lealor blushed. She hoped her hair wouldn't make her seem alien. For a moment, Lealor debated telling Rand about the mistake that brought her to Widdershins, but then she decided to wait. As nice as Fire Mountain Island was, she was not sure she should trust Rand's people with the gate secret. After she had stayed a few days, she would make up her mind about what to do. "Surely some people here must have red hair!"

"Oh, yes, we have some folks we call redheads, but their hair isn't half as beautiful as yours."

The compliment drove Lealor's next question from her mind. Which was just as well, for Rand started talking about his family.

"I haven't been home for a year, but I'm sure my mother and father will be glad to have you stay with us. My little sister Silanna will probably drive you mad with questions. My father says he would have named her Curiosity if he had known what she would be like as she grew. My married older sister won't be home for a visit until next year."

Lealor felt a little pang of homesickness as she listened to Rand talk about his family. For the first time she wished Seren and Argen, her brothers, were on this adventure with her. In a pinch, Argen and she could have trained Seren to help with the gate even though he hated to use his powers. Then they would have needed only one more person to stabilize the group and they could have fixed the gate. She thought that Baloo had done something to the Realm gate as she left. Why had the young Bright One wanted her on Widdershins? No wonder her mother sang him back to sleep when he awoke if he caused such trouble!

The guard on the battlements of the castle saluted them as they clattered into the courtyard. Servants hurried to take their horses. Everyone was very glad to see Rand, she could tell. He kept shushing them for some reason or other.

"The king and queen will be here directly," a man dressed in silver silks told Rand.

"We won't wait. We'll just go right in," Rand said as if he owned the palace.

Lealor tried to hide her astonishment. He must be one of the favored nobles, she decided. She watched as the doors of the castle opened. A tall, silver-haired woman dressed in purple came down the stairs and opened her arms to Rand. Lealor saw them embrace. The queen certainly was young, she thought. Her silver hair marked her as a user of moon magic. Just then a little woman in a stained gown bustled down the steps. She stuck a pair of garden gloves in her pocket as she came.

"It's been so long, my son," she said as Rand enveloped her in a bearhug.

A huge man lumbered out of the castle. "Where is that ne'er-do-well traveler?" His voice boomed so loudly in the courtyard that it echoed.

The servants bowed their heads briefly in respect. Lealor decided this must be King Erik.

Rand received a hug that would have crushed a smaller man. Their coming together reminded Lealor of films she had seen of two mountain sheep butting heads. Then King

Erik swung Rand to the side as if he were a small child. "And who is this?" he said, in quieter tones.

Lealor, for one, was glad King Erik had spoken quietly. If he had boomed at her, she would have died of fright. He was certainly an imposing figure.

"For shame, Rand. You have forgotten to introduce your friend," the gardening woman remonstrated, even as Rand wiped a smudge of soil from her cheek.

"This is Lealor." Just the way he said her name made Lealor's heart bump against her ribs. It sounded so official and proprietary, somehow. He pulled her out of the crowd she had faded into and to the forefront of the group. "And these are my parents, King Erik and Queen Alian." The woman in purple raised her eyebrows. "And my little sister, Silanna, of course."

Lealor curtsied and hid her surprise as well as she could. She hoped her mother never found out what she looked like when she met Rand's parents. Mirza didn't stand on ceremony often, but she had inflexible standards about a few things. "Your Majesties," Lealor said with a smile. "Silanna," she added with a nod. Little sister, indeed, she thought. She didn't fit Rand's description of her at all.

The look on Silanna's face would have soured milk. Lealor sighed inwardly. At least one person here on Fire Mountain Island didn't like her much. She wondered what she had done to make an enemy of Rand's sister at first meeting. She didn't have much time for wondering, because Rand's mother gave her a hug like those Lealor received from her own family.

"I'm so glad to meet you," the queen said, making Lealor feel truly welcome.

Lealor smiled at Queen Alian. She loved her already. The queen wiped her hands on her skirt, leaving stains. Lealor often forgot that she was wearing a skirt when she was gardening and did the same thing. It made a bond between them.

"Mother," Silanna spoke for the first time, "it's only a few hours until the noon meal. Don't you think we should allow Rand's guest time to—clean up?" Silanna's look at Lealor's sea-soaked outfit, dried by the wind far from the touch of an iron, said clearly she didn't care much for its wearer.

"I suppose I can plant those bulbs this afternoon," Alian announced with a smile. "Are you interested in plants, my dear?"

"Mother—" Silanna began.

Rand, who had been watching, broke in. "The answer to that is definitely. She's an herbalist, mother."

Alian looked at Lealor with delight. "Really?"

Lealor's eyes danced as she answered the queen. "Really and definitely."

"All that dirt—" Silanna began.

King Erik said, "Silanna, why don't you hurry lunch along a bit. All this greeting has made me hungry and I know Rand can always eat. After the sea air, I'll bet even Lealor has a great appetite. This afternoon I've a council meeting. Rand can give his official report then." A frown marred the king's face momentarily. Then he forced a smile. "I'm glad to have you home, son. Especially since you brought proof of your good taste." He winked at Lealor. "And she can blush!" he announced with a chuckle.

"Father, give her time to get used to you before you tease her to death," Rand said, obviously pleased with his father's opinion of Lealor.

"You two!" Alian said. "Behave yourselves or Lealor will be wishing she had never come." She turned to her daughter. "Please see to the meal, dear. Cook's so ingenious. Tell her in about an hour. I'm sure with your help she'll think of something. I'll take care of our guest."

Silanna nodded quietly and walked away.

Lealor wondered how Alian and her gruff but genial husband ever became the parents of such a regal daughter. Rand was very like his father in looks and his temperament matched his mother's. Silanna, however, seemed like a changeling. She certainly didn't resemble her parents.

"Be sure to give Lealor a chance to clean up before you drag her out to the gardens, mother," Rand said. "We'll probably have to take on extra help to keep the mud from the marble," he teased, sounding exactly like a harried housewife.

"Come along, my dainty cleaning maiden," his father said, clapping Rand on the back with a blow that would have felled half the men Lealor knew.

The queen led Lealor inside. No pictures adorned the walls of the wide corridors, but large windows allowed generous amounts of sunshine and flower-scented air to enter. Alian noticed Lealor looking out of the windows. "The bare walls seem to fit best on Fire Mountain Island. Although we haven't had an eruption in years, it's always so much easier to clean up with a fresh coat of whitewash, rather than worry about all those dusty wall hangings and ancestral portraits. I was never much good at sewing, although I can cook when I get the chance. As a girl, it always seemed so dreary to sit around sewing. Grace knows there are chests full of linens in reserve. When Erik found out how I felt, he allowed me to put the tapestries and portraits in the audience chamber to awe visiting dignitaries. At least there, they do some good." She ushered Lealor into a bedroom where a huge tub of water invited a guest to bathe. "Just give your clothes to one of the maids, and we'll soon find something to fit you."

"Thank you, Your Majesty." Lealor turned to find Queen Alian gone. "Is she always so—precipitate?" Lealor hoped the maids wouldn't be angry at her choice of words.

Both of the maids giggled. "Oh, no, mistress. She's just so happy Rand is home," the taller maid answered.

"We all are," her companion added.

Lealor could see from the maid's demeanor that Rand was a universal favorite among the ladies.

"Lady Berith will be especially glad he's home. She's Silanna's best friend, you see."

"Mitalla, don't gossip!" the larger girl said, turning to Lealor in the same breath. "If you'll give Mitalla your clothes, she can set about getting you some new ones."

"Unless you'd like me to stay and help you with your bath," Mitalla said.

The little maid's brown eyes reminded Lealor of a cocker spaniel she had once owned. She felt almost guilty at refusing help, but she didn't want to be waited on, and this wasn't the time to start a bad habit. "Sorry," she said to both girls. "I'll take my own bath, thank you."

The maids placed a screen around the tub and Lealor stepped out of her clothes, tossing them over.

"The green flask is for your hair," Mitalla called softly just before the door closed.

Lealor swathed herself in the oversize towel after her bath and stretched out on the bed. "Time for a nappy, Myst," she told her bracelet, which gave no sign of life. "I do hope you get over your sulks soon," Lealor said, enjoying the feel of the soft pillow at her head. She turned to look out of her window at the birds which glided past. She thought briefly of Fafleen, but realized there was nothing she could do for her friend. Then she dozed as she waited for Mitalla to bring her clothes.

She felt so comfortable, she didn't answer the knock on the door. It opened quietly. Mitalla and the other maid entered.

"Oh, isn't she pretty!" Mitalla whispered. "Much prettier than Lady Berith."

"Shhh! What if Lady Berith found out what you said?"

"Oh, Fia, the princess can't spend all her time spying on the servants."

"I'd curb my tongue if I were you. Lady Berith can be difficult to get along with as it is."

"Just because she's the special friend of the princess . . ."

"Your gossipy ways will get you in trouble yet," Fia warned as she straightened the room.

"Isn't it funny that Lady Berith has red hair and green eyes? Only Lealor's eyes are the soft green of moss and Berith's are harsh, almost a yellow green. Lealor's hair is such a rich color. Wait until they come face to face. Berith's hair will look like feather root compared to hers. The prince will never marry Berith now in spite of Silanna's plans."

"Just put the clothes at the foot of the bed. I'm afraid we'll have to waken her, or she'll miss lunch."

Lealor had been waiting for a chance to speak at some juncture that would not embarrass either maid. This innocuous speech seemed her best opportunity. She didn't care much for eavesdropping, but now she understood why Silanna disliked her. She yawned and turned over, giving her best imitation of someone waking from a nap. "Oh, are you back already? I must have dozed off. Are these the clothes you brought me?" She hitched her towel under her arms and swung her feet to the floor. "How did you ever find so many?"

Fia answered. "All of the ladies of the court sent you something to choose from."

Lealor picked up a bright pink dress with a neckline that plunged almost to the waist. She shook her head no and set it aside.

"Lady Berith sent that one," Mitalla said. "She wore it only once. Someone said she looked like a lady from a joy house in it. Nobody ever saw her wear it again."

"Mitalla," Fia warned.

"I won't tell," Lealor said, earning Mitalla's loyalty forever. "Mitalla, you'd best be careful. I bet there's some folks that can hold a grudge over almost nothing."

Fia's smile showed her gratitude for Lealor's cautionary attempt.

"You've met Lady Berith?" Mitalla asked, unaware of the silent communication between Lealor and Fia.

"Hold your tongue!" Fia said, plumping pillows as if she had her companion under her hands.

A knock on the door interrupted them.

"Come in," Lealor said, pulling a soft yellow dress over her hair.

"Are you ready, child?" Queen Alian asked.

"Almost, Your Majesty," Fia said, running a brush through Lealor's mane and preparing to pull it to the top of her head.

"Nothing fancy, Fia. Just a couple of combs to pull it back so I can see where I'm going. I wouldn't want anyone to have to wait for me." She smiled at the maid. "And besides, I'm starving!" she added for Queen Alian's benefit.

"We'll soon fix that," the queen said, opening the door.

"Thank you both for everything," Lealor called over her shoulder as she followed the queen from the room.

Queen Alian began talking as they walked down the corridor. "I hope you'll have time to see the gardens after the council meeting."

"I've been looking forward to that," Lealor told her. "I enjoyed the flowers coming up the mountain to the castle. Some of the ones growing here I've never seen before."

"Everyone is so kind. They bring me starts of plants from all over. Almost every ambassador and trader brings me something or other. I hope the council meeting won't keep you too long."

"Am I supposed to attend the meeting?"

"Ordinarily, no, but you were a prisoner of the priests of Sardoom, our old enemies, and they'll want to question you."

"As a prisoner, you don't learn much, but I'll be glad to tell them anything I can. Those priests are no friends of mine."

"I suppose they're still squeezing every copper they can from everyone."

Lealor nodded. "That's them, all right." Just then they

passed a window wreathed in a yellow-flowered vine. "That scent is wonderful! What plant is this?"

"It's called maiden's glory. I've been especially lucky with it. Most places it's only a tiny shrubby vine, but here, at this window, it climbs two stories. It's magical, you know. If a maiden casts it into boiling water and wishes, it gives her a true vision of her beloved."

"Then it's a kind of farseeing herb?"

"I've never thought of using it for farseeing, but it should work. Most seers use a combination of other herbs."

"Clear sight, honesty, and evilbane?"

Alian's delighted look told Lealor she was correct. "I've taken you the back way," Alian said. "Once we get down these stairs, it's only a few steps to the main hall. The dining hall is likely to be full of hungry courtiers, eager to see Rand, of course, and to get first word of Rand's decision."

Lealor looked at the queen inquiringly.

"Yes. It must be his decision whether to sail north to find the cause of the sudden sea rise. Our captains say it must be caused by ice melt, but why would the ice melt now? Here on the island we're losing valuable feet of shoreline. And it threatens Fire Mountain if it rises much more." They turned a corner and entered a busy hallway. "Oh, dear, it's all so complicated. You'll hear all about it at the meeting."

In spite of Lealor's curiosity, she hoped the meeting would be short. She wanted to try to use the maiden's glory to see what had happened to Fafleen. She had a feeling that Fafleen might get into difficulty. Fafleen was a very brilliant dragon, but she was young. No matter how intelligent someone was, a certain amount of experience made one wise. Although Lealor felt relatively safe, considering she was on a volcanic island that might explode, her magical senses were on the alert, warning her of possible danger.

Chapter Nineteen

"**M**IND trap!" Fafleen's ejaculation sounded like a curse. The red dragon turned his head to find the smaller blue dragon right behind him. She could not see the amused twinkle in his eyes as he flew directly at the tall cliffs that rose before them. He flew so low that the spray from the immense waves attacking the cliffs wet them both. At the last possible minute, he turned his immense power from speed into a thrust to provide altitude. He flew straight up the side of the cliff nearest him and settled with a swish of his wings on the flat top of the escarpment. He felt, rather than saw, the breeze created by the blue dragon's landing behind him.

"Well done, little blue lady," he hissed in the ancient tongue of the dragons.

"My name is Fafleen von Fafnoddle, daughter of Ebony von Drak Fafnir and granddaughter to Fafnir von Fafnir," she answered in the mindspeech that dragons had used since the Beginning.

"Beautiful flying, Fafleen von Fafnoddle."

Fafleen ruffled her scales as she caught his mental comment that her title was longer than she was. "Thank you." Her nod of acknowledgment was curt, showing him that she had not yet forgiven him for his transgressions.

"And why do you consider yourself the protectress of the young human with the fiery hair? I can sense no magical spell which binds you to her."

"The bonds between us are of our own choosing."

"Since when has a dragon made compact with mere Widdershins humanity?" The sun struck scarlet fire from the male dragon's scales when he stretched his neck upward to look down his nose at Fafleen.

"I wouldn't know. We are not from Widdershins."

"I am Flare von Berdularion, last of my line. Do not tell me anything which is not true."

"Not lie, truth. Lealor—"

"She of the fiery hair?"

"Do you want me to tell you this, or not?" Fafleen did not wait for his answer. "We came through a gate long abandoned."

"An existing gate in Magilan?"

"Yes. Activated by a young Bright One called Baloo. We were pulled from our world to this one. Baloo has meddled once too often. Something must be done about him. Lealor's mother will be most unhappy with him. Did you not sense the mind net set to trap me as we journeyed here?"

Flare shook his head. "No. Escaping a blue fury who threatened to harm me took all my concentration."

"I'm sorry I lost my temper." Fafleen gritted her teeth. She hated to apologize, but she knew she owed the red dragon the courtesy. At least when she told her mother of her foolishness, she could say she followed the proper dragon rituals.

It would go far in mollifying her parent. She muttered the ritual words of dragonly abasement required by the *Dragon Code*.

"Accepted," Flare told her.

Fafleen considered his terse acceptance a gracious response. In a few words, she told the red dragon all she knew of Lealor's stay in Magilan and about the books in the cave system.

Flare nodded his understanding. "Now, it is my turn. You feared for the life of your friend. Those fears were not necessary. For many years my people have sent me to collect the priests' sacrifice." He backed up a pace as Fafleen barred her teeth and hissed.

"Human sacrifice is barbaric!" Her silver-blue tail slithered from side to side, indicating her readiness to attack if necessary.

"You do not understand. When we dragons fled Magilan, we brought with us—at their request—a number of humans who formed a colony in the valley below. At first, the sacrifices were very important because so many men chose to come with us. They needed mates, you see. Now their numbers have swelled. In a few short years, they will form a force to return to their homeland and free the populace from the priests' injustices."

"Now I truly mean my apology," Fafleen said.

"Let's forget past misunderstandings."

Again Fafleen was favorably impressed with Flare's graciousness. "Agreed," Fafleen said, watching as a group of dragons flew across the valley toward them. "Is this the welcoming party?"

"You might say it is. They are probably wondering why I did not land in the town square below. Usually the sacrifices are quite upset when I fly them here."

"Humans are emotional. You get used to it in time."

Flare didn't think he would ever get used to the screaming maidens he delivered to the townspeople. He had no intentions of admitting his weakness to this attractive female, who probably wanted a fierce mate to help rear her young.

"Is there any dragonmage who might help me see what has happened to Lealor? She needs to know about the mind net."

"Our Ancient One knows many things. She has stored the books we dragons brought with us in her cave. She can answer most of our questions. Perhaps she can aid you."

"That'll solve all my problems!" Fafleen's enthusiasm shone in her silver eyes.

"I said perhaps, pretty one." Flare returned her inquisitive look quietly. "The Ancient One is blind. She can no longer use her books. If what you seek to know is not in her mind already it's lost to you."

"Not ssso! For I can read!" Fafleen hissed proudly.

"One so youthful can read?"

"Of course. In several dragon tongues and also in some human languages."

"And why would a dragon have need of human scratchings?"

Fafleen stretched her neck to look Flare in the eye. "Some humans are wise. The lore in human books is no mere scratching on parchment."

Flare decided to avoid argument. Instead, he said, "Here comes the welcoming party." Fafleen and he watched as four dragons landed on the cliff top near them.

All four lowered their heads in dragon obeisance. "Sire, have you news we should carry?"

"Indeed, yes, heralds," Flare said. "This year's sacrifice"—he paused, carefully selecting his words—"was diverted elsewhere. I shall inform the humans in the valley below in good time."

The heralds bowed again and flew back across the valley to the dragons' home caves high in the surrounding mountains.

Flare turned to the astonished Fafleen. "And have you

nothing to say?'' He waited, but Fafleen remained quiet. ''A rarity, I'll wager. Well, now we go to the Ancient One.'' With no further word, he rose into the air and angled toward the northernmost peak in the valley.

Fafleen tried to gather her scattered wits as they flew. Royalty, for scales' sake. No civilized planet had seen a royal red dragon for thousands of years. The dragons believed the royal line had died out. If she didn't manage to translate the old books, she'd still have news of great value to redeem her foolishness in winging into that gate so blindly!

As they neared the mountain, Fafleen saw a dragon-sized opening about one-fourth of the way down. Now that they were closer, she could see an almost invisible plume of steam rising from the top of the peak. She flinched as Flare trumpeted out a call before they landed.

''Who comes to the Ancient One?'' The thin hiss made Fafleen's blood run colder than usual.

''I, Flare von Berdularion,'' her companion answered in High Dragon.

''Welcome. You may enter.''

Flare disappeared through the opening. Fafleen gave herself a mental shake, and followed him. The inside was nothing she could have imagined. A thin beam of light entered from a crack high in the ceiling of a vast cave. A million slivers of light answered the single ray, turning the vast cavern into a fairyland of delicate colors as it reflected from the surface of the interior walls. A vast geode formed the entire cave.

Fafleen's first thought was, *and she can't see this? A tragedy.* As her eyes adjusted to the light, she saw the Ancient One. A giant of dragonkind, age had turned her scales to purest white. Where Fafleen's scales were hand sized, the old dragon's were small, no larger than teardrops, a mark of royal lineage.

The Ancient One turned her raised head in Fafleen's direction. ''And who is this you bring to visit me? She is not of our world.''

"You are well-deserving of your reputation for wisdom, Ancient One," Flare said respectfully.

Fafleen shifted into her best High Dragon, hoping she wouldn't mispronounce any of the words. No one on Realm ever spoke it except for ceremonial occasions. Her mother would scale her if she didn't show proper respect. She carefully crossed two claws, hoping the good-luck gesture worked for dragons as well as humans. "Greetings, Ancient One, Mother of Knowledge, Keeper of the Laws and Lore."

"Ahhhh." The old dragon's answer was a hiss of pure pleasure. "Come, daughter, and speak to me of your quest."

"You—you know her?" Flame said, as astonished as Fafleen had been earlier.

"Yesss. She has come to me in dreams. The Silver Seeker has a task to perform here on Widdershins."

"She's blue, Ancient One."

"Then her youth hides her true color which will come at her maturity. She shall stand, a silver dragon, a blessing on Widdershins dragonhood. Since you bring no sacrifice for the human colony below, you have done well in choosing her as a substitute guest."

"I shall need to inform them, Ancient One." Flare's tone showed his respect as did his lowered head. His gesture reflected itself in the million facets of the cave's crystalline walls.

Being discussed as if she were not actually present felt distinctly odd to Fafleen. She certainly didn't feel as if she were a seeker. The idea had never slithered through her mind—a Silver Seeker! Well, they were legendary. The last one had died centuries before she was born.

"We have things to discuss. You may go," the Ancient One told Flame.

Flame went.

"Now, daughter, you wish to see those who are absent?"

"Yes, Mother of Knowledge." Nothing had awed Fafleen as did this ancient dragonmage. Her form of address showed it. For once, she was glad her mother had been such a martinet about forms and protocol.

"Well-reared, a credit to your parents," the Ancient One hissed, pleased with the ceremony Fafleen knew that young Widdershins dragons hadn't learned since leaving Magilan. "Through there, you will find my scrying place." She gestured to a narrow fissure in the rock at the back of the cave.

Fafleen stifled a squeamish twinge. How she hated narrow openings! Especially those which led deeper into a volcanic mountain. She crossed the cave slowly, positioning her wings as tightly to her body as possible. The diamond shards were capable of ripping scales from flesh, she was sure. Just before she entered the crack, the Ancient One spoke.

"Ask to see those you know who are on the world of Widdershins."

Mercifully, the fissure was short. Fafleen gasped as she came to an immense pool of liquid fire, clearly fueled by the volcano itself. Fafleen paused on the edge, hesitant about disturbing such a magical place.

"Ask, daughter." The old dragoness had entered silently and stood behind the younger dragon.

"I would see those I know from Realm who are here with me."

For a second, the pool bubbled fiercely, then smoothed into a red mirror, showing the crystal form of Myst trapped within the silver strands of pure force that created the mind net.

"Myst, can you hear me?" Fafleen had experience with the mind net, but her brush with it had given her no idea that Lealor's talisman was trapped in it.

Behind Fafleen the Ancient One moved her head in a series of magical passes.

Myst opened her mouth to speak, then remembered her father's command. The twitch of her tail showed her anger. She nodded.

"Where is Lealor?"

A shrug of crystal shoulders answered Fafleen.

"Not trapped with you?" Fafleen continued without waiting for Myst's negative gesture. "Baloo put you in there, yes?" Fafleen answered her own question. Her talons clenched. "Then Lealor is unprotected!" Myst's head drooped. Fafleen's slow breath of realization fogged the pool. When the mist cleared the scene had changed.

The dragon saw Lealor standing in a garden admiring the flowers with an older woman. "Lealor!" Fafleen called, but she got no response. She quickly described the scene to the white dragonmage.

"It is no use, daughter. Queen Alian has bespelled Fire Mountain Island. All mind communications must come through the seers."

"But—"

Daughter, your friend is safe on the island. I shall cast a spell to tell us if she leaves. Now I would hear your story." She led the way back to the other cave.

Behind them in the empty cavern, the red magma formed yet another image. In it, Mirza and Jarl stood in the gate.

Chapter
Twenty

BERDU watched the gate, wide-eyed, as an older version of Lealor materialized with a tall, blond man.

"Well, I hope this is Widdershins," Mirza said with a sigh.

"It had better be. It was hard enough to force entry here. Now to find Lealor." Jarl stepped out of the gate, pulling Mirza with him. He stamped on the ground. "Nothing like a solid world under you," he muttered.

"You seek the flame-haired one?" Berdu asked, peering from behind a tree.

"Yes," Jarl said, hiding his surprise.

Berdu paled around the edges. The man sounded very fierce.

"Let me handle this, dear," Mirza whispered, giving her husband's hand an admonitory squeeze. "My name is Mirza and I am Lealor's mother. This is Jarl Koenig, her father.

She and her friend disappeared some time ago from Realm, where we live. It has taken us all this time to find where she went. Her absence even now worries us. Can you help us, please?"

Berdu slowly solidified and pointed. "Follow this path, cross the river, and wait at the cottage in the clearing," he said before disappearing.

"Well, milady," Jarl said, offering his arm to his wife. "The cottage awaits."

"What a strange little man. How can a wizened creature like that remind me of Old Fafnir from home?"

"I haven't the slightest notion, but he did give us some advice, even if it sounded like an order. If a building awaits us at the end of this path, it's worth checking out." He dropped Mirza's arm. "The path is too narrow to walk abreast. I'll lead the way."

Mirza followed, watching the woods around them with bright eyes. She saw some familiar plants and many that were not. After they found Lealor, she wanted to speak to a person who knew about local herbs. Some interesting remedies might turn up.

"All right. I could use a hand here," Jarl said.

Mirza smiled to herself. Jarl acted so helpless about magic. He had learned much since he first wore the dragon bracelet and arrived in Realm. Yet, with all their adventures, when it came to something magical, he always deferred to his wife. Mirza wondered if he understood how powerful a mage he actually was.

"The fact I don't want wet feet, requires a little magic here," he said, looking down at the swiftly flowing current of the river.

Mirza muttered a spell and the river obligingly hardened. "Come on," she said, starting to cross the water. "I don't want to expend much magical energy. We might need it later."

Jarl raced across like a long distance runner making a sprint for the finish line. He puffed ostentatiously. "I'm across," he told her.

"Not any too soon." Mirza laughed at the look on his face as he turned to find the river behind him.

"You weren't going to hold it for me until I was safe on this side!"

"You're wearing hiking boots. They'd dry," she said over her shoulder. She took the lead in finding the cottage.

"Well, at least your strange little man didn't lie about this," Jarl said, pushing open the door.

"Feel the protection spell?" Mirza said. "I'd recognize it anywhere. It's one of Lealor's."

Jarl prowled around the room. "Yes, and these are her belongings. She's been here!"

Mirza noticed the thin layer of dust on the table. "Not for a while. Now what do we do?"

"We have no choice but to give your little friend a chance. I wonder where he disappeared to? I hope he went to get someone who knows what's going on."

Mirza sat at the table. "Sit, Jarl. There's nothing to do but wait."

Jarl sat and drummed his fingers on the table top. Mirza's thoughts whirled. Rescuing their daughter was not going to be as easy as they had supposed.

Fialla jumped when Berdu materialized beside her with a little *pop*. "Blessed be. You frightened me, Berdu."

"You didn't turn a scale—er, hair," Berdu told her. "Steady as a rock, you were."

"Do you have any news of Lealor?" Fialla finished pouring a distilled herbal remedy into a small jar. She covered it and wiped her hands on her apron.

"Not news of her, but news." Berdu helped himself to six cookies from a plate.

Fialla drew a short breath, sensing that Berdu would tell

her when he was ready. Her foot tapped impatiently on the floor.

"Humans. No patience . . ." Berdu mused absently before popping all the rest of the cookies into his mouth at once.

Fialla bit her tongue. Berdu was starting one of his rambling intervals. "Berdu!" she said sharply, hoping he wouldn't disappear, taking his news with him.

"Magic is dangerous," he said, looking around the room carefully, "but this is an emergency!" With these words he took her hand, and closed his eyes.

Fialla had no time to blink before she was at the door to Lealor's cottage. "Widdershins' sake, Berdu!" she said, making no effort to hide her exasperation. "You could give a body warning before rushing her hither and yon so rudely."

"Only hither." Berdu chuckled at his own joke. "Humans are so persnickety," he murmured to himself as he faded out.

"Berdu! You come right back here! I've got to walk all the way home without a wrap and this breeze is chilly!" Her words were wasted on the air. Berdu had vanished. "Maybe Lealor has something I might borrow," Fialla said, pushing open the door.

When she entered the cottage, Fialla, Mirza, and Jarl stared at one another.

Fialla recovered first. "That Berdu!" she said before she smiled at Mirza and Jarl. "You must be Lealor's mother." She sketched a blessing sign in the air and looked at Jarl.

"Like two peas in a pod," Jarl referred to his look-alike daughter and wife.

Mirza gave her husband a look, then said to Fialla, "Yes, of course. I'm Mirza. And this is Jarl Koenig, her father."

"My pleasure, I'm sure." Fialla offered the old courtesy with a smile. "I can guess that you are here to find your daughter." She didn't wait for confirmation. "I wish I could give you her exact whereabouts, but I do not know. The last time I saw her, Sardoom's priests had chained her to a post on Sacrifice Rock, and a red dragon flew towards her."

"What!" Jarl banged his fist on the table. "See if she ever gets a chance to use another gate"—he looked at Mirza's shocked face—"once we get her home safe," he concluded in a voice whose loudness compensated for his uncertainty.

"Where is this rock?" Mirza asked, leaning forward as if she were prepared to leave for it at once.

At the same time Mirza spoke, Jarl was asking, "Who's this Sardoom? How did those scurvy priests get her? Why hasn't anyone done anything? Someone's going to be sorry they chained my daughter to some rock!"

Fialla decided to answer Mirza's question first. "East of the city of Mancy." Fialla took pity on the distraught parents and added, "But I do believe she is safe—somewhere—because neither Pook nor Fafleen returned."

"Pook?" Jarl's gruff voice rumbled. "What's a pooka got to do with Lealor?"

Fialla looked puzzled by Jarl's use of the word *pooka*, but explained, "Pook is a bear she rescued and nursed back to health."

"I should have known," Jarl said. "Lealor's better than an Animal Welfare Division. So you sent a bear and a dragon to rescue her?"

"Not exactly. They insisted on going," Fialla said, sitting on the cot, since Mirza and Jarl were using both chairs. She rummaged on the shelf above it for the map she left the day Fafleen needed directions. "Here is where we are," she said, placing it on the table and using a spoon to mark the spot. "Here is Mancy." She pointed to it before she sat down again.

"How far away is that?" Jarl asked.

"Several days travel on a fast horse."

"If you will excuse us," Mirza said. "We must go now."

By the time Fialla followed them to the door, she was just in time to see Mirza's form shift to that of a horse with wings.

"Oh, my," she gasped.

Jarl mounted the winged beast. "Just like old times, isn't it? Notice I didn't even argue about this." He said to Fialla, "Thank you for the help."

The winged horse bowed to Fialla, snorted once, and sprang into the air with one beat of its henna-hued wings.

"Oh, dear me! I hope the wards will give them no trouble."

"Use your head, human! Of course they won't." Berdu materialized before the awed Fialla.

"And how can you know that?" Fialla bent over to look Berdu in the eye.

"Because they're not dragons! They're not even human!"

Understanding dawned. "Ohhh. I see!"

"Weren!" With this pronouncement giving him the last word, Berdu vanished once again, leaving Fialla to borrow a cloak and walk home alone. She wondered what Mirza and Jarl could do against the priesthood of Sardoom. Everything happened so fast she had not had time to warn them.

Mirza flew at top speed for hours before she allowed herself to sink to the ground.

"About time, Love," Jarl said. "As late as we are finding Lealor, a few hours one way or the other won't make much difference."

"Yes, but we don't know where she is. Perhaps seconds count," Mirza communicated mentally. Her wings vanished, but she remained a horse.

"Well, if I had known why you were hoarding magical energy for days, I might have tried to argue you out of it. You were using some kind of augmentation spell the whole time, weren't you?"

"And what if I was?" Mirza trotted down the road, intent on reaching Mancy before nightfall if possible.

"I don't like to take advantage of you. You seem to be doing all the work." Jarl resettled himself as Mirza slowed to ford a stream, blessing her for materializing a saddle. He had never been much of a rider, and without a saddle, he would have fallen off most horses. Of course his wife could always keep him astride by magic, but it always irked him that he couldn't do it alone.

"Don't fret, Jarl. Soon we'll come to Mancy. You can get yourself a pleasant room in the inn and put me in the stables. Mind you pick a nice one!"

"Now, wait just a minute! If you think I'm going to spend the night in a cold, lonely bed while you're standing all night in the stables . . ."

"Don't be silly! You'll spend time listening in the inn and I'll be listening to the stableboys. Some of the best information I ever got came from stableboys as they groomed me."

"And that's another thing—"

"All right. You groom me yourself, then."

"Better." Jarl whistled happily, having made his point, not realizing that he had conceded all of the important points to Mirza.

She whickered and settled to a walk. She was feeling pleased with herself.

Within the next hour traffic picked up on the road. Jarl talked to several farmers and merchants. He already disliked the priests, and what he heard from his informants did little to foster respect or affection for the priesthood.

Mirza's thought startled him. "No one has ever figured out why people set up governments and priesthoods and let evil men take over. It is a weakness of the human race."

Jarl nodded and reined her into the line that was passing inside the city gates under the watchful eyes of the guards. He felt her shiver. "What is it?"

"Can't you sense it?" Mirza paused, but did not wait for Jarl's answer. "Nasty magic. Evil. The priesthood of this city has a great deal to answer for."

"Lealor, for one." Jarl's voice sounded as if he intended to ask for some of those answers very soon.

The next morning, Jarl and Mirza pooled the information they had gathered. The yearly festival of Sardoom would be celebrated in three days' time. All of the priests were required to be present at the temple ceremonies which began on the next day. As Jarl's informant said, "The place is crawlin' with priests like buzzy bugs around a honey pot." Mirza's contribution was the fear of the stableboys. Children "disappeared" more frequently than usual at the time of the ceremonies. They stayed inside the barn as much as possible. Their master was a kind one and did not send them on errands out of the inn yard. She concluded, "For ceremonies, read sacrifices."

"What do you propose we do now?" Jarl asked, an admission that her plans so far had been good.

"Let's find a secluded spot where I can change into a rich courtier. You had better be an emissary from the kingdom of Realm, on the other side of the great desert."

"What desert?"

"How am I to know? I've never been here before. There must be one someplace."

"Right," Jarl said, guiding her down a street lined with imposing houses.

Mirza caught the bit in her teeth and turned into an alley that led to the rear of one of the houses. When they reached a door in the side wall, she stopped and Jarl dismounted.

"Thanks," she told him. "I do believe you've been putting on some weight, dear." The air around her shimmered with magic.

"You certainly look as fetching as ever," he replied. Swept into an imposing style and decorated with diamonds and emeralds, her long red hair glistened. Her dress was gold which matched her opulent jewels. Jarl noted that every finger wore a ring, and a series of huge emeralds formed a necklace which almost covered the skin revealed by the low neck of her gown.

"Don't you think you're—um—" Jarl paused for thought. Even though he had been married to Mirza for years, he hesitated to be undiplomatic about articles of dress. After all, she was a powerful magic wielder in her own right and he didn't fancy spending the rest of his days croaking and hopping. "—Perhaps overgilding the lily as it were?" he said after suitable thought.

"Not at all, my dear," she said with a giggle and a gesture.

Jarl glanced down to see himself resplendent in rubies and silver. "Mirza—" he began.

"No, this is not a whim on my part. We must look very rich indeed. We are seeking an audience with the king, after all."

"We are?"

"We are," she echoed him positively. "I do hope you're saving your magic. It will take me hours to recharge after this little display." Before them on the ground a flying carpet appeared.

"Ye gods and little fishes!" Jarl said.

"Necessary disguise," Mirza replied, seating herself on the carpet. "Are you coming or not?"

It was well that Jarl wasted no time in joining his wife, for in seconds the carpet was airborne, heading for the palace.

Is this really going to work? Jarl asked himself as Mirza landed the carpet in front of the castle.

Evidently it was, because he and Mirza were duly escorted into the throne room of King Yve by an awed functionary.

"See? Wealth impresses royalty."

Jarl nodded, thinking royalty were not the only ones susceptible to the clink of gold. He turned his attention to the much bedecked functionary who introduced them, word-forword as Mirza had told him. At least he had a good memory. Jarl himself couldn't remember half of what Mirza had told him about their titles.

King Yve motioned them forward. Mirza took Jarl's arm

and advanced. Which turned out to be a good thing because the high priest in attendance on His Royal Majesty captured Jarl's whole attention. Jarl had learned enough about Sardoom and his priests to know that any priest left in the kingdom was Sardoom's. The unhealthy pallor and general demeanor of the priest shouted self-righteousness and cruelty to Jarl. In Jarl's eyes, the priest might as well have worn a sign saying: *Evil*.

Mirza and King Yve made diplomatic overtures to one another while the priest and Jarl glowered at one another in mutual animosity. The king's next words caught Jarl's full attention.

"Your daughter Lealor?" King Yve repeated Mirza's words as a question. "Er—I—"

The high priest hurried into speech to assist his floundering monarch. "An unfortunate incident occurred, milady. Lealor herself volunteered to be the spring sacrifice, but before the red dragon king could carry her away, a huge bear pushed her into the sea." He neglected to mention the fact that she had been chained to the post on Sacrifice Rock.

"Into the sea?" A muscle twitched in Jarl's cheek. No one but Mirza knew it masked his anger.

The priest looked sad. "She would have made a very acceptable sacrifice," he said with a sniff. "However, we were unable to recover her. A smaller blue dragon chased away the red one. We are searching the texts of Sardoom to see what such events mean."

"Then she is dead?" Jarl's tone showed clearly how he felt.

Mirza said nothing, but she placed her hand on her throat and tears glittered in her eyes.

"Quite likely," the priest said. His unfeeling attitude chilled the room as much as Jarl's anger heated it.

"And you can tell us no more?"

"No." The high priest was unaccustomed to being questioned by anyone. "We are planning a number of sacrifices to Sardoom so he will protect us from the dragons. This is the first time anything broke the pact between us."

"You have an agreement to sacrifice people yearly to the dragons?" Mirza's voice tinkled like ice.

"Just maidens, milady," the high priest told her, attempting to propitiate her.

"Oh, Jarl!" she said, turning to her husband for the first time.

Her stricken look released something in him. His anger, which had grown greater by the minute, was almost palpable. Jarl willed magic to him. Those who watched saw him acquire a green aura. "Begone!" he commanded as he pointed to the high priest, who promptly vanished from the hall, black robes and all.

King Yve, white as the ermine fur on his robe, sat speechless. Jarl turned to him. "Where is the temple? Can you see it from this room?"

Wordlessly, the king rose and pointed to a window. Jarl crossed the floor in a dozen steps. He looked at the vast marble edifice rising above the rooftops across the town. He raised both hands, paused a moment as green fire flared, and clapped them once.

Mirza turned as pale as the king. She knew what Jarl had done. That flash of fire destroyed the temple and its grounds, including all its devil priests. The truly powerful wielders of magic had not joined with the amoral priesthood so they had only the defense of their god Sardoom. Mirza would have hesitated before attacking the temple of a god. If he existed, even Sardoom must have felt disgusted with his worshippers, for he did nothing to protect them. Mirza never could have unleashed such power, and if she could have, she would not have dared. But Jarl, acting instantaneously, was an outraged father and he desired to punish by obliteration. She worried about how he would feel when the extent of his power actually registered on him. He was angry still.

"Do you have farseers here?" Jarl asked as if nothing had happened. His voice swept through the room, cold as a winter that kills every living thing exposed to it.

"That is magic," King Yve explained, trying to sound unafraid, although his hands gripped the arms of his throne tightly so they would not shake. "No one but Sardoom's priests may work magic. I shall send for one."

"That's not necessary, Your Majesty," Mirza said, attempting to break the news gently. "Sardoom's priests are no more."

"You mean, they're all gone? Vanished like their temple?" The king's eyes goggled at the news.

Mirza nodded.

"Very well," he said, quite courageously, Mirza thought. "Am I to retain my life and my throne?"

Jarl gazed at him. He seemed dazed at the devastation he had unleashed. Surely he was not so powerful a mage! His anger shielded him from full realization.

"You may," Mirza spoke for them both. "So long, of course, as you rule justly and redress the woes the priesthood has inflicted on your subjects."

"They're really gone?" The king allowed a relieved look to form on his face when Mirza said he was correct.

"Now what?" Jarl asked Mirza. He grew paler by the minute as he realized what he had done without thinking.

"To Fialla. She can help us best now." Mirza felt weak, but she knew she had to get Jarl and herself away before full realization of what he had accomplished with his wrath registered on Jarl. After such a use, it might well be that he could never summon power again. Some of Sardoom's followers might take revenge on a powerless pair of magic users.

Mirza summoned the carpet, hoping the magic that remained to her would be adequate for the demands she was making. She and Jarl sat upon it, unhindered by anyone in the court. The destruction of the temple occurred in a moment. It took time for human minds to comprehend what had happened. The carpet sailed out the window towards the west. If it wobbled a bit, no one noticed.

Chapter
Twenty-one

HE Ancient One sat quietly after Fafleen finished her tale.

The young dragon repeated herself, hoping the old white dragonmage could help her. "So that's why I need someone to work with me to decipher the books in the old dragon tongue."

"I would gladly teach you, but I cannot see the symbols. So what will you do now?"

"Lealor is unprotected. I must go to her. Perhaps she will be able to help you see again. She knows both Earthly science and Realmish healing. Surely she can do something. Then you can help me translate the books I will bring here."

The Ancient One indicated an old chest sitting against the back wall of the cave. "Open it for me," she commanded.

Fafleen crossed the cavern and did as the old dragon told her. Within the chest, ropes of pearls lay over layers of gold, rubies, emeralds, sapphires, and gems of every imaginable color. The whole cavern scintillated with the shades of the rainbow, reflected thousands of times by the faceted diamondlike gems that lined the cave. Fafleen expelled her breath in a long hiss.

"Beautiful, are they not?" The Ancient One arched her neck. "Over the centuries I gathered them, not by force of claw, but through the gifts my magic won for me. Dig down to the bottom front right-hand corner and bring me the stone you find there."

Fafleen followed directions and discovered an ordinary piece of obsidian. Perhaps the Ancient One was growing senile. Fafleen had been around her grandfather, Old Fafnir, enough to know that elderly dragons developed quirks of personality. "This is just volcanic glass!" she said, voicing her disappointment.

"Do you not find it strange that in a vast chest of jewels, each more beautiful than the last, I hoard such a keepsake?"

Fafleen tried to be as tactful as she could. "I'm sure you have a reason," she lied politely.

"What you hold in your talons is an Odyssey stone."

"An Odyssey stone?" Fafleen had read the Greek Homer's story of the sailor's attempts to return home. It was exciting, but she couldn't see how the Ancient One knew of the book.

"When the gates still functioned on Widdershins, stories traveled between worlds as well as goods. The Odyssey stone is a fitting name for what you now hold. It is the greatest of my treasures."

"How so?" Fafleen looked at what she held, searching for enlightenment.

"Two times only in the life of the owner it may transport anyone or anything to any location specified."

"Then what happens?"

"It renews its energy by being given to its next owner."

"Have you used it yet?" Fafleen peered at the stone, trying to see if it looked used.

"Only once, therefore I may use it to speed you to Fire

Mountain Island." The Ancient One held out her claw for the obsidian.

Fafleen placed it in her talons. "Can you send me now?"

"Such haste! The young are always in a hurry. One tends to forget, you know." The ancient mage hissed her amusement. "One thing before you go. To return here, you fly east from the island, then north along the coast. Eventually you will reach these mountains."

"Yes," Fafleen said, stretching her wings. "I already know where the landing spot is." She didn't try to explain her method of instantaneous travel, since the Ancient One could not see.

"Very well."

Fafleen blinked. She stood atop a flat rock overlooking a large garden area. Lealor and the woman with her had identical looks of surprise on their faces.

Lealor broke the stillness. "Fafleen!" she cried, running to her and rubbing the nose the dragon obligingly lowered to the ground.

"I take it you know this dragon?" Queen Alian said, adding soil to the pot she was holding.

"Oh, yes! Queen Alian, this is my friend Fafleen from Realm—you remember I told you about her. And Faffie, this is Queen Alian, Pook's mother!"

Fafleen decided to overlook her friend's use of the childish nickname. The dragon stared rudely for a moment before saying, "Doesn't look a bit like him."

Lealor and the queen burst into laughter. Fafleen hissed her distress. She thought they were laughing at her.

The queen saw the problem before Lealor did. "Oh, Lealor, why didn't you tell me how clever your friend was?" Then she turned to the dragon. "She told me how learned and intelligent you were, knowing so many languages and all. She never mentioned your sense of humor. I'm sure we shall be great friends."

"No doubt," Fafleen replied as she reached out a talon

and rescued the partially transplanted herb that was ready to fall out of the pot.

"And you like flowers, too." The queen beamed while making a mental note to strengthen the wards of the island.

Lealor rushed in with her questions, wanting to spare them both a botany lecture on the habits of herbs. "Are you all right? What happened to the red dragon? Where have you been all these days?"

Fafleen answered the questions, explaining about the need for the Ancient One to see.

Lealor promised to try to help.

Then Fafleen wanted to know all about what happened to Lealor and Pook. Lealor and the dragon had forgotten all about the queen, who sat down on a convenient rock and prepared to listen to Lealor's version of events.

". . . So after we got here, the council held a meeting."

"It must have been pretty boring," Fafleen said, knowing something of the human propensity to talk a problem to death instead of acting.

"Not really," Lealor said, ignoring the queen's nod of approval. "It's been an interesting two weeks although I've been concerned about Rand. The seers of Fire Mountain Island have visions of the mage who is causing the ice to melt far to the north on Misty Island."

"Why is it important to the seers here?" Fafleen fluffed her scales and settled her head on a different spot of ground. "Sharp rock," she explained. She closed her eyes to double-check the feel of the ground, then opened them, indicating she was ready to continue listening.

"The ice melting from all those glaciers has caused a rise in the sea level. If it rises another couple of feet, it will pour over into part of the volcano through a crack on the other side of the island."

"Ohhhh." Fafleen's eyes grew round. "All that steam wouldn't be very good for humans."

"Not only that," Lealor said. "The volcano might explode from the cold water. Then there would be no more island at all!"

"What are you doing about it?" Fafleen asked the queen.

"The council has sent my son Rand—you know him as Pook—to visit the island. He left two weeks ago."

"Didn't you want to go with him?" Fafleen asked Lealor.

"Of course, but Rand's sister said she didn't see me in her vision about the trip, so I stayed here. When Rand returns he will take me back to my cottage."

"By then, we believe some of our magicians will have studied enough to be able to renew the gate," the queen said.

"Then we can go home?" Fafleen didn't sound very happy at the news.

"We have to let our parents know what happened to us, Fafleen." Lealor smiled to take the sting from her remark.

"Oh, sure. It's just that I want to stay a while and work with the Ancient One on those translations."

"Once the gate is open, your mother will probably come here to see those old books you found."

"If I know father, he'll come too. Then my brother will show up. He can't stand missing anything." Fafleen sighed. "Probably grandfather will come as well." She rolled her eyes and covered her snout with her talons.

Lealor hid her smile with her hand. Widdershins would never be the same once the Realmish dragons arrived. "Well," she said, "now you know all my news and I know yours."

"Not all of it, you don't." Fafleen shot a triumphant smoke ring into the air. For once, she knew something Lealor needed to know. She was aware of how often Lealor prevented her from telling everything she knew about some subject. What sense was it to know tons of facts and not be able to share the information with someone?

"What else can there be?"

"Have you tried to communicate with Myst lately?"

"Yes, but you know how stubborn she is. She's been sulking ever since I was in the priests' power."

"She's not sulking," Fafleen told her. "She's caught in Baloo's mind net."

"Poor Myst." Lealor frowned. "Baloo's made a mind net? I've read of them, but never actually seen one."

The queen said, "Once they were used here on Widder-shins. Whenever someone with power wanted to remove an enemy for a while, he would create a mind net. It isn't too difficult to do if you can manipulate the power. A mind net is a portion of another plane, bounded by magical force. No one but the creator can release anything placed within it."

"That settles it. We must do something about Baloo. Bright One or not, he's still a child. He can't whisk beings into mind nets willy-nilly." Lealor's clenched fists showed her determination. "Baloo!" she called.

"Don't waste your time trying to get his attention. After he does something naughty, he always hides for a while. He's dreadfully afraid your mother will find out what he's done." Fafleen chuckled at her mental picture of Mirza castigating the immensely powerful Bright One.

"It's not funny."

"You're right. It's not." Fafleen looked suitably grave. "You now have no talisman to protect you."

"Oh, I'll be all right. I have you and Fialla—"

"And us," the queen added.

"Hasn't it dawned on you yet?" Fafleen gave the two humans an exasperated look. "Add things up: powerful mage, dramatic changes with no thought of what those changes may do to people, secrecy, a shadowy figure, removed from humanity—"

Lealor's eyes registered her horror. "The Shadowlord!" she gasped.

"The one who caused so much trouble on Realm and Achaea?" the queen asked.

Fafleen gave her an approving look. "The same."

"We must go help Rand. Will you carry me to his ship?" Lealor asked the dragon.

"Wait." Queen Alian's expression was grim. "If the mage we detected is your Shadowlord, the visions of my daughter should have seen Rand and Lealor facing him together. I must talk to my daughter before you go. Lealor, will you take our guest to the kitchen for some refreshments before you leave? Ask someone to prepare you a satchel of food to take with you. Just don't leave until I speak with you again." The queen looked at each of them. "Promise?"

Lealor and Fafleen agreed. When the queen left them, she heard Fafleen say, "I am a bit hungry." Alian hoped there would be enough in the kitchen to feed a dragon. It had been years since one visited.

Queen Alian wasted no time in finding her daughter, Silanna. She found her within the seer's vision room. She thought her daughter looked disturbed by her presence, which confirmed her idea that Silanna had not been honestly reporting her visions.

"Silanna." The single word dropped into the silence like a stone into a pool. The spreading ripples were Silanna's hurried explanations.

"I'm sorry, mother. The mist distorted the visions so that I wasn't certain who Rand's companion was. He is only going to reconnoiter. He won't actually face the mist mage until he confers with the council and father."

"Have you searched the mists for your brother today?"

"Yes. Some spell keeps him from going farther north. He will try to return here and take our magicians with him when he returns."

"You are fortunate nothing worse has happened. Look once more into the scrying bowl. Seek to see Rand's companion on his quest."

Alian and Silanna positioned themselves around the magic container. Since the question was Alian's, she poured the herbal liquid into the bowl. Silanna spoke the words of summoning. The liquid turned grey. It roiled within the sides of the container, resisting Silanna's summoning.

"The mage thwarts our clear vision with his magic."

Silanna placed her hand on the silvery stone she wore on a chain around her neck. She repeated the summons. Then for an instant, the roiling ceased, showing them Lealor and Rand in a room made of ice. They saw a shadowy figure in a robe. For one second the image clearly revealed the mage. The watchers blanched. He had no face. The magical liquid turned to icy vapor which rose into the room until it dispersed in the air.

Alian and Silanna looked at one another. Alian spoke first. "Your father and Lealor must know of this."

Lealor had fed Fafleen and introduced her to King Erik, who came to see what the commotion was. The servants were fascinated to see a real dragon. They had heard old tales of the days in Magilan, but no one on Fire Mountain Island had ever seen a live dragon until Fafleen arrived. Fafleen was on her best behavior, carefully answering any questions that were put to her. No one would be able to say she had been anything but a perfect dragon lady—if her mother should ever inquire.

Alian heard Lealor's last words as she entered the huge area behind the kitchen garden where a table, covered with empty dishes, proved Fafleen had eaten.

"That's all there is to tell, I guess," Lealor said to King Erik. She turned to Fafleen. "Unless I've left something out."

"Not a thing," Fafleen managed to say, licking the last of the icing from the top layer of the four-tiered cake she had politely divided with her tongue. Unable to resist, she gulped it down in two bites. She caught Lealor's look. "I'm sorry."

"You won't be able to get off the ground if you eat much more," Lealor warned, pretending she did not see the look on the cook's face as the dragon finished off the last cake in the castle.

"Don't worry. I know exactly where we're going. We'll fly Air Fafleen."

Lealor hid a shudder. The business of climbing on a dragon, closing your eyes, and being there always unnerved her.

Queen Alian waved the servants and gawkers away to their places. "Erik, I have news. Silanna and I managed to get one clear vision of the mage. Lealor and Rand were facing him together."

"This slip of a girl?" Erik's loud rumbling remark showed his astonishment. He modulated his voice and added, "When?"

Silanna appreciated her mother's tact. She understood her dereliction of duty would not become public knowledge. So she answered rather humbly for her. "Soon, father."

"Well, what should we be doing to help?"

"Lealor and I need to consult with the Ancient One. Perhaps her magic will aid us," Fafleen said.

"Fafleen and I will find Rand," Lealor promised. "He won't have to face the Shadowlord alone."

"Ready?" Fafleen asked.

Lealor nodded, knowing dragons were notorious for abrupt departures.

Fafleen unfurled her wings to get the kinks out. She took Lealor firmly in her talons and warned, "Careful!" as she gave a tremendous wingbeat to move Lealor and all the food she had ingested into the air. Once aloft, Lealor had time to cry out, "Goodbye!" before Fafleen used her magical power to travel instantaneously and took them to the cave of the Ancient One.

* * *

"So you have returned, daughter." The ancient dragon-mage hissed her pleasure.

"Yes. Lore Mistress, this is my friend, Lealor."

Lealor was stunned by the rapidity of the trip, the vast cavern with its crystalline walls, and the old dragon who stood before them. "Greetings to you, Lore Mother," she said, remembering that Fafleen told her the Ancient One liked ceremonial address.

"A most interesting human," she murmured to Fafleen as if Lealor had no feelings. The Ancient One turned toward Fafleen. "You believe this one knows enough to restore my sight?"

Impressed as Lealor was, she knew better than to allow a potential patient to expect too much from her. For the millionth—or was it the billionth—time she wished she dare turn herself into another form. If she wore dragonshape she would not be so dwarfed by her surroundings. "I can but try if you so wish it," she said, hoping it sounded acceptable in dragonish.

"Bend down your head, Ancient One, so Lealor can see."

A jet of warm air blew over Lealor, who was thankful that this dragon was so old her fires would not light.

"For the first and only time, I bow before a human," she hissed.

Lealor walked up to the dragon and looked at her eye. Then she walked around the dragon's snout to view the other one. "Yes, it is as I thought from Fafleen's description. You have growths over your eyes called cataracts," she told her patient, for she now believed she could cure her.

"Do I need to return to the cottage and find your medical supplies?" Fafleen asked.

"I don't think so. Since dragons are mystical creatures, I can use my knowledge of surgery to help in the magical removal of the cataracts."

"What will you need?" Fafleen asked.

"Although I will remove the cataracts magically, you will feel some pain. It will take several days for your eyes to heal completely," Lealor told the Ancient One.

"I agree," the old dragoness hissed.

"Have you some painease?" Lealor asked the dragon.

"Yes. The people in the valley keep me supplied with herbs. Sometimes I can bespell illness for them." The dragon held her head still, afraid she might hurt the human who could restore her vision. "Daughter, beside the chest is a rack holding my herbs. Bring the ground leaves in the small bag made of rabbit fur."

Fafleen found the bag and handed it to Lealor. "Do you need boiling water to make a tea?"

"Yes." Lealor waved her hands to make glowing patterns over the eyes of the Ancient One.

By the time she had finished, Fafleen had filled a bowl with hot water. The Ancient One drank it to the lees. That the dragon drank the steeped leaves as well surprised Lealor, but she said nothing.

"Please don't move," Lealor said.

The old dragon's eyelids closed while they watched.

"Fafleen," Lealor said softly, "I'll need your help."

"What should I do?"

"Lift me onto her nose."

When Lealor was safe on her patient's snout, she said, "Now raise her eyelids for me—gently!" Lealor reached into the pouch she had tied around her waist to replace her magic bag. She took out a container filled with a creamy substance. A green glow formed around Lealor's hands as she chanted. Lealor rubbed the substance over the old dragon's eyes. Fafleen watched, fascinated, as the cataracts became first translucent, then transparent. In the next few seconds, they disappeared!

"I never heard of that spell before. What did you use?" Fafleen asked.

Lealor, seeing her patient cured, giggled. "Vanishing cream!"

"I hope you can come up with as good an idea when you face the Shadowlord."

"I wish I knew what was happening to Rand," Lealor said.

"While the Ancient One finishes her nap, let's go see," Fafleen said, leading the way to the lava pool.

Chapter
Twenty-two

THE sight of the pool awed Lealor.

Fafleen formed her question carefully, hoping she would be able to bend the magic to her desire. "We would see Rand, the prince of Fire Mountain Island." To the young dragon's relief, an image formed instantly.

The ship lay becalmed in the middle of an icy sea filled with bergs. Lealor saw Rand's frosty breath as he looked to the north.

"You did well, daughters." The Ancient One's hissed words at their backs startled both Fafleen and Lealor.

"Thank you," Lealor said, noting that the old dragon had called her "daughter." "Can you see the image?" she asked.

The old dragon nodded. Lealor could feel her pleasure.

"Look," Fafleen said, "someone's talking to Rand. Can you fix it so we can hear?"

The old dragoness hissed a word and the figures in the image began to speak aloud.

"Prince, how long must we wait here? The bergs grow more numerous daily."

"Captain, this is no ordinary calm. Some magic keeps us from sailing northward."

"We didn't take the time to get provisioned for a long wait. If we do not leave in two days we will not have food or water enough to return home."

"Let your wizard study possible ways to get through for one more day and then we shall return," Rand said.

"Very well, sire," the captain said.

Rand nodded his dismissal, turning his back on the captain to look north again. He pulled his cape about him, for the air stung with cold, although no wind blew.

Lealor watched, wishing she could speak to Rand. She turned to the Ancient One. "Can we speak to him?"

"It is long since I wove that spell. Let me see . . ." Strange noises came from the throat of the Ancient One. Lealor supposed the sounds to be words, but they formed no language she could recognize.

"Speak now," the Ancient One said.

"Rand! It's me, Lealor!"

"Lealor? Where are you?" Rand's face lit with joy.

"Safe with the dragons. I'm using a magical mirror."

"The two who swooped down at Sacrifice Rock?"

"Waste no time. The spell weakens," the Ancient One hissed.

Lealor hurried. She was sure Fafleen, at least, would help. "We'll come, if a dragon can fly through the magic shield."

"The ship's wizard says that whoever designed this spell did it to stop all human magic and shape-changing. That's why I can't change into a whale and swim to the island."

"We'll be flying on dragonback, and that's perfectly natural," Lealor said. "Get ready. We're coming."

Rand nodded as the image disappeared into the bubbles formed by the slowly boiling lava.

"You will take me, won't you, Fafleen?"

"Of course, but I can't carry double in that cold. I can probably fly you to the island, but I'll have to come back here and warm up before I can return and get Rand."

"Come, daughters. The answer to your problem lies in my cavern."

Fafleen and Lealor exchanged puzzled looks, but they followed the old dragoness back into the main cave.

"Ancient One, have you seen—Fafleen!" the red dragon said.

The Ancient One chuckled. "Did I not say the answer to your problems awaited?"

Fafleen and the red dragon were busy talking. Lealor watched the three saurians. The Ancient One waited quietly, certainly an unnatural behavior for so powerful a being. Lealor smiled. Why, the old one was matchmaking! Fafleen and the red dragon made an imposing pair. Now, however, was not the time for romance. Lealor drew a deep breath and said, "Fafleen, will you introduce me to your friend?"

Fafleen jerked her head around and looked at Lealor as if she had never seen her before. Then she said, "Oh. I forgot. This is Flare."

A heavy fur coat and a pack materialized on the cavern floor. The Ancient One said, "This is for you, Lealor." Then she turned to the younger dragons and spoke some words. A pale golden shimmer surrounded each of them. "You will be warm. This spell will last for three days, no more. By then you must be on your way home."

"How—" Fafleen began as Lealor put on the coat.

"I am in contact with the magic users in the human colony below. They prepared the pack with things humans find necessary." The old dragon had a smug look on her face. She could still show the young ones a trick or two.

"I know a rock four days' flight from here. It's in the middle of the sea. If you can follow me, we can save some time."

"I followed you here, didn't I?" Fafleen answered Flare with fire in her eyes. "Lead the way."

"Let's leave from the ledge outside. Are you ready, human?"

Lealor winced at the word. Flare was clearly willing to participate, but only because the Ancient One and Fafleen were taking an interest. She felt very small and powerless as she crawled to her place on Fafleen's back.

"Farewell—" blackness cut off the Ancient One's hiss. The transition had been almost instantaneous. Far below, Lealor could see a single spur of rock sticking out of the roaring sea. If Rand's ship was becalmed, it must be magic, she thought to herself. Look at those waves!

"Do you need to rest?" Flare roared over the noise below.

"Let's go!" Fafleen answered, shooting past him toward the north, watching for Rand's ship.

After the first three or four wingbeats, Lealor's stomach caught up with her, and she started to feel the cold. She pulled part of her cloak over her face and, forsaking the view of the wild sea, rested her face against Fafleen. Just like a dragon, she thought. The warmth spell covered Fafleen, but not her.

After a day of flight, Flare swooped down to the sea and returned with a large fish, which he fed to Fafleen. Fafleen's hiss of pleasure reminded Lealor of her mother's reaction when her father presented her with a box of candy. She wondered what Mirza would say if Jarl gave her a big fish on Valentine's Day. Lealor felt the stiffness in her face when she tried to smile. She changed position enough to rub her mittens on her face. She had no desire for frostbite now. The moon shed cool beams on the three.

She felt Fafleen lurch slightly. "Faffie! What is it?" she asked in mindspeech.

"The calm place is this way," the dragon replied. "I can feel the magic."

Several hours later, Lealor could see the moonlit ship. The

deck was too small to hold both dragons and their tails, so Fafleen draped hers over the mast.

Everyone who could find a dragon-free inch or two of deck crowded around to watch as Rand heaved a pack containing supplies on the deck. Lealor introduced Fafleen and Flare. Rand wasted no time climbing aboard the red dragon.

"Hold on," Lealor warned.

"We go," Flare announced as he and Fafleen winged their way aloft.

The captain, the ship's wizard, and the crew watched as the dragons flew northward. They reached the magical barrier which shimmered as they passed and disappeared. With the barrier gone, a cold wind tore down from the north. The captain gave the order and the crew hurried to set sail for Fire Mountain Island. The wind filled the sails and the ship fairly flew southward to warmth and safety.

The moon sank and the sky lightened. Noon passed and Lealor and Rand could feel the dragons tiring. Rand had never carried on a mental conversation with a dragon, but when he yelled to ask Flare if he could do anything to help, he felt the dragon's chuckle in his mind.

"Human eyes are not as keen as a dragon's. I can already see the patch of fog that surrounds Misty Island. This wind has vapor streaming for miles."

Rand squinted, wishing he could change to hawk form for long enough to see, but in a few minutes the foggy air passed them in ragged wisps, then formed a solid cloud around them. "How are we going to see it when we get there?" he asked.

"Dragons know what kind of terrain is below whether they can see it or not. We are superior hunters because of our magical senses."

Rand wisely kept silence. He was only a passenger, after all.

"Ready?" Flare asked.

"Yes," Rand answered, knowing they were going to land when and where it suited the scarlet dragon.

Even with the prior warning, Rand's stomach lurched as the dragon's plummeted to earth. They landed on a sandy beach, wind scoured and snow free. Rand and Lealor dismounted hastily—Lealor, because she knew the dragons needed to return home before the heat spell expired and Rand because he was following her lead.

"Thank you, Faffie," Lealor said. "Take care going home."

Rand thanked Flare, who merely nodded before turning to Fafleen. "Can you follow me, Seeker?" Seeing Fafleen's nod, he rose into the air so rapidly that he almost blew Rand over.

Fafleen was beside him. "Be careful," she warned mentally as both dragons winked out of sight.

"Was that normal?" an awed Rand asked Lealor.

"'Fraid so," she answered, fitting her pack to her back. "Let's go. We have to find shelter before night falls."

"Lealor, if dragons can travel like that, why didn't they just zip us here?" Rand settled his pack and kept pace with her.

"They have to visit a place at least once before they can travel there instantaneously. Sometimes dragons can whisk themselves to places they've never visited, but they have to study or read the mind of their riders if they know the place. It's a pretty risky way to travel. Only great need would cause a dragon to do it. Misty Isle is somewhat off the beaten track in case you haven't noticed." Her words came in short bursts.

Rand saw how hard it was for Lealor to move in the knee-high snow they encountered as soon as they left the shore, so he took the lead. "Let me break a path," he said. "Do you have any idea which way we should go?"

"Your mother told me a mountain ridge forms the northern half of the island. If the Shadowlord is here, he would create his castle on the south side of the mountains sheltered from the northern gales."

"If we are going to find a safe place to stay for the night, we should look for shelter somewhere off this flat plain," Rand said.

An hour or so later, Lealor spoke. "It's not as windy here as it was when we landed on the beach. Perhaps we're already approaching the mountains."

The light faded until they were slogging through a grey landscape. Both Lealor and Rand felt the cold beneath the layers of clothes they wore. Rand had tried to get Lealor to agree to stop several times. Thick snow fell from the night sky. It was impossible to see more than a few feet ahead. Lealor staggered on through sheer willpower. When Rand stopped without warning, she ran into him.

"Look!" he whispered to her.

The bulky form of a huge white beast rose up before them in the snow. Rand reached for his sword, ready to protect Lealor.

"No," she told him. "Wait."

"For what?" He expected the beast to charge any moment.

The mouth of the gigantic form opened, showing sharp fangs.

"Carnivore," Rand thought, placing his gloved hand on his sword.

"A plant eater would starve to death here." Lealor's gentle mental answer surprised him.

"We're talking mind to mind," he thought to her.

"I never really tried before. When you were a bear, I didn't think of it, and later, it was habit to talk to you out loud."

Their mental voices were joined by the voice of the beast. "I, Sleet of the Snow People, am glad you know our tongue."

Rand looked at Lealor in puzzlement. "How does he speak our language?"

"Mind speech uses raw ideas, not words, for communication," Lealor told him. "I am Lealor of Realm and he" —she gestured to her companion—"is Rand of Fire Mountain Island. It is an honor to speak with Sleet of the Snow People."

"A great storm comes," Sleet said. "Would you guest with my people until it is over?"

"Yes," Lealor and Rand thought in unison.

"Follow me," the beast said and lumbered off into the snow, leaving a path for the humans who trailed after him.

The walking was much easier with someone else breaking a pathway through the snow. Lealor and Rand could sense how much the speed of their travel picked up as they followed Sleet. The hope of being sheltered refreshed them enough so they could keep going.

Without any warning, a cliff rose up from the plain. Sleet turned to make sure his guests were still with him and gestured. After a few minutes of walking, he paused for Rand and Lealor to come close to him. "Come," he thought to them, and disappeared into the cliff.

"Illusion," Lealor murmured to herself as she advanced with her hands held before her. When she disappeared, Rand followed blindly. He blinked in the soft light that illuminated a great cave. The walls seemed cut from solid ice which glowed.

Sleet led them forward into the center of the cave. From the openings in the wall a number of huge snow beasts emerged and gathered around Sleet, Rand, and Lealor.

"The small ones are my guests," Sleet said.

"They are like the Evil One," a smaller snow beast said, growling.

"No. Sense their thoughts and know their hearts," another beast said.

Lealor and Rand stood very still, trying to project friendly thoughts. It didn't seem to be making much of an impression until a tiny snow beast toddled through the circle and held up his arms to Lealor.

"Hello, small one," she said, unable to resist picking him up.

A chorus of mental chuckles broke the silence. They were accepted.

Sleet took the baby from Lealor. "My son," he said.

Within a few minutes they were settled in a small alcove within the cavern. Sleet offered them food, but Rand and Lealor opened their packs and retrieved their own. Sleet's nose quivered when he scented the fruit in Lealor's pack.

"It is long since I tasted fruit. When I was a cub, sometimes ships would come to trade with my people, but none come now. When the Evil One took the castle for his own, things changed. Now we are the hunted." Sleet's eyes gleamed red with his rage. "The Evil One poisons my people to remove their will. Only our power over illusions and magic has saved some of us from bondage."

"We are here to see this Evil One. I believe he is a mage I have met before. My people call him Shadowlord."

Sleet looked at them. "What can such small ones do to the Evil One? His magic is great."

"My people drove him from Realm, our home. Later we helped drive him from Achaea. Perhaps we can defeat him again." Lealor spoke quietly, hoping her fear did not show.

"Sleep. Tomorrow I will take you to his castle," Sleet told them.

The caverns were somewhat warmer than the outside, but not warm enough for Lealor and Rand to take off their coats or sleep comfortably. Lealor woke the next morning with her head pillowed on Rand's chest. Rand smiled at her. She sat up quickly. She hoped he didn't notice the flush on her cheeks. She rummaged to find something in her pack for their breakfast. She set aside the rest of their fruit for the little snow beast.

Just as they finished, Sleet came. He took them through a series of underground passageways. When he led them to an opening, they could see the grey walls of a forbidding castle. Someone had cut it from solid rock.

Sleet pointed across the valley where moving white figures were barely visible. "My people, captured to be slaves to the Evil One."

Lealor nodded her understanding. She remembered tales of the Shadowlord's behavior on Realm. Fafleen's mother, Ebony, had been enslaved by a magical chain.

Sleet said, "If you have need of our illusions, we will aid you. Think of me and I will speak in your mind." He raised a paw in farewell and disappeared into the mountain.

Rand looked at the wide expanse of snow before them and said, "Well, how do you propose we cross that unseen?"

"If you can turn yourself into a bear again—a white one, preferably—you can move unnoticed in the snow."

"What about you?"

Lealor thought how simple it would be to change herself into a white bear. Silanna had enjoyed telling Lealor that Rand could only marry a shape-shifter. Lealor felt the familiar pang as she remembered she could never marry Rand. Then she thought what it would be like to stay in bear form forever. While she was thinking, she searched through her pack. Inside was a square of white cloth. She thought it was a sheet, but it didn't matter to her why she had it. She opened it and draped it over her head, covering her flame-colored hair. "How will this do?" she asked.

Rand answered with a woof. He had already changed into a great polar bear. She felt his grin. "I forgot I'd have to mindspeak when I was in bear form. Now you get on my back and I'll give you a ride to the castle."

"I can walk."

"I suppose you can. How will it look if the Shadowlord's servants see human boot tracks in the snow? A bear is easy to explain. In fact, my paw prints look a little like Sleet's."

Lealor stifled her wish to be independent and got on. Rand set out across the snow at a lope in spite of his rider. In a little over an hour they reached the castle. Lealor felt uneasy. Everything was working out too well! The snow beasts wore silver collars and seemed intent on nothing but their tasks, although Lealor and Rand couldn't figure out the purpose of their leaden comings and goings.

The guards were visible on the main gate to the castle, so Rand and Lealor started walking around the castle's perimeter. Finally, they came to a small door in the side. They expected to find the door locked, but it opened easily. Once inside, Rand changed back to human form before he and Lealor looked for a place to hide.

Rand drew his sword and led the way. A short distance down the passageway he found a stairs cut into the rock. He started upward. When they came to the first landing they saw a door. "Up or in?" Rand asked.

"Let's take a minute to rest. We need to talk. In," Lealor whispered.

They entered a windowless room. Lealor risked a small sphere of mage light. Rows of barrels filled the floor space. Rand peered into an uncovered barrel near the door. He wrinkled his nose. "Fish—and none too fresh. It must be what the slaves eat."

Lealor made a face. Rand helped her climb on top of a barrel and sat on one himself. He unlaced the neck of his shirt and pulled out a stone on a chain. Lealor watched silently. Within seconds, the stone began to glow. Queen Alian's worried face peered at them. "Children," she said, "are you all right?"

"Fine, so far. We're in the castle. We don't know yet what the Shadowlord is doing to melt the ice, or why, but when we find out, I'll try the earth stone."

"Be careful," Alian said as her face faded from the pendant.

"What's an earth stone? All stones come from the earth," Lealor said.

"It's a magical artifact that uses the forces of nature to restore the balance when someone disturbs the proper order of things. This is probably the only one left in existence. We have lost the knowledge the power wielders used to make this."

"How does it work?"

"If we knew that, we could probably make another."

"That's not what I should have asked. I meant what do you have to do with it to stop the Shadowlord?"

"I'll know when the time comes. You can just take that look off your face. I know it's crazy, but that's what our wisewomen told me. Speaking of wisewomen," Rand said, "just what is it you're going to do to drive the Shadowlord away?"

Lealor hid her worry with a smile. "Oh, I'll know when the time comes," she told him.

The walls of the room began to shimmer. Lealor felt a moment of vertigo, then she and Rand were in a huge chamber. She saw the Shadowlord standing before them on a raised platform. "Welcome," he said. "My trap worked very well, didn't it?"

Lealor bit her lip in chagrin. "I should have known things were too good to be true."

"I remember you, although you were a good deal younger when last I saw you. And more destructive," he added as an afterthought.

"I remember too," Lealor said, keeping her voice steady with an effort. She had too much pride to let him know how frightened she was.

The Shadowlord motioned her aside. She looked behind her and saw Rand, frozen in time, his sword drawn, one foot ready to take his first step to battle the Shadowlord.

"And who is your warlike young companion?" he asked.

Lealor hesitated. Should she tell him or would it put Rand in more danger?

"You might as well. I can take it from your mind if you don't."

"This is Prince Rand from Fire Mountain Island."

"Oh, you've found yourself a weren all of your own. How clever. You shape-shifters will probably be very happy together—if you cooperate with me."

Lealor's instinctive reply quivered in her throat. *Never,*

she wanted to shout, but she wisely decided to wait and see what she could learn before she had to act, although what she could do against so powerful a magic worker, she didn't know.

Lealor took a deep breath. "Do you know you are melting the ice and raising the level of the sea?" she asked.

"My castle is high," the Shadowlord replied.

"The volcano on Fire Mountain Island has one very low place. The cold sea water is almost ready to run into it!"

"That explains why the prince is here. What is their island to me?"

"You really don't care what happens to others, do you? Yet when I look at you I see a golden sparkling rod shape hiding under some kind of—grey covering." Lealor bit her lip. She didn't know the right words to discuss what she saw within the Shadowlord. If there were ever a time when she needed to be eloquent, this was it!

"Womanly foolishness!"

Lealor felt a familiar ruffling through her mind. She recognized the touch of Baloo, the Bright One. She allowed her thoughts to expand until she touched him. "Baloo, can you help me?"

"It's such fun to watch you have adventures, Lealor."

"This is serious! I need you to tell my mother and father where I am. Can you bring them here? And release Myst from the mind net, too."

"Okay."

For the first time in weeks, Lealor felt Myst tighten on her wrist. It was surprising how much better she felt.

"Who are you communicating with now? Another companion?" The Shadowlord's words cut into Baloo's and Lealor's thoughts like a sharp shard of glass. He waved a hand and muttered a word, but nothing happened to Lealor. He stopped to look at her and tried again. This time Myst flared into incandescence. His eyes peered at the dragon talisman. "You have gained a dragon guardian. This proves that I am right. Your abilities are the key. Now, if you will not aid me to save yourself, perhaps you have an interest in this young man. He has no dragon talisman!''

"Bad man!" Baloo said before disappearing from Lealor's mind, leaving Lealor alone, remembering that Fafleen said the Bright One always ran and hid when he was afraid.

Lealor watched in horror as the Shadowlord raised a bony finger and pointed it at Rand. Blue fire outlined Rand's body and encased him in ice which continued to thicken.

"Now answer me! Who aided you?"

"It was the small Bright One from Achaea. The one you almost destroyed when you meddled with the sun there."

"Not very brave, is he? I give you credit, Lealor. You have courage," the Shadowlord admitted grudgingly. "I hope you are not as stubborn as your mother was. I want you to lend me your magical power so I can complete my plans here. If you want Rand to survive, you will join me. The ice spell kills if it encases someone too long. I give you five minutes to decide. I shall return for your answer." With these words, the Shadowlord disappeared.

Lealor's thoughts scurried like mice. What could she do to stop the Shadowlord?

Chapter
Twenty-three

AS Baloo fled through the planes of existence, he worried. It was his fault that Lealor faced the Shadowlord alone. He slowed, then stopped. He would return to Mirza and confess.

He scintillated brilliantly for a moment, the Bright Ones' equivalent of a sigh, then raced for Mirza on Widdershins. Before he could reach the plane where Widdershins was, he saw a great golden light materialize before him.

"Stop, foolish child!"

"Who are you?" Baloo asked, filled with wonder at so powerful a being.

"I am Oron, an adult Bright One."

"Please let me get by. I have to tell Mirza what's happening and take my punishment. I did a bad thing." Baloo's golden form drooped in shame.

Oron's form grew larger and larger, becoming white-hot. "Who dares punish a Bright One?"

"Mirza never actually punished me, but I know I deserve to be. Lealor wanted an adventure and it was so easy to have the gate take her to Widdershins. The Shadowlord was there and she could have an exciting time and convince her mother and father that she was really a grown-up being and—"

"Stop!" Oron winced. "Child, you are very young to be out of the nest alone."

"That's why I hide from Auntie Mirza. She catches me and sings me back to sleep. She thinks I'm too little to be out, too. Please let me go. The Shadowlord is a very evil being. He hurt me once and Auntie Mirza saved me."

"Auntie Mirza indeed!" Oron roared.

Baloo extruded hands and covered his mental ears. He sobbed and two drops of molten gold dripped down his column.

Oron saw and relented. "The humans must do without your help, child. I despise them because the Shadowlord is one of their race. Why they have not destroyed him long before this, I cannot understand. Years ago, I made a vow. If the Shadowlord wins, all the worlds with humans on them are forfeit to the Black Universe. I shall see to it myself as I promised."

"But—" Baloo began.

"If you are quiet, I will allow you to watch with me."

Baloo fell silent.

Lealor rushed over to Rand. She tried to rouse him, but quickly saw it was no use. Then she remembered the earth stone. She could pretend to join the Shadowlord to get a chance to use it herself. She tried to undo the shirt pocket where Rand kept the stone, but the ice was already too thick.

"I'm back," the Shadowlord announced.

Lealor kissed Rand through the ice, hoping the Shadowlord would not find out about the stone.

"And what is it you work so hard not to think of? Hmmm?"

"A pendant he wears," Lealor admitted, trying to look subservient.

The Shadowlord held out his hand and the pendant materialized within it. "Simple device of no real value," he murmured, glancing at it before dropping it to the floor. "I take it this means you do intend to assist me," he told Lealor. "I chose this place because it is the heart of all the most powerful magic on Widdershins. In this world, the dragons control most of the old magic, so I need to wear a dragon's shape. All is ready to forge a universal gate that will take me and my armies to any gate world at any time I wish. Holding this power in control is melting the ice, so when you aid me, you stop the sea from rising."

"What do you want of me?"

"First, I wish to change shape. You gave me the answer when your dragon bracelet flared. On this world only a dragon may wield the powers I need. You will change shape first to teach me how."

"If I change, I'll have to remain in that form forever. You told me so yourself."

"Yes, that's right. I did. So you've remembered all these years."

"How could I forget?" Lealor's simple question let the Shadowlord know how grieved she had been.

"Well, then, I'll be magnanimous. I'll let you choose the form you change into. If I learn to change into one beast, I can become another, can I not?"

"Yes. The process is the same."

"Do you choose to be a bear like your weren friend? Or perhaps a bird to sail the skies or a fish to swim the waters of Realm forever." His eyes sparkled maliciously as he watched Lealor's face.

"If I may never be human again, I choose to be a dragon," she told him.

"Fortuitous. You'll be the very queen of dragons, I'm sure. Let's begin."

"We must hold hands so you're in contact with me. It's been a long time since I shape-shifted. You'll have to follow my thoughts as I change." Lealor didn't try to hide her grimace of disgust. She sent a mental call to the snow beast for help. "Sleet! Create an illusion. We must both seem to be dragons!" She broke mental contact before the Shadowlord touched her. He would have to be sharing her mind to change, she knew.

The Shadowlord advanced and took her hands. His bony fingers were gnarled with arthritis and icy cold. Except for his forcing her to give up her human shape, Lealor might have found it in her heart to pity him as she noticed the brown age spots on his hands. How old was he, anyway?

"One more thing. You promise not to harm the people here and you will free the snow beasts after I have aided you?"

"The sun will be cooler, for I must steal some of its energy. I will not harm the people and I will free my slaves if I am successful."

"How much cooler?"

"Eventually they will have an ice age here. The water from the seas will turn to ice and snow. This will free large portions of the sea beds for human habitation."

Lealor shrank from the Shadowlord in horror. "But—"

"Begin!"

As Lealor watched, she saw the Shadowlord take on dragonshape. She looked down at her hands and saw dragon's talons. Sleet had heard. The illusion was perfect.

The Shadowlord-dragon rose to the ceiling, intending to break through and be outside, but as his head hit the stone, he dropped back down beside her.

He was so angry he could hardly speak. "You agreed to help me. None of these tricks, or Rand will suffer for them." The dragon illusion vanished. The Shadowlord pointed toward Rand and this time the blue fire doubled the thickness of the ice block which encased him. "You have cut his survival time in half with your foolishness. If you wish him to live, begin the transformation now, Dragon Queen!''

Lealor cast one despairing look at the ice that held Rand captive and began.

While years had passed since Lealor had changed her shape, she remembered the sensation as she initiated the process. She took great care to think of what she was doing. First, her neck must lengthen, her skull must reform with sharp teeth along the lengthy jawline. Next, a long tail to balance, a larger body, strong hind legs, and front legs with long talons to hold her prey. And now, scales to cover her body from snout to tail tip. Last of all, she formed the strong wings that would carry her aloft. Her eyes watched as the Shadowlord followed her gradual transformation, shifting himself slowly, then more rapidly as he understood the process. While Lealor waited for him to complete his scales, she used all her magical senses to make certain he was truly shifting and not merely creating the illusion of a dragon.

''Lealor, look! He's just like me!'' Baloo's voice broke the stillness.

''Quiet, young one! You were supposed to watch and nothing more.'' The tall golden plume that was Oron joined the slighter form of Baloo.

As the grey veil disappeared from the Shadowlord, Lealor could see him more clearly with her magical senses. She gasped as she realized what she was seeing. Baloo was right! A gout of hot flame burst from her nostrils.

''Why have these two meddlesome entities arrived here?'' the grey dragon who was the Shadowlord asked.

Excited by her discovery, Lealor failed to notice his question. ''You're like Baloo, only dimmer. You're a Bright One yourself!''

''A being of such power? Of course I'm not. I'd know if I had the powers of an energy being.''

''You are! You're a Bright One! You must be the Bright One who disappeared so many years ago when the great dragonmage Wyrd was experimenting with a sun!'' Lealor became so excited that she forgot she was in dragonshape and almost knocked a hole in the wall of the castle, solid as it was.

"You lie, human!" Oron's golden column shook with outrage. "I am Oron of the Bright Ones! This creature cannot be one of us!"

"Yes, he is." Baloo's tiny voice protested unheard by any of the others. Oron's mental voice was so loud Lealor held her talons over the place where her ears would have been if she was in human form.

"Use your power to look at his essence," Lealor told Oron, so excited by her discovery that she gave orders to the Bright One as if he were a child. "Can't you sense he is one of you?"

Oron's golden column expanded until it encompassed the grey dragon.

Baloo's childish mindthought broke the stillness. "Oh," he said, "look at the dragon! Just like I said! He's one of us, too!"

Under the tutelage of Oron, the former Shadowlord was gradually assuming the pure energy form of a Bright One, except he was silver, rather than gold.

"Are you going to destroy the human worlds of the gate, Oron?" Baloo asked, with no conception of what his question did to Lealor.

"No, Baloo," Oron's mental voice was as gentle as it had been harsh before. "It has been millennia since I was in error, but this time I was wrong. The Shadowlord was not a human problem. I should have looked into this more deeply."

"Why is he silver?" Baloo asked as he watched the grey dragon turn into shimmering energy. "You and I are golden."

"Because his development has been repressed by being in a material form so long."

"Is he going to be good now?" Baloo asked.

Lealor sensed that Oron was fast nearing the end of his

patience, so she answered. "Of course. He didn't mean to be evil. Whenever we try to be something we're not it makes us miserable and selfish. Now that the Shadowlord knows who he is, he'll be happier."

"More to the point, I shall be watching him," Oron added.

"He isn't Lord of Shadows anymore," Baloo said to Lealor. "He's all silvery light."

"Perhaps I should choose another name," the silvery column said. Turning to Lealor he continued, "May I call myself Lor after you, Lealor? You saw me for what I really was even when you were a child."

"Of course," Lealor said. "Would you free Rand now?"

As she spoke the words, the ice surrounding Rand shattered into a thousand pieces and he stepped over to her side.

"You have my word that I shall teach these young Bright Ones. They will not meddle with you humans again," Oron promised. "Baloo, Lor, follow me." The golden column that was Oron diminished rapidly until it was an incandescent light which winked out abruptly.

Two tears rolled down Lealor's snout. The defeated Shadowlord was a Bright One and she was prisoner in a dragon's form forever!

"What are you crying for?" the silver column asked as it stopped dwindling.

"While we are both happy that you have found your true form at last, Sha—er, Lor," Rand answered for the dragon, "Lealor, here, is condemned to be a dragon forever! I heard you talking about it while I was under your spell."

"I really fooled her, didn't I?" Lor's form quivered with his mirth.

"Fooled?" Lealor fluffed her scales. "What do you mean?"

"You remember when I told you about changing? You had taken baby dragon form and destroyed my laboratory, upsetting my plans. I was very angry at you, so I told you if you changed, you'd stay that way. I didn't actually form a spell. I had no time and I didn't know how to effect such a spell. I'm not sure anyone can keep a shape-shifter from changing if he wishes. You can be in human form any time you choose!'' Lor winked out abruptly.

"Wait for me!'' Baloo called, starting to dwindle erratically. Then he stopped. "Oh, I forgot. I'd better send you to your parents. They've really worried!'' He grew and solidified as Lealor said, "Rand, what about the earth stone?''

In answer, Rand walked to the window and tossed the stone to the ground far below. "That should do it,'' he said.

Before Lealor could look to see what happened, she found herself and Rand at the door to her cottage.

"Mother! Father!'' Lealor cried as they rushed out to greet her.

Rand stood quietly to the side. Finally, Lealor remembered him. She introduced Rand to her parents.

They smiled at him politely, but he could tell they needed to hear about Lealor's adventures before they seriously considered anything else—like a wedding.

Berdu and Fialla materialized in the clearing. "See! I told you she was back!'' he said. "And I was able to transport us both here in spite of your doubts.''

The cottage did not have enough seats for everyone, so Mirza waved a hand and created some chairs and refreshments. They were all listening to Lealor and Rand tell their adventures, when Fafleen arrived.

"Now where can he be?'' she said.

Seeing the dragon, Berdu jumped from his chair, but Jarl took hold of his arm. "Don't wink out now,'' he told the little man.

With a gout of flame, carefully aimed upward, Flare arrived. He took one look at Berdu and said, "The Ancient One was right! Father, don't you remember me?'' Then, without waiting for an answer, he shook powder from a bag he'd brought with him over Berdu. As the silvery motes settled on the tiny man, he began to change until a mighty dragon joined the other two.

Jarl backed away from the dragon. The clearing remained crowded although the three dragons had snaked their tails through the trees.

"That's Berdularion, the dragon king," Fialla whispered to the other humans in the clearing.

"Look out below!" called a familiar voice as Young Fafnir, Fafleen's brother, materialized over the clearing.

The humans hurriedly vacated their seats as the young dragon made an awkward landing, crushing two of the chairs into kindling. "Humph," he said. "They don't make chairs very well here."

Fafleen forgot a good bit of her new-found dignity as she told her brother, "I've found some important volumes of dragon lore and I'm staying here to translate them. You can go home and tell mother and father. Besides, there's no gold for you here."

Flare and Berdularion watched the spirited exchange between brother and sister, but the humans were busy sharing information that was important to them.

Rand turned to Jarl and Mirza. "How long will it be before you can repair the gate?"

"Now that Berdularion has returned to his proper form, he has released the old magic that was fettered so long ago," Fialla said. "Probably all those transformed so long ago have returned to their original forms."

Rand looked a little puzzled by the information.

Mirza explained to him. "You see, now that things are being set right, the gate will return to its old form as well. I just don't understand what magic is working to fix everything."

Lealor said, "Rand fixed it."

"How?" Jarl asked, taking another look at Lealor's friend.

"He threw the earth stone," Lealor said, too happy to

realize her answer was not clear to anyone but Rand and her. "I don't understand why you want to know about the gate, Rand."

"Our parents should meet before our wedding."

"What makes you think—" Lealor began.

"Oh, I remember a certain indication I had when we were in the Shadowlord's power—"

Lealor blushed and didn't say another word when Rand took her hand in his.

Jarl put his arm around Mirza and they smiled, misty eyed.

The dragons turned their attention to the humans. Young Fafnir took one look, and said, "Oh, yuck!" He reared his head as high as it would go and looked Flare in the eye. "I suppose you're going to tell me you and my sister—"

Berdularion sent a jet of fire at Fafnir's tail as Fafleen ruffled her scales in a dragon's blush.

Fafnir waved his warmed tail to cool it before he gave the couples a disgusted look. "I hate mush!" he said, and disappeared.

Epilogue

LEALOR looked down at her bracelet as Myst continued explaining. "So, Wyrd finally admits he was in error when he commanded me to silence."

"I've always been rather envious of my brothers. They had Soladon and Nyct to talk to, and we couldn't share our thoughts," Lealor said. "Now, all that's changed."

"The Shadowlord is no longer a danger to you or the gate. Wyrd created me to protect you. You no longer need me as a talisman."

Myst's musical voice was so pleasant, Lealor almost missed her message. "You mean you won't be staying with me?"

"No. I have other things I wish to do. It isn't as if you actually need me as a companion. You will be busy preparing for your wedding to Rand. Then he will come first with you as is only right."

"But—"

"However," Myst's voice added, "I will leave my material form with you. If you ever have need of me, you have but to call and I will come." The dragon's form began to coalesce in the air before Lealor.

Myst's shape dwarfed the size of the other dragons Lealor had met. She realized how great a being she had worn as if Myst were a simple piece of jewelry. "Thank you for your care all these years," she said, removing the bracelet from her wrist.

"May you be happy," Myst said, fading from view as Lealor watched.

Cibby, Mirza, and Jarl watched from a window.

"Well, that's a relief. Our problems are over, witch," Jarl said to his wife.

"Lealor will always be my baby." Mirza sighed. "I hope she isn't too badly hurt by Myst's leaving."

"She couldn't have had much of a bond. They couldn't talk to one another," Jarl said, thinking like all fathers, that he understood his daughter perfectly.

Cibby shook her head. "The pain will fade. Rand will see to it." She watched Jarl and Mirza stroll away like lovers without a care in the world. "No problems?" She repeated Jarl's words, remembering all the worrying she had done since Mirza and Jarl met. "They still have a lot to learn about parenting." She chuckled as she went to tell Andronan.

"Are you content to leave, Baloo?" Oron said from the far spaces where he and Lor, the former Shadowlord, watched with the youngest Bright One.

"Perhaps we should stay to keep an eye on them," Baloo said. "I have this funny feeling—"

"He's right, Oron. I sense the faintest of evil shadows gathering." Lor shimmered silver between the stars.

"Enough!" Oron's words flared through the ether. "The first lesson you both have to learn is that Bright Ones have no interest in the doings of material beings! Now come!'' he commanded, streaking away.

Lor and Baloo streamed after him, but Baloo looked behind him as he followed, leaving a trail of golden teardrops to mark his passage.